T0171183

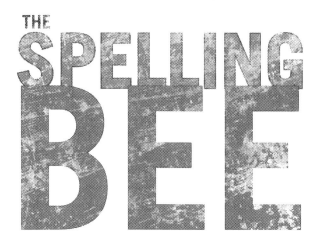

THE SPELLING BEE

DON BOZEMAN

iUniverse, Inc.
Bloomington

The Spelling Bee

Copyright © 2011 by Donald G. Bozeman

All rights reserved. No part of this book may be used or reproduced by any means, graphic, electronic, or mechanical, including photocopying, recording, taping or by any information storage retrieval system without the written permission of the publisher except in the case of brief quotations embodied in critical articles and reviews.

This is a work of fiction. All of the characters, names, incidents, organizations, and dialogue in this novel are either the products of the author's imagination or are used fictitiously.

iUniverse books may be ordered through booksellers or by contacting:

iUniverse
1663 Liberty Drive
Bloomington, IN 47403
www.iuniverse.com
1-800-Authors (1-800-288-4677)

Because of the dynamic nature of the Internet, any web addresses or links contained in this book may have changed since publication and may no longer be valid. The views expressed in this work are solely those of the author and do not necessarily reflect the views of the publisher, and the publisher hereby disclaims any responsibility for them.

Any people depicted in stock imagery provided by Thinkstock are models, and such images are being used for illustrative purposes only.

Certain stock imagery © Thinkstock.

ISBN: 978-1-4502-9767-7 (sc)
ISBN: 978-1-4502-9768-4 (ebk)

Printed in the United States of America

iUniverse rev. date: 02/11/2011

Dedicated to all the children of the world who have suffered at the hands of the ones they trusted the most.

"Pandora opened the box. All the evils it contained spilled out. When the last had escaped, she looked inside. A single gift remained. The gift of _Hope_."

THE SPELLING BEE

———

Chapter 1

M innie was about to throw the dirty shorts into the wash pot when she saw the bloodstain.

"Miss Julia, you better come out here."

My mother got up from her chair on the back porch. She brushed scraps of potato peelings from her apron and walked down the steps to the path that led to the smokehouse and the wash shed.

"What is it Minnie? Has Derek torn his britches again?"

"No ma'am. They seems to be some blood in this pair of shorts." Mama took the shorts from Minnie. She turned them inside out and looked at the label.

"These must be Derek's. He's the only one that wears BVDs. It's probably just a case of the piles. They run in the family you know. Dr. Sumner's had to cut on two of the boys already.

* * * *

MINNIE LEE CICERO HAD WORKED for my family for over twenty years. She lived in a small, two-room shack that my father built for her just across the road from the Antioch Negro Baptist Church—not to be confused with the Antioch Missionary Baptist Church just a quarter mile away where the white folks went. The little house had just two rooms. It had electricity but no running water, and it wasn't finished on the inside. Minnie plastered newspapers to the bare walls to keep out the insects and the winter winds.

Minnie had one daughter. Della had moved to Detroit during the war. She got a job in one of the factories making airplanes. Minnie got occasional post cards from her. I never knew what happened to Della's father—I never asked. That morning Minnie had gotten a card.

"Derek, read this card to me," she said. "I ain't heard from Della in over a month. Hope nothing ain't wrong." I read it to her.

"Dear Mama,

I'm sorry it took so long to write. You know I got married a while back. Well, you are now a grandmother. Baby Maurice is doing fine, and Lester just got a promotion down at the Ford plant. I hope to be able to send you some money soon.

"Love, Della"

"Well, if that don't beat all. Me a grandma. I didn't even know she was expecting no baby. Unhh! Unhh! I sure do hope they'll be able to bring him down here to see me. Ain't that something? Me a grandma. Derek, I want to send her a card right back. Will you write one for me?"

I got a card from Mama's dresser and wrote the message that Minnie dictated. She always insisted on paying for the penny postcards. She said it wasn't our place to have to provide them for her. She had a real independent streak. She reached into her bosom and pulled out a handkerchief that was tied in a knot at one corner. That's where she kept her money. She untied the knot, counted out two pennies, and handed them to me. Then she retied the knot, stuffed the handkerchief back into her bosom, and took the card out to the mailbox. She raised the flag for the mail carrier to stop.

"There!" she said with an air of satisfaction, "If you does things right away when they needs doing you won't never have no regrets." She headed back to the laundry shed to stoke the fires under the wash pots.

I headed for the toilet. It was a fine two-holer out behind the smokehouse. The holes were shaped properly, with smooth edges, and there was a vent stack. That didn't help much though. With the size of our family, we had needed those two holes. At times, we could have used more.

The path to the toilet ran between the wash shed and the smokehouse. The wash shed was made of corrugated tin on three sides. The front, facing the pots, was open. The shed had two washtubs for scrubbing the clothes and two others for rinsing. Coloreds and whites.

*   *   *   *

THROUGH A CRACK IN THE door I could see Minnie walking back and forth from the pots to the tubs. She picked up a pile of clothes to throw into the scrubbing tubs. She was sorting them by color when she stopped suddenly. I heard her call to my mother who was sitting on the back porch peeling sweet potatoes. My daddy loved sweet potato pies.

I reached for the remains of an old Sears Roebuck catalog and ripped out a few pages. I crumpled them up to wipe myself. I always avoided the women's lingerie section. Those pages were printed on slick paper, and they didn't wipe so good. I looked at the paper when I finished. There was a smear of blood on it.

"What were you and Mama talking about?" I asked Minnie as I passed her on the way back to the house.

"That's for me to know and you to find out," she said. She took a good-natured swipe at my backside with the paddle. "Ask your Ma if you want to know, Mr. Smarty-pants." I walked back to the porch.

"Derek, Minnie found some blood in a pair of your shorts. Have you been having trouble with the piles?"

I stopped dead still. How would I answer her? I knew I couldn't tell her the truth.

"Yes'm. A little bit, I guess."

I had never lied to my mother before.

"Well, if it keeps on I'll ask Gordon for some of that ointment he gave your daddy." Dr. Gordon Sumner was Mama's cousin on the Thornhill side. "You let me know if they keep bothering you."

"Yes'm. I will."

"You better hurry up and finish getting ready for school. The bus'll be here in a minute. Don't forget your lunch bucket."

We didn't have an indoor bathroom, but Daddy had installed an electric pump on the well so Mama could have running water in the kitchen and on the screened porch. The spigot on the porch drained into a big funnel, and the water ran through a pipe under the house that fed the fish bait bed on the other side. I washed my face and hands and slicked my hair down with Wildroot Cream Oil.

"I'm going on up to the corner Mama. I'll catch the bus when it comes back around." On my way out the door, I grabbed the gallon syrup bucket that served as my lunch pail.

The bus came by our house then made a big loop to pick up the McCrary kids. That gave me plenty of time to join the other kids up at the corner before it returned. Several of them were already there when I arrived.

*   *   *   *

WE LIVED IN ANTIOCH, ABOUT three miles north of Shiloh. Antioch was the county seat before the Civil War. Some of the older folks called that "The War of Northern Aggression." They had already started building the railroad through Antioch when the war started. You can still find sections of the track bed down in the woods behind the sawmill. After the war, the railroad was moved to Shiloh and that became the county seat. Antioch kind of dried up afterwards. Most folks figured that the carpetbaggers were in cahoots with the railroad men. They said that lots of people who bought up the land around Shiloh got rich.

Julia Grimes was Daddy's second wife. His first wife died in childbirth with my half-sister Esther. They tell me he nearly went crazy when she died. Daddy sent Esther and my half-brother Elton to live with his sister Lizzie in Poulan while he went off to work on the railroad. They say he got heavy into drinking after that. A few years later, after he straightened himself out, he married Mama and moved her and the kids to Albany.

Around 1930 Daddy bought a small farm, and him and Mama moved back to Antioch from Albany. Five of my brothers were born in Albany: William, Harold, Tom, Roger and Larry. Jim and me were born in Antioch. My four oldest brothers all served in WWII. During the war, Mama had a white flag with three blue stars hanging in the front window. Those stars were for William, Harold and Tom. She couldn't find a flag with four stars when Roger was drafted, so his was the flag with a single star. There were two flags in Antioch with gold stars. Those boys never came home.

*   *   *   *

ANZA GARNER WAS ALREADY AT the bus stop. She lived on the other side of the old courthouse that sat in the middle of a big square. She was a real tomboy. She was tall, skinny, and tough as nails. Besides her brother James, she had six sisters. James and my oldest brother, William, had run off to join the Marines in 1938. They got back just in time to finish high school and get drafted. Each Garner sister seemed to pair up with one of the Barton boys, age-wise. I don't think there were ever any romantic entanglements. Anza was a year younger than me.

It was unusually cold for January in South Georgia. Hoarfrost pushed up through the red clay of the roadbed and crunched underfoot as I walked to the corner. I had just gone back to wearing shoes a few weeks earlier. The calloused bottoms of my feet were as tough as whet leather from running barefoot through the fields.

Anza was looking in her lunch box. Miss Lola was always making peanut butter and jelly sandwiches for her. About twice a week, she'd offer to trade with me. Especially if I had a pineapple or banana sandwich.

The bus came by a few minutes later, and we all climbed on board. Henry Thornhill, another of my mother's cousins, was the driver. I could still remember my first day of school when Mama had waited for the bus with me and Jim.

"Well, Henry. This is my last boy," she said. "You take good care of him for me." Mama had wanted a girl. She had already decided to name me Rachel. She quit trying after I came along.

Jim took me to Mrs. Russell's first grade classroom and sat me on the first step outside the door.

"You stay here until your teacher comes," he said. Then he just walked away. That was my introduction to school. I would spend the next seven years at McPhaul trying to master reading, writing, and arithmetic.

Those would be my last years of innocence, the time when I still believed in the basic goodness of people.

Chapter 2

This was my last year at McPhaul. I was almost thirteen. I had gone from an awkward underweight kid to a robust, five-foot six, one hundred ten pound, physical specimen. Good farm cooking, hard work and plenty of exercise worked wonders. Like all six of my brothers, I had my mother's features: dark hair, heavy eyebrows, deep brown eyes and long eyelashes. We had dark skin. I was told my mother had some Indian blood in her. It was like our father had nothing to do with our creation.

I was in Miss Burch's homeroom. There was a boy named Henry Tillman in our class. He was even poorer than I was although neither of us knew we were poor at the time. Henry was always getting into trouble. One day Miss Burch asked me if I would help her with Henry.

"Derek, Henry is really trying my patience. If I move him up to the side of the room near my desk, would you mind sitting by him?"

"No ma'am. That'll be all right with me."

So Henry and I spent that year as buddies, and I kept him out of trouble. On the other hand, come to think of it, maybe he kept me out of trouble. Miss Burch was pretty smart.

One time Henry and I were supposed to run the three-legged race at spring Field Day. He was really looking forward to it. He didn't get many chances to shine. That morning the bus stop gang decided to meet over at another kid's house a half-mile closer to Shiloh. We were playing King of the Hill on the little island where the road forked. Someone pushed me off, and I caught my bare foot on a metal spike that was sticking out of the bank. It opened a two-inch gash in my instep. I hobbled home where Mama cleaned it out with turpentine and wrapped it up with a piece of old bed sheet. No one went to the doctor in those days unless it was a matter of life and death. It's a wonder more of us didn't die of lockjaw. I was still able to catch the bus. Henry and I ran that race, and we came in second, bloody foot and all. I still have the scar.

After the war, the government began funding a lunch program at the high school cafeteria. There was so much surplus food I reckon they figured that was a good way to use it up. Every day we had to line up to march over there. Lunch cost a dime. If you had a dime.

"Come on Henry, it's lunch time."

"You go ahead, Derek. I'm not hungry today."

I knew better. Sometimes Henry brought his lunch, but as often as not he didn't have anything to eat.

"Come on," I said. "Mama gave me an extra dime to buy a Coke and candy bar on the way home. I'll buy your lunch with it."

"Naw. You go on," he said. "I ain't hungry."

"I'm not going if you don't," I said.

"Well, okay. I don't want to see you go hungry on my account." That had to be the best lunch I ever ate.

Another time we had an awful stink in the classroom. Miss Burch finally couldn't take it anymore. She marched all the boys down to the basement where the bathrooms were located. She called to Primus, our Negro janitor. He came out from the furnace room.

"Yes'm Miss Burch. Whut can I do for ya?"

"I want these boys to go in there and check each other's underpants. Someone has soiled himself, and I want to know who it is. Primus, you make sure they do a proper inspection."

"Yes'm. I sho will. You boys come on with me."

I was embarrassed beyond belief. Thank goodness, it wasn't Henry or me. It turned out to be one of the boys from the Bloody Ninth, down near Scooterville. He spent the rest of the day in the basement with Primus until the buses came. Miss Burch sent a note home to his folks. I doubt any of them could read it.

That was the year that Georgia decided to move from eleven school grades to twelve. My class would be the first to go twelve years. That meant there would be one year with no graduating class. A few years later, all the high schools in the county consolidated, and Shiloh High became Wyatt County High, and we went from being Eagles to Rams. Jim was in the last class to graduate after eleven years. He was three years older than me, but he stayed back a year to play football. Him and some of his buddies joined the navy right out of school. They later wound up serving during the Korean War. That next year I moved to the high school. That's when I first met Miss Daniel.

Miss Sara Daniel was what folks called an old maid or spinster in those days even though she couldn't have been more than forty. About the only work that women could get was nursing or teaching, especially after the boys came back from the war. I thought she was the most elegant woman I had ever seen. She wore her reddish hair rolled up on the sides and in back with big pins to hold it in place. She wore just a touch of rouge and a light red lipstick. She and several of the single women teachers took rooms with folks in the big Victorian houses along Antioch Street. Miss Daniel lived with the Cone family. Their son, Warren, was in my class.

Miss Daniel was the school librarian. She also taught English Literature. She introduced me to the world of books. In so doing, she changed my life. She encouraged her students to make the most of their natural-born talents. That first month, she assigned several books for us to read. I fell in love with MacKinlay Kantor's little hunting dog, Bugle Ann, and I never looked back. After the first few weeks, she called me aside. It scared me to death.

"Derek, I'm extremely proud of your progress in my classes. I wonder if you might be interested in entering the school spelling bee."

I had never thought of myself as an especially talented speller, but if someone like Miss Daniel thought I was then who was I to say no.

"Miss Daniel, if you think I can do all right, and you'll help me, then I'd like to try it."

"That's wonderful, Derek. I'm going to begin by giving you a list of words that were used in the last three contests. I'm sure they won't use the same ones again, but it will give you an idea of the types of words to prepare for. I want you to take them home with you and study them. I'll give you a test on them next Friday."

She handed me a half-inch sheaf of papers. There must have been at least twenty words on each page along with their definitions and pronunciation keys. I could see this was going to be a busy week.

Chapter 3

I saw Red Crawford coming out of the old store building on the corner when I got off the bus. Daddy ran a small grocery there early in the Depression. He had given so much credit to our kinfolks—we were related to half the families in Antioch—that the store finally had to close. Nobody could pay him back. Once, when we were playing hide-and-seek, I found an old ledger hidden way up on top of the shelves. The names of most of our neighbors and kinfolks were listed in it. Practically none of them had *paid* written by their account.

"How you doin' boy?" Red called. "I ain't seen you for a month of Sundays. You been too busy to say howdy?"

"No, Red. I guess you've been down at the sawmill every time I came by."

* * * *

RED SHOWED UP ON OUR doorstep a few years back, just after the war was over. He was eating at the old table on the screened porch when I got up that morning. He just looked at me and kind of grunted as I came through the door.

"Mama, who's that Negro man on the back porch?"

She was in the living room by the window where she sat each morning combing out her hair. Shafts of light from the early morning sun angled past her. She rhythmically pulled the brush through her long, graying hair.

When she finished, she would wrap it in a bun and pin it to the back of her head. She was a tall and angular woman. She had a weariness about her that was common to all the farmwomen who were struggling to raise their families while trying to make meager ends meet. Bearing seven sons and raising Daddy's first two children had taken a lot out of her. She was in her mid-fifties but aged beyond her years in every respect but one—her face. Her beautiful, dark, brown eyes and long, black eyelashes looked like they did in the picture I had hanging over my bed. It was a sepia photograph taken when she was sixteen. She was beautiful then. She was beautiful now.

*   *   *   *

"HE JUST SHOWED UP YESTERDAY looking for work," she said. "Your daddy hired him to work at the mill. His name is Red Crawford. He said he had worked some in timber down near Cairo. We're a hand or two short at the mill now that one of the men has started sharecropping on the Blizzard place."

"What's he doing eating on the back porch?"

"He doesn't have any place to live. Hiram said he could stay in the old store building. He's going to help out around the house and in the garden to pay for his eats and a place to stay."

Red was the color of what was called *high yellow.* His skin looked like a white person with a bad case of yellow jaundice. His hair was a dirty, sandy, red color. Some called it strawberry blond. It was not very long. He had it marcelled in waves to the back of his head where he wore a short ponytail. His hair wasn't as kinky as most Negroes I knew. It was a little smoother. You could tell he had a lot of white blood in him.

Red was not real tall, but he had a powerful build. He reminded me of the Negro workers I saw loading pulpwood onto the flatcars down near the depot. They went shirtless in the hot summer sun. Their ebony muscles glistened with sweat, and they rippled like steel as they heaved the hundred pound logs onto the rail cars. Red had obviously done work like that in Cairo.

Red moved into the back of the store where he had a cot, chair, table, and potbellied stove. He had a little black and yellow terrier that he called Pee Wee. There were no lights in the store, but he had a kerosene lamp. I don't know where he went to relieve himself—it never occurred to me to ask. I do know where he bathed though. All the Negro establishments in Shiloh were located below the railroad, south of downtown. There was a Negro barbershop there with a public bath, and Red would go there every Saturday afternoon to shave and bathe. Sometimes he wouldn't come home before Monday morning.

"Red, I didn't see you all day Sunday," I said as I went past the store on Monday morning. "Where were you?"

"I was just cattin' around downtown," he said with a big grin. "I found me a nice little woman, and we had us a good old time."

"Yeah, but what did you do?"

"Derek, ain't your daddy or none of your brothers ever told you about the *birds and the bees?*"

"No," I said. "What are you talking about?"

"You know. What men and women do when they get together?"

"Oh, you mean sex and stuff like that? I see what goes on with the farm animals. It doesn't take much to figure out that stuff. We studied a little bit about it in Mr. Tyler's science class."

"Well, let me tell you Derek, if you could be a black man for just one Saturday night you'd never want to be white again." He winked at me and laughed.

*   *   *   *

RED TAUGHT ME A LOT about life over those next few years. Him and me became almost inseparable. I would go with him and Daddy to *cruise* timber. That's where we would walk through the woods and try to figure out how many board feet of lumber could be cut from the trees so that Daddy could make an estimate. He was good at that even though he had only a fourth grade education. He could look at a stack of lumber and tell you how much it contained to within a few board feet.

One day we were *cruising* a wood lot near Doles. Daddy was looking up at the trees trying to estimate their yield when Red started to stammer.

"M-m-m-m-ister H-i-i-i-ram, look out!"

Daddy looked down to see a six-foot long rattlesnake lying across the path. It must have been five inches thick across the middle. Daddy already had his foot in the air when Red yelled, so all he could do was to go ahead and jump over the snake. We didn't understand why it didn't strike until we saw the big knot in its belly. Red killed it with the bushwhacker he was carrying. He cut the snake open, and we found a big fat rabbit that it had swallowed whole. I guess it was just too stuffed to coil up and strike. Anyway, I always kept my eyes glued to the ground after that.

Shortly after Red came to work for us, Daddy got a contract to cut the timber on the Strangward place. The Strangwards were the richest farmers in Wyatt County. They lived in a big mansion at the end of Antioch Street where it dead-ended into Lundy Road. The house was two stories tall, and it had big white columns out front. To me it looked like Twelve Oaks where the Tarleton twins lived in *Gone with the Wind*.

It was summertime, and Red would take me with him to cut the trees and snake them out of the river bottoms. He would get on one end of a crosscut saw and me on the other, and we could cut down a two-foot thick pine in less than ten minutes. He'd stop every so often and shake turpentine onto the blade from a Coca-Cola bottle to keep the blade from binding on the resin.

We had a big team of yellow oxen hitched to a cart with wheels that must have been eight feet tall. Red would back that rig over the cut log and ratchet it up with a come-along pulley. Then those two huge beasts would drag it up to the clearing where it could be loaded onto a truck. Harold got his leg caught between two of those logs once. It took the skin off his shin right down to the bone. That sore never did heal right. He had trouble with it for the rest of his life. That was the first summer I was allowed to work at the mill. Daddy paid me fifty cents a day.

"Derek it's time you learned your way around this mill," he said. "You may find yourself running it one of these days, and you'd better know how

to do everything that needs doing. I'm gonna start you out *doodling* dust."
He could have been speaking a foreign language as far as I was concerned.
"Come on back here and I'll show you," he said.

The mill was steam driven. There was a big brick boiler off to one side.
My job was to *doodle* sawdust into the firebox so it could burn and generate
steam. A chain belt ran from under the sawpit up to a tall pole sticking out
of a big mound of sawdust. The belt carried the sawdust up the mound and
deposited it there. It was hot, dirty, work, but that two dollars and fifty
cents I got on Saturday made up for it.

There were pulleys and belts flying all over the place: one to drive the
cutoff saw, one to pull the log carriage into the main saw, one to carry
away the sawdust, one to drive the main saw blade. They were all driven
by the steam engine's heavy flywheel. The three-ball governor on top spun
around and rose up and down. It let steam escape or held it in depending
on the load on the engine. I now understood where Rube Goldberg got
his inspiration for those cartoons that Daddy showed me in the Sunday
edition of the *Albany Herald*.

When the groaning log trucks pulled into the wood yard, the side
braces were dropped, and the logs came tumbling off, cascading down
the hill toward the carriage. Three men with peaveys would wrestle the
logs onto the carriage and jack them into place. Daddy would look at the
log and decide how many two by fours, four by eights or whatever else he
could get from that log, and then he would tell Red to cut it. Red would
push the lever that powered the carriage, and it would roll up to the saw.
He would make whatever last minute adjustments were needed and send
the log through. Sawdust flew everywhere. To this day, my favorite smell
in all the world is fresh-cut pine sawdust.

*   *   *   *

THE SEASONS MELDED INTO ONE another as I worked with Red at the
mill and on the farm. It was a hard but rewarding life. My skinny frame
filled out. I became more muscular. I started to take on some of the more
strenuous jobs.

I drove the wood and burlap tobacco sled back and forth from the barn to the field where the men filled it with the cropped leaves. Later, when all the leaves were strung onto sticks, I would climb up into the barn and hang them across the rafters for curing. Several of the boys would stay up all night stoking the furnace. Tobacco season always coincided with the maturing of the peanut crop. We'd boil a batch of peanuts in an old wash pot and eat them all night long while telling ghost stories.

The last year of the war, Daddy won a contract to dehydrate sweet potatoes for the army's C-rations program. We had over a thousand bushels of potatoes in that barn. They were being cooked for dehydration when the barn caught fire. The walls of the barn were insulated with sawdust, and the fire spread like crazy. The aroma of baked sweet potatoes hung over Antioch for a week. Us kids would snake potatoes from the smoldering ashes and eat them. I don't know what the consequences of that fire were to Daddy. He never did talk about it. After that, he built a new tobacco barn closer to the house with an automatic oil fired furnace. It worked real well, but it sure took all the fun out of tobacco season.

Chapter 4

Three weeks had passed since Miss Daniel gave me the first words to study. She asked me to stay after my study hall. I had study hall in the library.

"Derek, the county wide spelling bee will be held here next Friday. In addition to you, there will be two other contestants from Shiloh. There will be one each from Doles, Bridgeboro, Sumner and Warwick; a total of seven. Do you feel as if you are ready?"

"I don't know Miss Daniel. I've studied all the words you gave me, and I've been going through the dictionary at night. I think I'm probably as ready as I'm ever going to be."

"Good. I think you'll do very well. Miss Kuhn is coaching Mary Kate, and Mr. Tyler is coaching Jimmy Earle. They'll be stiff competition, but I have every confidence that you'll come through with flying colors."

Mary Kate and Jimmie Earle were friends of mine. They lived in town. Town students were looked up to by most of us country kids. What we didn't understand was that their lives were, in most instances, just as desperate as ours.

"Thank you, ma'am. I hope I don't let you down."

"Don't worry about that, Derek. You just do your best If you win, that's great. If you don't, then we'll move on and try again next year."

The next week went by in a blur. I studied words until they were coming out of my ears. The only book my family owned, besides the bible, was an old, cheap, Funk and Wagnall's dictionary. Someone had written across the edges of the pages, "This is a good book." They were right.

The day of the spelling bee dawned cold and blustery. All the contestants arrived by ten. We were shepherded onto the stage of the small auditorium and seated off to one side. A small lectern was placed in the middle. The judges sat on the other side. Mrs. Person, the teacher chosen to read the words, walked up to the lectern.

"Welcome to the annual Wyatt County Spelling Bee," Mrs. Person said.

"We are fortunate to have seven extremely competent scholars today vying for the title of best speller in Wyatt County. The winner of today's contest will move on to the district meet in Albany next month." Our district was comprised of twenty counties in southwest Georgia.

During the first round, two contestants were tripped up by the word *minutiae*. Doles and Warwick dropped out. *Connoisseur* eliminated Mary Kate and the girl from Bridgeboro. Sumner faltered on *cataclysm* leaving me and Jimmie Earle to duke it out. We sailed through six more words before we came to *asymmetrical*. Jimmie Earle, who was sporting a black eye and a cut on his cheek, went first. He included only one *m*. I got it right on my turn. I had just won something for the first time in my life.

*   *   *   *

JIMMIE EARLE COULD HAVE BEEN forgiven for messing up his word. He'd had a very bad weekend. He went on a local version of the infamous *snipe hunt*. The older boys had developed an elaborate prank that they delighted in springing on unwitting lower classmen.

There was an old abandoned barn just north of Antioch. It was well back in the woods behind a small private cemetery. From the cemetery side, in the moonlight, its tin roof could be mistaken for a house. The victim was told that a certain girl of easy virtue lived there, and it just so happened that this night she would be home alone. Saturday night's victim was Jimmie Earle. Dan McCorkle was in charge of preparing Jimmie Earle for this, his first sexual encounter.

"Now, Jimmie Earle," he said, "we've been told that her daddy and mama will be gone until after ten o'clock, but just to play it safe we're gonna park up on the main road and walk in the back way by the cemetery." He handed Jimmie Earle a silver, tinfoil package. "Now, do you know how to use this?"

Jimmie Earle cleared his throat and managed a high-pitched nervous response.

"Of course I do."

"Okay then, I reckon we're ready to go."

It was about seven-thirty. Only a sliver of moon lit the path around the fenced cemetery. I was allowed to tag along. A bunch of us were lying in a patch of broom sedge behind the cemetery fence when Jimmy Earle passed by. We could hear them talking.

"Now you have to be real quiet when we get close. Just in case. When we get through the gate, I'll go up on the porch and call for Nadine. If everything is okay, then you and Ted can come on in." Ted Parsons was an accomplice. A few minutes later, we heard Dan's voice.

"Nadine. It's us. Is it all right to come in?"

The front door burst open and a booming voice shouted.

"You boys have messed with my Nadine for the last time."

That was followed by a loud shotgun blast. We could hear Dan thrashing about and yelling as he ran back to where Jimmie Earle and Ted were waiting. The front of his shirt was shredded and bloody and he was carrying on something awful.

"Come on Jimmie Earle, we gotta get him outta here," Ted said. When he turned around Jimmie Earle had already cleared the cemetery fence and run headlong into a marble angel. It was all we could do to keep from bustin' out laughing.

When they got back to the car, they threw Dan in the back seat and headed for the hospital. Jimmie Earle was all scratched up and near fainting. Dan kept moaning. The rest of us hopped into another car. We pulled up to the hospital just as the first car drove up to the emergency room door. It was only then that Dan took off his tattered, ketchup stained, T-shirt, and Jimmie Earle knew he had been had. He jumped out of the car cursing and took off running for home which was only three blocks away. Needless to say, the next school day was quite interesting.

*   *   *   *

"CONGRATULATIONS TO DEREK BARTON," MRS. Person said. "It was a hard fought contest, and we wish Derek continued success as he moves on to the districts in Albany. Our thanks to the other contestants. We hope to see you back here again next year. Good spelling."

Miss Daniel came over and gave me a big hug.

"I knew you could do it," she said. Then she handed me another stack of papers.

"Start on these. I'll have more for you on Monday."

No rest for the weary; or is it the wicked.

I went back to studying words, doodling dust, weeding tobacco and milking cows. Mama and Daddy were proud of me, but that didn't cut any ice when it came to shouldering my part of the workload. Life went on. Work had to be done.

One Monday morning, Miss Daniel called me up to her desk.

"Derek, Miss Kuhn and Mr. Tyler have graciously and unselfishly agreed to help us get ready for Albany, and since Mr. Tyler is the only one with a car he has generously consented to drive us over. The contest starts at ten, so we'll leave as soon as school takes in that morning."

I never knew there were so many words in the English language. I spent every spare moment looking at words, spelling words, sounding words, dreaming words. Miss Daniel, Miss Kuhn and Mr. Tyler took turns drilling me during study hall on the most arcane words they could uncover in the dictionary. I had words running out of my ears.

I stumbled up the lane toward the bus stop, my nose buried in a list of words. I bumped into Red as I rounded the corner of the store.

"Where you been, boy. I ain't seen hide nor hair of you for days."

"I won the spelling bee at school last week. I've been spending every spare minute studying."

"That's good, Derek. I always knew you wuz smarter than most of the young'uns around here. I'd sho like to help you, but you knows I cain't read or write." He scratched at the stubble on his chin. I could tell he wanted to say something more but was hesitant to do so.

"What is it, Red?" I ventured. It wasn't often that he was at a loss for words.

"I'm going back down to Cairo for a while. My mama's sick, and it don't look like she's gone make it. I was wondering if you'd take care of Pee Wee for me while I'm gone."

"Is that all? Sure I will." His face lit up like the Fourth of July.

"Thank you, boy. I knew I could count on you."

Red was gone for two weeks. Pee Wee and me had a grand old time. He was the only dog I had been responsible for since Spot got run over three years ago. I swore then I would never have another dog. Losing him had hurt too much. After keeping Pee Wee for those two weeks, I began to change my mind.

"I'm sorry about your Mama, Red."

"It's all right. She done lived a good, long life. She gone to see my Daddy now. He been dead near five year. I don't gots to go back to Cairo no more. All my family's gone now. You and Pee Wee is about the only family I got left." Tears welled in my eyes. I was sad for Red.

During those two weeks my workload at school increased by the day. Every extra minute was devoted to drilling on every conceivable word that the three teachers could conjure up.

The annual high school choral competition was set for the next Friday in Thomasville. Me, Bryce, and Charles, my two cousins, were scheduled to take the bus with the other members of the choir. At the last minute, Mr. Tyler approached the three of us.

"How would you boys like to keep me company on the way to Thomasville? I'll be driving down so that I can stop in Moultrie on the way back and pick up a suit I bought last Saturday at Friedlander's. They're altering it for me. It was a little snug around the middle. Probably all that cake and pie Miss Kuhn's been feeding me." There was a hot rumor going around school that the two of them were sweet on each other. Bryce was first to speak.

"I'd love to Mr. Tyler, but I promised Johnnie Merle I'd ride on the bus with her." The two of them had been an item since Christmas. "I thought Miss Kuhn might be going with you."

"No, she has to chaperone the girls. Otherwise, she would have. How about you two? Can you make it?"

"I can't," I said. "Miss Daniel is chaperoning the boys, and she wants to go over some new word lists with me. I'm sorry."

"Well, I'm not in the spelling bee, and I don't have a girlfriend, so I guess I'll ride along with you, Mr. Tyler," Charles said. "How long will you be in Moultrie? I have to be back home by five o'clock."

"Oh, that won't be a problem. Besides, we come right past your house on the way back, and I can drop you off. Probably faster than the bus too. That way, no one will need to pick you up in Shiloh. I'll welcome the company."

"Okay, it's a deal," Charles said.

Shiloh's combined choirs came in third behind Albany and Camilla. Neither the boy nor the girl choir placed. The buses pulled away from the auditorium about three thirty in the afternoon. I saw Mr. Tyler's car pull out just ahead of us. It was parked on the courthouse square across from Friedlander's when we rolled through Moultrie. We were back at the school before five. I caught a ride home with my cousin, Jack Paul, who worked at the Chevrolet place across from the Blue Moon café. The Woodfins ran the Blue Moon. They were my oldest brother Bill's in-laws.

I had just walked in the front door at home when the phone rang. It was close to six o'clock. Mama was in the back yard, so I answered it.

"Hello."

"Derek, is that you?"

"Yes, ma'am." I recognized the voice. It was Charles' mother.

"Have you seen Charles? He was supposed to be home by now. We have to go to Albany tonight."

"He rode down to Thomasville with Mr. Tyler. They had to stop at Friedlander's to pick up a suit on the way back. I saw Mr. Tyler's car when we came through Moultrie. It was parked near the store. They must've not had his suit ready, so it took a little longer than he expected. I'm sure they'll be home soon."

"Thank you, Derek. I hope you're right. Buck's mother gets real upset when we're late for Friday night supper."

Buck was Charles' stepfather. He worked at the Ford place in Albany. I didn't hear any more from Lillith that night, so I reckon they got to Albany on time.

Charles wasn't at school on Monday or Tuesday. I told Mama, and she called Lillith. She had a strange look on her face when she hung up the phone.

"What is it, Mama? Is something wrong with Charles?"

"No," she said real fast. "You go on and eat your supper now. I left it in the warming oven for you."

I walked down the hallway. The loose boards creaked underfoot. I was reaching for the knob on the back porch door when I heard my mother crank the old magneto telephone in the front room.

"Hello. Mary Lou? Please connect me with Naomi Hatcher."

Mary Lou Kincaid knew every Wyatt County subscriber's number by heart. I closed my eyes and could see her as she pulled up two plugs from her tray and inserted one in the jack for our phone and one for Naomi's before pressing the ringer button. I saw her do this on one of our field trips. I stood there listening, curious as to what was going on.

"Naomi, this is Julia. Did Bryce get home all right last Friday?" I could only guess at her answer, but it had to be yes since I saw his grandpa pick him up at the school.

"I don't know if there's anything to it," I heard Mama say, "but I just talked to Lillith, and Charles has been acting peculiar since he got back. She kept him out of school the last two days. She said he was moping around, and he wouldn't eat. Stayed in bed all day Monday. It may be some kind of flu or something. Derek seems to be all right. How about Bryce?"

I heard mama hang up the phone. I quietly opened the door to the porch and crossed to the kitchen. When she came in, I was busy shoveling peas and cornbread into my mouth.

"Derek, did you notice anything funny last Friday when you went to Thomasville?"

"What do you mean, Mama?"

"I mean, was Charles acting strange? Did he seem sick to you?"

"No ma'am. He seemed fine when him and Mr. Tyler pulled out just ahead of us. Why?"

"I just talked to your cousin Lillith, and she's worried about him. He must have caught the flu or something down there. I sure hope you didn't get it."

Charles was back in school on Wednesday. He didn't seem any worse for the wear. I did notice that he was quieter and kept more to himself. By Friday, he seemed to be back to his old self. Whatever ailed him had passed with little more fanfare.

Chapter 5

I was studying like mad for the district spelling contest. It was scheduled for the following Monday. Today was Friday, and Daddy had just come in from the mill.

"Derek, come here a minute," he called to me from the screened porch. I was lying on the front room sofa listening to *The Lone Ranger* on the radio. All the fifteen-minute serials started at four o'clock in the afternoon when most kids got home from school.

"What is it, Daddy?" He was bending over the funnel washing his face and hands.

"Hand me that towel." When he finished drying off he said, "I want you and Red to take some corn up to Mercer's Mill tomorrow, and have it ground up for cornmeal. Mr. Mercer will take ten percent as payment for himself. Make sure we get our own meal back and not someone else's. On the way back, I want you to stop by your Cousin Lester's house. He's making syrup this week. He'll trade you five gallons of syrup for three pecks of corn meal. I expect it'll be pretty late when you get there, so you may need to spend the night and come back home on Sunday morning."

"But Daddy, I'm going to the spelling bee in Albany on Monday. I'm supposed to be studying this weekend."

"You weren't too busy to listen to the radio. You do what I tell you, boy. You can get Red to do most of the driving. That'll free you up to study on the way. I'd do it myself, but Roger's gone and I have to do all the mail runs."

"Yes sir," I said in resignation.

*   *   *   *

Daddy had a part time job picking up the mail at the Atlantic Coast Line Railroad depot. He met three trains a day and took the mail to the post office that was just two blocks away. For this, he received the handsome sum of $100 per month.

My middle brother Roger came back from the Pacific where he had helped MacArthur pacify Japan. Jobs were scarce, so he took over running the farm from Daddy. He was a 52/40 man. He attended a few hours of class every week down at the high school agriculture building for a year, and the government paid him $52 a week. It helped to ease the returning GI's back into a job scarce society.

*   *   *   *

That Saturday was my morning to light the fires. I had put kindling in the kitchen stove and the front room fireplace before I went to bed. When Daddy called me at five o'clock, I jumped out of bed, lit the fires, and I was back in bed before the sheets could get cold. I hated getting out of that warm bed on cold mornings.

I saw Red's lantern as I passed by the kitchen window. He was down at the barn feeding the mules. He had already milked the cows and turned them out to pasture. I drifted back off to sleep. The next sound I heard was the shrill crowing of our old bantam rooster. I knew I had to get up for real, now.

Mama fixed eggs, bacon, grits, and biscuits for breakfast. I slathered butter on my biscuits and drenched them with cane syrup. Red had come in from feeding the mules and was finishing his breakfast out on the porch when I walked out of the dining room.

"You ready to go, boy?"

"I reckon so."

Red hitched Ada and Queen to the wagon while Mama packed our lunch buckets, and I filled the water jug. She put in some biscuits and fried fatback. That would hold us until we got to the mill. It was about a twelve-mile trip that took four or five hours by mule-and-wagon. We headed north on the Warwick Road. We swung left at Blue Springs, just below Providence Primitive Baptist Church. That's where Mama and Daddy went to church. An hour or so later, we passed Giddens' store. Red stopped to buy us a cold drink.

We stopped to water the mules at Cousin Lester's place. The cane grinding was almost over when we got there. An old mule harnessed to a long pole walked around the mill in a big circle turning the gears that crushed the sugarcane. Bobby, Cousin Lester's youngest son, was feeding the last of the cane stalks into the rollers. The thin, gray-green juice flowed into a wooden barrel that was covered with a strainer cloth made from feed sacks.

"How you boys doin'?" Cousin Lester asked. "I've been expecting you. Uncle Hiram called and said you were on the way."

Cousin Lester was a heavy smoker. After every few sentences, he had to stop for a deep breath. He'd draw it in real quick like. All the tendons in his neck would stand out as he sucked the air in. He got tired real easy and had to rest a lot.

"We're doing all right, Mr. Lester," Red answered. "We just wanted to stop to let the mules get a little water. Derek and me'll eat our dinner before we head out again if you don't mind."

"That'll be fine Red. Bobby and me already had something, so you go right ahead."

"Mr. Lester, if you don't mind, I'd like a little cup of that cane juice to drink."

"Why, sure thing, Red. Bobby, fetch two of those tin cups over there for Red and Derek."

Bobby held the cups under the spout where the juice poured out. He handed me the half-filled cup. I had never drunk raw cane juice before. It was the sweetest thing I had ever tasted. That wasn't surprising seeing as how it was basically liquid sugar. You couldn't drink much of the stuff without getting sick. We finished our biscuits and fatback and re-harnessed the mules. Bobby was hauling the cane juice over to the syrup boiler as we drove away. When we got back later that evening, the boiled juice would be condensed into golden syrup.

Mercer's Mill was just off the road from Albany to Cordele. The millpond covered several acres and was fed by a small creek. It was over twenty feet deep at the dam. The water passed over a spillway and through the millrace into the Flint River a few miles away. The water was so clear you could see the bass and blue gills swimming near the surface and several huge catfish scavenging near the bottom. The mill straddled the dam with a sluice running along one side. When the sluice gates were opened, the water cascaded onto the big wooden wheel driving the mill machinery.

"You boys can back that wagon up to the side door and just shovel that corn down the ramp there," Mr. Mercer shouted over the thrum of the mill. Two other wagons were parked alongside with their mules grazing under a grove of sycamores.

I knew Mr. Mercer. He was a lay preacher who sometimes came to my folks' church. Like most Primitive Baptist ministers his sermons were full of fire and brimstone and went on for hours. The church didn't allow any musical instruments, and there were no notes in the hymnals. It was called "Sacred Harp" singing, referring to the human voice as a special instrument from God. Sometimes my parents would take us to church with them, but the services were strictly for the grownups. There was no Sunday school or any other accommodations for the children. That probably explained why it was a dying denomination, but that sure didn't bother us kids any. We would play tag among the gravestones or slide down the steep bank behind the outhouses which was always covered with fallen magnolia leaves. You could get up a big head of steam going down that hill. One of my uncles is buried in the cemetery. Colored marbles set into the cement gravestone spell out *Doc Barton*.

Sometimes we would sneak off across the woods to Blue Springs and go swimming. Blue Springs had the coldest water I ever saw. You couldn't stay in longer than a few minutes, and when you got out your teeth were chattering like mad. Someone always had to stand guard for snakes.

My brother Bill and me were fishing there once, and there was a huge water moccasin sunning on a tree root way out in the water. Bill sent me back up to the churchyard to get his shotgun out of the truck. He shot that snake and then fashioned a grappling hook to fish it out of the water. Biggest moccasin I ever saw. Made me think twice about ever swimming there again.

We unloaded the shucked corn and fed it into the shelling machine. Golden kernels poured out of the hopper in an endless stream filling several large baskets. Corncobs spewed out the other side into a huge pile, destined to be ground up as roughage for Mr. Mercer's dairy cows.

"You ever seen a grist mill in operation, Derek?" Mr. Mercer asked me.

"No, sir. Not up close."

"Come with me." He led me up the stairs while Red went off to water the mules and turn them loose to graze.

"You see that conveyor belt over there?" he said. "That brings the corn up to the holding bins on the floor above the mill. We feed the corn down through a hole in the middle of the top stone. The faces of the stones are grooved in such a way that the corn gets ground finer and finer as it moves out toward the edges. We watched the corn trickle down through the floor and could hear the crunching noise as the kernels fed into the wheels. Mr. Mercer motioned for me to follow him. We went back down the stairs to the collecting room. There were more gears, belts, and pulleys than we had at the sawmill. I wondered if Mr. Goldberg had seen this operation.

"I liken this to what Jesus said in the bible about the fields being white unto harvest," Mr. Mercer shouted above the roar. "Them kernels of corn is the lost amongst us. They have a hard shell, and you can't get through to 'em. God gets aholt of 'em and starts to working on 'em. He tests 'em and grinds 'em down till they comes out the other end white and pure as snow." He caught a handful of the meal and poured it into my hand. It was warm, and it smelled like bread baking in the oven.

"You saved, boy?" he asked.

"Yes sir. I joined at Antioch when I was ten."

"That's good. You gotta trust in Jesus and believe in God's salvation."

The load of corn yielded well over a hundred pounds of cornmeal. After giving Mr. Mercer his toll, we loaded the remainder on the wagon and headed out. It was close to dark when we got back to Cousin Lester's house. The smell of syrup hung in the air, and the glow from the boiler fire bounced off the white trunks of the sycamore trees. Bobby was still skimming the dross off the syrup and pouring it through a cloth into a wooden barrel. After a few days of fermenting and distilling, that juice would produce a fiery rum with the kick of a mule. A hundred-eighty proof they said. The Negroes called it "cane buck". They usually got a gallon or two for their services. Red and me sat around the boiler while Bobby finished off the syrup. When the dripping mass formed a circle off the paddle blade, it was ready.

Cousin Lester had gone back up to the house. He looked awful tired. Bobby asked Red and me if we'd help him fill the buckets before the syrup got too thick to pour. After all the water had boiled off, there were twenty-five gallons of syrup left. We filled the cans and stacked them off to one side to cool. We would come back to get our five gallons the next morning.

Supper that night was biscuits, fatback, buttermilk, and fresh syrup. Times were still hard following the Depression and the War. Cousin Annie put the food on the table and asked me to say the blessing. I mumbled a few words of thanks and said amen. The meager meal tasted pretty good after the long day we'd had. After supper, Red went to check on the mules. He said he was going to bed-down in the corncrib when Cousin Annie spoke up.

"Red, why don't you just sleep here on the porch? I can put down a pallet, There's a lot of rats running around in that old barn."

"Why, thank you, Miss Annie. That's mighty decent of you."

"Derek, why don't you and me sleep out here on the porch with Red?" Bobby said. "I've got a bunch of new stories to tell you."

By ten Bobby was running out of stories. Through the open window I could hear Cousin Lester's wheezing.

"Bobby, what's a *queer*?" I asked. I heard Red rise up on his elbows. Bobby hesitated. He was a year or two older than me. I could tell he was embarrassed.

"What do you know about *queers*?" he responded.

"Somebody at school was talking about it. I couldn't hear much of what they were saying. They shut up when I got near. Like it was something they didn't want me to hear."

"Well, best I know it's when one man starts messing around with another man. You know, instead of a woman."

"Well that doesn't make any sense to me. Why would a man do such a thing? It doesn't seem natural."

"It ain't natural. And it's a sin in the eyes of the Lord. It says so in the bible," Bobby added. I could tell he didn't want to talk about *queers* anymore, so I pulled my covers up and went to sleep.

Chapter 6

My school bus dropped us off before eight that next Monday. I went straight to the library. Miss Daniel was packing her book sack with things to take to Albany. Miss Kuhn walked in a few minutes later.

Poor Miss Kuhn. The dark circles under her eyes made her look like the animal that her name sounded like. The kids in her classroom tormented her something fierce. When her back was turned, Warren Cone would let go with a big spitball hitting her in the behind. She'd whip around to see who did it, but everyone's eyes were glued to their books. This would happen two or three times before she'd run out of the room in tears and get the principal to come in. Mr. Gear would read the riot act to us, and things would settle down for a few days before Warren would start up again.

Mr. Tyler came in a few minutes later. He was brushing the crumbs of a doughnut from his vest. A little piece of white icing clung to his mustache. He was about six feet tall and a little paunchy. He always wore dark suits with vests and a gold watch chain that draped across his front. I think he was about forty or so. He was real nearsighted. His horn rimmed glasses looked like the bottoms of Coke bottles.

"You ladies ready to go?" he said. "The contest starts at ten, and I need to stop for gas."

"I believe we're all set," Miss Daniel said. "Derek, do you need to go to the restroom before we leave?"

"No ma'am. I'm all set," I said, turning beet red at the suggestion.

We stopped for gas at the Pure Oil station in Acree. Mr. Tyler asked the attendant to clean the windshield and check the radiator and the oil while he walked around and kicked the tires. Satisfied that everything was in good order, he paid the attendant and got back into the car.

"Either one of you ladies want this candy dish?" he asked. That was the premium that week for buying ten gallons of gas.

The spelling bee was to be held in the city auditorium. We parked on a side street. I could see car tags from counties all over southwest Georgia. We parallel parked between Terrell and Mitchell. I was very nervous.

A sign outside the side door said, "All contestants and teachers enter here." When we passed through, we were at the back of the auditorium near the stage. The first four rows were roped off for advisers, teachers, dignitaries and visitors. A smattering of onlookers trickled in and took the seats farther back. The stage was arranged like the one in Shiloh only there were two extra tables and lots more chairs. There was also a microphone. A reporter and photographer from the *Albany Herald* were there covering the event for the *Atlanta Journal,* which sponsored the statewide contests. They would send the results out to other papers in the state.

The superintendent of schools from Colquitt, in Miller County, was elected to conduct the contest. He sat at a table with the two teachers chosen to certify all the spellings and record the outcome. He rose to speak.

"Ladies and gentlemen, teachers, advisers, contestants and visitors, welcome to the Southwest Georgia District Spelling Bee. My name is Osage Jones. I am Superintendent of Schools from Colquitt, down in Miller County. It is a great privilege to be selected to chair this important contest. Nothing is more valuable to society than the education of its children, and I believe a good education begins with an appreciation for reading and spelling. I compliment all you young people who have earned the privilege to be here. You have proved to be the best spellers in your home counties. I know that only one of you can prevail here today, but those who do not claim first prize should not be disheartened. Hold your head high, and go on back home to begin preparing for next year." He turned to address the tables on either side.

"Now," he shuffled and straightened the stack of cards in his hand, "Mrs. Jane Arbuckle from Bainbridge and Mrs. Ann Seavers from Pavo will alternate in the reading of the words. We will call each county by name, and the representative will be called to the microphone. The word will be read and clearly enunciated. The definition of the word will be given from <u>Webster's Unabridged Dictionary</u>, latest edition. Each contestant has two minutes to spell the word correctly. Misspelling will disqualify a contestant. All contestants will have an opportunity to spell the chosen word. Those spelling the word correctly will move on to the next round. Each round will become progressively more difficult. The last student standing at the end of the last round will be declared the winner. Now, without further ado, Mr. Phillips will you please escort the contestants to their waiting room?"

We were sequestered in a soundproof room behind the stage and seated in two rows of ten chairs. We were instructed not to talk to each other. There were two proctors in the room. I was in the last seat of the second row. Alphabetically, Wyatt is the last county in Georgia. I would be called last. The girl from Baker County went first. We couldn't hear what was happening, but when Mr. Phillips called for the boy from Brooks County the girl from Baker didn't return. One down.

Brooks came back and Calhoun went. Thirty minutes passed as the procession of spellers went and came before Mr. Phillips called my name. Only ten had returned. I walked out on stage trembling. Nothing in my life previously had prepared me for this moment. I could see Miss Daniel, Miss Kuhn, and Mr. Tyler seated in the second row. Miss Daniel smiled her encouragement.

"Mr. Barton, the word is *colloquial*. *Colloquial* is an adjective. It is appropriate to, used in, or characteristic of spoken language or writing that is used to create the effect of conversation. You have two minutes to spell *colloquial*."

I didn't hear a word Mrs. Arbuckle said, but I did remember studying the word.

"Colloquial. C-o-l-l-o-q-u-i-a-l. Colloquial." I finally breathed.

"That is correct, Mr. Barton. You may return to the waiting room.

Please ask Mr. Phillips to send out the Brooks County representative for the beginning of round two."

I stumbled back to the room in a daze. I couldn't believe I had survived the first round. My knees were knocking so hard I was sure everyone in the room could hear them.

At the end of the third round there were five contestants left. Amazingly, I was one of them along with Dougherty, Miller, Seminole and Randolph. It was a little past noon. Mr. Jones called a recess for lunch. Miss Daniel met me at the bottom of the stairs.

"Derek, I'm so proud of you. Come on. We'll buy your lunch."

I had never eaten in a restaurant, and I was terrified. We crossed the street to the Davis Brothers Cafeteria where we fell in line with others from the auditorium. I watched what Miss Daniel did and just followed along. First a tray, then silverware. Next, we had to choose a meat. I took the hamburger steak. I added mashed potatoes and snap beans. Cornbread, butter, and iced tea completed the meal. Mine came to fifty cents. I'm glad I didn't have to pay for it. I think I had a quarter in my pocket.

We were back in the auditorium a little after one. Mr. Osage Jones called us to order, and we resumed the contest. We went back to our room with stomachs full of food and dancing butterflies.

When Dougherty didn't come back, I knew it must be a very tough word. Five minutes later, Miller came back and Seminole left. She didn't come back. Randolph did. It was my turn.

"*Garrulous. Garrulous* is an adjective. It means excessively or pointlessly talkative. *Garrulous.*"

"*Garrulous. G-a-r-r-u-l-o-u-s. Garrulous.*" Again I exhaled, fearing the worst.

"Congratulations Mr. Barton. You are one of our three finalists," Mr. Jones said.

As I left the stage, I caught a glimpse of Miss Daniel out of the corner of my eye. She was beaming. We went through three more words before we came to *sycophantic.* Miller went first and didn't return. Mr. Phillips called Randolph. An agonizing three minutes passed before the door opened again. No Randolph. This was it then. If I spell this word correctly, I'll be district champion. Sweat popped out on my forehead. My hands were clammy. My underarms were drenched. Here goes.

"*Sycophantic. Sycophantic* is an adjective. It means the act of being servile or obsequious, flattering somebody powerful for personal gain. *Sycophantic.*"

My mouth was dry. I tried to swallow, but I couldn't. I knew I had seen this word among the thousands I had studied. I summoned up all that I knew about phonetics and began.

"*Sycophantic. S-y-c-o-p-h-a-n-t-i-c. Sycophantic*". I actually felt faint. I grabbed the microphone stand and hung on. The pause felt like an eternity.

"Congratulations, Mr. Barton. You are the new spelling champion for the Southwest Georgia District. We wish you the best of luck next month in Macon at the divisional semi-finals. As you know, the two top finishers there will go on to Atlanta for the finals against North Georgia's two best."

Miss Daniel was running up the steps, closely followed by Miss Kuhn and Mr. Tyler. She threw her arms around me and nearly squeezed the breath out of me. Everything after that was a kind of blur. It was almost five when we got on the road home.

"Derek, why don't you ride up front with me on the way home?" Mr. Tyler said. "Give the ladies some time to celebrate your victory."

I looked at Miss Daniel and she nodded okay. The trip home was uneventful. Miss Daniel and Miss Kuhn jabbered away in the back, and Mr. Tyler just grinned. He kept clapping me on the back and squeezing my leg. He seemed more excited than Miss Daniel did.

Chapter 7

I had just taken my seat in homeroom on Tuesday morning when the public address system began to crackle and buzz. Mr. Gear's bass voice boomed down the hallways.

"Attention all classrooms. I have called a special assembly for the first ten minutes of the first period. All teachers and students will please gather in the auditorium immediately."

"Must be some news about the upcoming school carnival," I said to Henry.

When my class marched in, Miss Daniel grabbed my arm and steered me toward the stage. Mr. Gear, Miss Kuhn, and Mr. Tyler were already there. I couldn't imagine what this was all about. She led me onto the stage. Mr. Gear rose and walked to the lectern.

"Good morning," he began. "Some of you may not have been aware that one of our own went to Albany yesterday to represent Wyatt County in the district spelling bee. I am delighted to report that Derek Barton not only competed, but won. Next month he will represent our district in the semi-finals in Macon."

I was dumbstruck. Never in my life had I been singled out like this for an honor; much less in front of the entire school. I was proud and embarrassed at the same time. I felt like that prize heifer I entered in the FFA livestock show last fall. I just prayed I didn't do to the stage what the heifer did to the show ring. Now that would be real embarrassment.

"Derek, I can't tell you how proud I am of you. I'm sure the whole student body and the teachers feel the same way. (Tommie Person obviously didn't as he was making faces at me from the second row). "We all wish you the best as you go up to Macon in a few weeks. Our hopes and prayers will go with you. Now I'd like you and Miss Daniel to say a few words." He stepped back from the podium, and I felt Miss Daniel grab my arm as she rose. I think she knew I was paralyzed, and I could never get up on my own. I stumbled to the podium behind her.

"I'm so proud of this young man," she said. "I've never seen anyone work so hard to achieve a goal as Derek has over these last few weeks. It's been a distinct pleasure for Miss Kuhn, Mr. Tyler and me to work with him. Now, Derek, do you have a few words for your adoring audience."

I wished she hadn't said that. I was going to catch it from all the other boys. Teacher's pet was already ringing in my ears. My mouth felt like cotton again. I didn't know if any words would come out.

"I'd like to thank Miss Daniel and the others for all their help. I couldn't have done it without them. I look forward to Macon, and I just hope that I can continue to represent you well." I waddled back to my seat as a burst of applause rose from the assembly. I began to feel pretty good about myself.

If I had any high and mighty opinions, the other kids brought me down to earth in a hurry. We weren't out the door good for recess before Bryce, Charles, Tommie, Warren and all the other boys were razzing me to death. Two of them held me down while the others gave me *noogies* until my head ached. I knew they were secretly proud that one of their own had done something notable, but they could never let it show. They finally let up, and we played our usual touch football game until the bell rang for our next class. On the way back to class Charles stopped me.

"Mr. Tyler is taking some of us to the movies Friday night. They're showing *Gentleman's Agreement*. He said the show has to do with the unfair treatment of Jews in our country, and he's going to be teaching about that in Social Studies next month. He wants everyone in the class to see it. Do you want to go with us?"

"I don't know if I can. I have to go home after school to get my work done. I guess I could get back to town in time, but I don't know how I'd get home."

"Mr. Tyler said he'd drive any of us home who needed a ride." Charles said.

"I don't know. I'll have to ask Mama. I'll let you know tomorrow."

Daddy was still down at the mill when I got home. Mama was in the back yard. She was holding a young Rhode Island Red rooster. She swung the bird around a couple of times, popped its neck, and dropped it to the ground. The chicken flopped around for a while before dying. Mama carried the bird up onto the porch where she dunked it in a bucket of scalding water and began to pluck its feathers. I figured we were having fried chicken for supper.

"Mama, Mr. Tyler wants us to go see this picture show Friday night. Charles and some of the other boys are going. He wants to know if I can go. Mr. Tyler's gonna be teaching about it next month."

"I don't know Derek. Your daddy won't want to go down and pick you up that late."

"He won't have to, Mama. Charles said Mr. Tyler would give us a ride home if we didn't have one."

"You'll have to ask Hiram when he gets home. If he says it's all right, I guess you can go. What's the show about?"

"It's called *Gentleman's Agreement.* Gregory Peck's in it. Something about the way Jews are treated up north. I don't know much about it."

"I know there are a bunch of Jews living up there," Mama said. "Mostly in New York, I think. We don't have many down here. The Hirschs and the Steins are the only ones I know. They run that dry goods store on Front Street. They seem to be good people. Somebody said Don Green, who owns the Famous Store is a Jew, but his name sure doesn't sound like it. They keep to themselves mostly. Is Mr. Tyler a Jew?"

"I don't know Mama. If you want, I'll ask him tomorrow."

"No! Don't you do that! It's not polite to ask people about their religion."

Daddy was late coming in from the mill. He was washing up on the back porch when I asked him if I could go to the show.

"I don't know, Derek. Will it count against you if you don't see it?"

"I don't think so, but I think those who do see it will have an advantage when the exam comes up."

"Let me think about it. There's your work to do and gettin' to town after school."

He went in to supper leaving me to wonder what he'd say. After Mama had served the banana pudding he looked at me. "I guess it'll be all right for you to go. But make sure you've got your work done."

I was busy all week studying and trying to learn new words. It was Thursday night, and Daddy was in the front room as usual. He was listening to H. V. Kaltenborn on the radio. Every night after supper he would pull his cane bottomed, straight-backed chair up to his old Philco and sit hunched over with his hand cupped behind his ear. He had done this every night of the war, listening to the crackle and pop as the foreign correspondents reported from places named Anzio and Bastogne and Iwo Jima. I don't think he knew exactly where his boys were, but I reckon he felt closer to them in this way.

He asked me to cut his toenails. He was getting a little fleshy around the middle and found it hard to bend over to reach his toes. Besides his nails were real thick. You almost needed steel shears to cut them. Daddy had a strange toenail on the second toe of his right foot. He had hurt it someway when he was a boy. The nail came off, and when it grew back in it was split down the middle and grew in as two nails. Sometimes he'd give me a dime for cutting his toenails. I told him he ought to give me eleven cents since he had eleven nails. He didn't think that was so funny. When I finished I could tell he wanted to say something. I was afraid he was going to tell me he had changed his mind about the show.

"Derek, after school tomorrow why don't you just go on down to your Uncle Gordon's office at the courthouse. You can study there until it's time to go to the show. I'll get Red to do your chores for you. He reached into his pocket and handed me fifty cents. "You can go over to Pop Gullett's for a hamburger and a Coke. You should have enough change left to get into the show." I was flabbergasted.

*　*　*　*

GORDON PAUL WAS MARRIED TO my daddy's sister, Annie. They lived across the woods behind the Negro church. Some Sunday nights when we visited them and sat on the front porch, we could hear the choir singing.

Uncle Gordon was Judge of the Ordinary Court for Wyatt County. He was a very small man of limited formal education, but he was the smartest person I knew. His office was on the main floor of the courthouse. There was a big vault in the back where he kept all the county legal records. I once looked up my birth date in the old newspaper archives. I found out I was born on the same day that Will Rogers was killed in a plane crash in Alaska.

Uncle Gordon always wore green eyeshades and arm garters to keep his shirtsleeves clean. He could "hunt-and-peck" on his old Underwood as fast as Miss DuPree, the typing teacher at school. When it came time to buy a fountain pen for our penmanship class, I didn't have the money. He went out and bought a Waterman pen for me. I was never so proud of any possession in my life.

*　*　*　*

I WAS SURPRISED WHEN DADDY said I could go to Pop Gullett's for a hamburger. Pop's wasn't much more than a beer joint. It was located on Liberty Street, an alley running parallel between Front and Kelly. Some Saturdays, when we'd go to town early, he'd slip off and go there. I never knew for sure, but I expect he had himself a beer or two. Funny thing was I could never smell it on him. I still don't know how he managed that. Bryce and Charles were standing in front of the Ritz when I got there.

"Who else is coming?" I asked.

"I don't know for sure," Charles said, "but I think Tommie, Warren, and Jerry will be here."

Jerry Laird was the son of the owner of the Ritz. Bryce lived in Gordy. Charles lived in Tempie. All the others lived in town. I wondered why none of the girls in the class were coming. Their parents probably didn't like the idea of them being out at night with a bunch of boys.

Several Negroes came up to the ticket window while we stood there waiting. They bought their tickets and walked around to the side of the building. The Negroes had to sit in the balcony. They had a separate entrance off the alleyway and a separate concessions counter. After a few more minutes, the rest of the boys arrived. Mr. Tyler drove by in his 1942 Chrysler sedan and honked. It was one of the last cars built before the country geared up for the war. He parked just up the street in front of the Chamber of Commerce. It was located in an old house next to the post office. It was almost time for the show to start. We bought our tickets and hurried inside, stopping just long enough to buy some candy or popcorn. After the hamburger and ticket, I had enough left for a box of popcorn and a Coke. Mr. Tyler led us down the second row from the back. There was no one sitting in the last row. Mr. Tyler sat in the middle with Charles on one side and Warren on the other. We were hardly seated before the lights dimmed.

The previews for the coming week were *Captain of Castille* and *Life with Father*. A double feature was announced for Saturday. Two westerns. One with Roy Rogers and the other with Lash LaRue. I didn't know if I'd be able to come back tomorrow. I had already spent fifty cents today. I really liked Lash LaRue. He wore all black and carried a bullwhip. The bad guys always got a taste of that whip before the movie was over. His sidekick was Fuzzy Q. St. John. Fuzzy made a personal appearance at the Ritz last summer.

The newsreel came on. It showed a terrible explosion at an oil refinery in Texas City, Texas. Several hundred people were killed and hundreds more hurt. Babe Ruth was speaking at Yankee Stadium following his throat operation. Some man named John L. Lewis with real bushy eyebrows was talking about a coalminer's strike.

I hadn't been to very many serious movies like this one. It started out with Gregory Peck working as a reporter for some magazine. His boss wanted him to write a hard-hitting series about discrimination against the Jews. Gregory Peck's character didn't think the same old stories would work, so he pretended to be Jewish to find out how he would be treated. Boy, did he find out! He wasn't allowed into certain hotels or restaurants. He couldn't go to certain country clubs or swim in certain pools. His girlfriend's family shunned him when they found out he was "Jewish." The movie uncovered the racism that was lying just beneath the surface of polite society. Racism that was covered up by the unwritten *gentleman's agreement.*

When we came out of the show, there was a glow in the sky to the west. We heard sirens and horns blaring in the distance.

"I wonder what that's all about," Mr. Tyler said. "Come on boys. Let's walk up to the corner and see."

The police had roped off Kelly street between the courthouse and the telephone office. They wouldn't let us pass. We could see flames shooting through the roof of the jailhouse at the corner of Kelly and Washington Streets. Firemen were lugging hoses in from hydrants all around, and the pumper truck was going for all it was worth, but the fire was out of control. They finally backed off and just tried to save the other buildings around the jail.

"I wonder what happened to the prisoners," Bryce said. "I hope they got them out." A policeman on the other side of the barricade answered Bryce.

"They got'em all out," he said, "but just barely. The fire started in the Parks Body Shop behind the jail. They sounded the alarm real fast, but with all the wood and sawdust in that building, it went up like kindling. Somebody said one of the workers on the night shift had pulled a metal strap out of the forge and was moving it over to the bending machine when he dropped it into a pile of shavings. Place went up like a firecracker after that."

"What are they gonna do with the prisoners?" I asked.

"Heard one of the deputies say they were taking them out to the County Farm until they could figure out what to do with them."

The County Farm was where they kept all the prisoners that weren't sent to state prisons. Mostly they were in jail for a few years for minor offenses and not considered a big threat to the community. They were also a cheap and convenient labor force for maintaining the county roadways. The County Farm was located half way between Shiloh and Antioch. Several families that attended Antioch Missionary Baptist Church lived there. The men worked as guards or drove the road grading machines.

"Come on boys," Mr. Tyler said. "I'd better get you home before your parents start worrying."

Bryce's daddy was outside the Ritz waiting for him. Jerry and Tommie lived close enough to walk home.

"Warren I'll drop you off on the way out to Antioch to take Derek. Then I'll loop back and take Charles home."

When we rode past, the crowds were already beginning to thin out around the fire scene. A couple of the fire trucks were rolling back toward the firehouse. Several of the remaining firemen were coiling up the tangle of hoses while another crew tamped down the last few embers.

The '42 Chrysler headed north on Antioch Street. Mr. Tyler stubbed out his cigar and put it in the ashtray. When we reached the Cone house, I could see there was a light in the upstairs apartment. Miss Daniel must still be up. Probably grading the test she gave us this morning. The pavement ended a couple of blocks from there right after we passed Dr. Sumner's house. The red dirt road rattled our teeth. It felt like we were riding over one of Minnie's washboards.

"I wonder if the new inmates at the County Farm will be put to work soon to smooth out these bumpy roads," I said.

"I don't think so," Mr. Tyler said. "I don't think those fellows have been convicted of any crimes yet. They'll have to find some other place to keep them until a new jail can be built."

I wondered where that might be. We got back to my house about ten thirty. There was a light on in the old store when we drove by. It was unusual for Red to be up so late. There were no lights on at home, and I could hear my daddy snoring in the front bedroom. I was tired and went right to bed.

Bryce was standing on the front steps of the school when I arrived on Monday.

"What time did you get home Friday night?" he asked.

"Oh, about ten thirty I think. Why?"

"Charles' mama called my mama Saturday morning. She said Charles didn't get home until after midnight. She was up waiting for him, and she was worried to death. She said she had called the Ritz and no one answered, so she called Mr. Laird at home. He told her the show let out before ten o'clock. When she asked Mr. Tyler why they were so late getting home, he said there was a big fire in town, and they'd stayed around to see what happened."

"Well," I said, "it probably takes at least a half-hour to get from Antioch to Charles' house. Could take more if you drove real slow."

"Lillith was pretty upset. This is the second time Charles has been late coming back with Mr. Tyler. I don't think she's gonna let him go on any more trips with him."

When I got home that evening, there was a car parked in our yard. I recognized it. It belonged to Marvin Arnold. He was married to my half-sister Esther. Her mother died when she was born. That was before Daddy married Mama. It seemed funny that his car was here on a Monday. The Arnolds rented a farm near Sasser, a little town in Terrell County on the way to Dawson. Mama was sitting in the front room with Marvin.

"I sure do appreciate you doing this Miss Julia. I don't know how long she's gonna be down, but the doctor says she's gonna have twins, and she's plumb wore out. I'll try to get back on Sunday to pick them up."

Marvin left their two youngest children at our house for the rest of the week. The two oldest were staying with a cousin that lived nearby in Sasser.

After Marvin left, David Arnold and me walked up to see Red. A strong smell of tobacco filled the old building. Daddy stored tobacco there after we took it out of the barn to let it take on moisture.

"Now who's this young man, Derek?" Red asked.

"This is David Arnold. He's my nephew. My half- sister Esther's boy. He's staying here while his mama's having a baby."

"Derek says you've got a little dog," David said.

"I sho do," Red said. "He's around here somewhere." He whistled for Pee Wee. I looked toward the bark, and I could see a nose peeking out from between two sheets of tobacco. That was his favorite hiding place.

"Come on over here, Pee Wee. I've got somebody I want you to meet." Pee Wee ran up to Red wagging his stump of a tail.

"Pee Wee, this is Mr. David Arnold. He's Derek's nephew. Now, ain't that something. David's about as old as Derek is."

David reached down to scratch Pee Wee between the ears. Pee Wee loved to have his head scratched. He rolled over on the floor and begged for more.

"You boys see what's going on over at Mr. Powell's place?" Red asked.

"No. What do you mean, Red?"

"They's two trucks from the County Farm over there. It looks like they's working on the old jailhouse."

Before the county seat moved the jail was located near the old courthouse. The Powells bought the property and built their house next to it. They used the old building to store hay and fertilizer.

"Come on, David," I said. "Let's see what that's all about. You want to go over Red?"

"Naw. I got to go tend to the livestock. You boys go on ahead. You can fill me in later."

Cousin Lester's oldest son, Graham, was the warden at the County Farm. He was leaning against one of the trucks when we got there.

"Hey, Derek," Graham said. "Who's this young man?"

"This is David, Graham. He's Esther's boy. He's staying with us while she has a baby."

"Hey there, David. I know your daddy, Marvin. We used to go double-dating together. What are you boys up to?"

"We heard this racket over here, and we were just wondering what's going on."

"I'm sure you boys know about the jail in town burning down. The county commissioners decided to fix up the old jail out here until they can build a new one. It was originally built out of brick and plaster. It's still in pretty good shape. The slate roof is fine. The bars on the windows are still strong enough to hold in the prisoners, so they felt this was the cheapest way to go. Especially since the county work gang can do the repairs. We have to get a phone installed and some electricity run in, but that won't take long. We're supposed to have it ready to go by the end of next week."

We wandered back to the house. I was thinking it was going to be a little strange having prisoners living just a few hundred feet away from us.

Chapter 8

Marvin Arnold came back on Sunday morning. The two older children and a friend of theirs came with them. His name was Gobbler Thompson. I don't think Gobbler was his real name, but that's what everybody called him.

"Esther's doing a lot better," Marvin said. "The doctor thinks she'll be able to go full term now. It was nip and tuck there for a while." There was a sudden bright flash of lightning followed immediately by a deafening clap of thunder.

"That was close," Daddy said. "Sounds like you'd better stay for dinner. Doesn't look like this storm's gonna blow over anytime soon."

"I believe you're right, Mr. Hiram," Marvin said.

All the kids piled out of the car and ran into the house. We went into the back bedroom where we played games while the grownups talked up front. A few minutes later, Mama walked past the door on the way to the kitchen to finish up dinner.

"Now you children behave yourself. Don't go breaking anything." I don't think she'd counted on four more mouths to feed, but she was used to last minute company, what with the sawmill and all.

We finished dinner around one o'clock. Daddy wanted to drive Marvin over to the Blizzard place to show him the new tobacco. He was trying out a new type of hybrid tobacco seed that was recommended by Mr. Ladson in Tifton. We rented the Blizzard place that was next to our property on the road to Red Rock, just past the cemetery. Sharecroppers lived in an old shack there. The Smith's had a boy about my age, Jack, and twin girls about eleven. They sharecropped the fifty acres with Daddy.

The rain had stopped, and the boys all headed down to the creek below our house to see if it was running over the road. There was a culvert at the bottom of the hill. It drained water from the cypress swamp on the north side of the road. That property belonged to our neighbors, the Sikes. Gene Williams was old Mrs. Sikes' grandson. After a rain like this, it could get to running real fast.

"Boy, look at that water gushing out of the pipe," Carl Arnold said. "It must be going a hundred miles an hour through there."

I picked up a pine knot and threw it into the whirlpool on the swamp side. We ran over to the other side of the road. A few seconds later that knot popped up and took off downstream.

"I dare you to go through that pipe," Gobbler said. Carl didn't hesitate for a second. He was a daredevil anyway. He shucked off his clothes down to his shorts and jumped in the water. He stood there for a few seconds then grabbed his nose and went under. We could see his feet kick before he disappeared into the muddy water. We ran to the other side.

"There he is," David shouted with a look of great relief. Carl climbed out shivering and put his clothes back on.

"Okay, who's next?"

We all looked at each other. We were scared of the water but more afraid of being called chicken.

"I'll do it," David said.

He didn't seem all that sure of himself, but he stripped off and jumped in. A minute later, he popped out the other end. He took a second to catch his breath. Gobbler and me stared at each other. I was about to volunteer to go next when Gobbler spoke up.

"It's my turn," he said. "This ain't nothing compared to swimming in the Kinchafoonee when it's running fast."

Our backs were to the swamp. We didn't see the big stump spinning in the whirlpool before it was sucked under. Gobbler jumped into the creek, took one last look around, and dove in headfirst. We waited for his head to surface on the other side of the road. Thirty seconds went by and there was no Gobbler. We began to panic.

"Derek, run up to the house and get help," Carl said. "Me and David'll try to get him out."

I ran as fast as I could. I started yelling as I hit the front steps. Mama ran out the door with the girls.

"Mama, Gobblers caught in the culvert. He didn't come out."

"Run get Red," she said. She ran toward the barn with the two girls in tow. She was coming out of the barn with a rope as Red and I ran past. Red grabbed the rope, and we ran down that hill as fast as we could go. When we got back to the creek, David was holding Carl by the ankles, and he was trying to reach Gobbler.

"Here," Red said to me. "You and Carl hang onto this rope. I'm going in. When I yank on it, you pull me out."

Red tied the rope around his legs and went head first into the water. The rope paid out for about fifteen feet and then stopped. A few seconds passed before Red tugged on the rope. Both boys started pulling with all their might. First Red's legs appeared, and then his head popped up. He was gasping for air. He had Gobbler by the legs. Gobbler was blue. He wasn't breathing. Red pulled him up on the roadway and turned him on his back. He started pushing on Gobbler's chest. Brown water spurted out of his mouth. Red kept at it for five minutes or so before he turned to Carl.

"I'm done tuckered out. You boys take over."

Carl pumped on Gobbler for what seemed forever. He didn't respond. About that time, Daddy and Marvin came back by from the Blizzard farm. They jumped out of the car.

"What happened?" Daddy asked, looking down at the still blue form of Gobbler Thompson.

"Gobbler tried to swim through the culvert," Carl said. "He got caught on something. He ain't breathing."

"Quick, put him in the car," Marvin said. "We'll take him down to the hospital emergency room."

The car sped off slinging mud on those of us left behind. We were standing there in the middle of the road muddy, cold, and bewildered. Some of us were staring at death for the first time in our lives.

"All of you come on back to the house," Mama ordered, "and get out of those wet clothes before you die of pneumonia. Red, I'll put a tub of hot water in the smokehouse in case you'd like to get warm and clean up."

"Thank you, Miss Julia, I'd 'preciate that. I'm sorry I couldn't save the boy."

"Twasn't your fault Red. They knew better than to try a fool stunt like that. They'll answer to their fathers when they get back. I just hope the doctors can revive Gobbler."

About an hour later, Daddy and Marvin came back from town. Gobbler was not with them. The doctor on duty pronounced Gobbler dead at the hospital. Accidental drowning the official papers said. Marvin said the funeral home had already taken his body away.

Mama and Daddy followed Marvin back to Sasser. They felt responsible and wanted to be there to offer comfort to Gobbler's folks. The drive took an hour. David told me later that Gobbler's mother fainted and they had to carry her into the house. Mr. Thompson just walked away toward the barn with his head in his hands. Daddy went for a doctor in Dawson. It was a sad day all around. Daddy and Mama went back that Saturday for the funeral. I didn't go. Our folks were not too happy with any of us for what happened that day.

Chapter 9

The regional meet was coming up in three weeks. I had a hard time concentrating on getting ready for it. I had never been so close to death before. It really tore me up, seeing someone die before my very eyes. One minute we were laughing and playing in the road, and the next minute Gobbler was dead. It didn't make much sense to me. I had been taught in Sunday school that God was good, and that we were like his sheep, and that he would take care of us. The Sunday before, my teacher had read to us the bible passage about how the shepherd had left the ninety-and-nine to go and look for the one lost sheep. Wasn't Gobbler a lost sheep too? Why did God let him die? Why was God letting bad things happen to good people? I didn't have any answers, and no one else could explain it to me. At least, not in any way that I could understand. "It's God's will," Brother Jordan said in his sermon the following week. "We'll all understand it better in the great by-and-by." That wasn't a good enough answer for me.

I really believed in God and Jesus. I joined the church with Anza and two of the Ford girls when I was ten. I tried to attend all the services at the church even though my parents didn't go there. I took part in as many of the church activities as I possibly could. I always went out each year to get the church Christmas tree. I sang in the choir. I helped the smaller kids at vacation bible school.

I tried to be a good Christian. I cut and hauled firewood for Mr. and Mrs. Clark. Mr. Clark was born with no legs, and he had a deformed body.

Mrs. Clark pulled him around in an old Red Flyer wagon. She had been taking care of Mr. Clark even before his parents died. They got married shortly after that. She said it was the respectable thing to do, seeing as how they were living together. It seemed like such a huge sacrifice on her part, but she always had a smile on her face. If she could be so good, why couldn't God. I wondered why Mr. Clark had to be born like that in the first place.

We were a small church. The weekly attendance at Sunday school was probably no more than forty. Not many more came for the sermon. I felt bad when Brother Jordan would issue the invitation, and no one came down. He would stand there through all four verses of "Softly and Tenderly" or "Bringing in the Sheaves," pleading for the sinners to come home. Most Sundays no one came. Many times I wanted to answer the call again just to make him feel better. Slowly the numbness faded. Everyone kept saying that life had to go on. I guess they were right.

That next week, Daddy bought two new coonhounds. He said I could have one of them if I'd like. I had never wanted another dog since Spot got run over. Not until I had to look after Pee Wee, while Red went back to Cairo for his mother's funeral. I picked the smaller one. She was black and white with a little tan patch on her face. The small black and white specks along her back and stomach mingled together and looked blue from a distance. She was a Blue Tick. She looked like what I thought Bugle Ann would have looked like, so I named her Bugle Ann. I didn't think Mr. Kantor would mind.

"Derek, I'm going to take the new dogs out for a run tomorrow night. Want to come along?"

"Yes sir! I'd like that."

I was looking for something to take my mind off what happened last week. A romp through the woods at night listening to the dogs baying after a coon seemed like the perfect tonic. I believe Daddy felt that way, too.

"You want to ask any of your cousins to go?"

"Yes sir. Maybe Bobby and Bryce. If their folks will let them. It's a school night."

"Well, you call them up, and if it's all right with their folks, ask them to join us. Tell them we'll have you boys back and into bed by midnight. Shouldn't interfere with your schoolin' any. Red's gonna run the dogs. Cousin Marion and Cousin Sim are going."

Marion and Sim were Uncle Tommie's boys and Cousin Lester's brothers. Since they were my first cousins, they were a good deal older than me. Marion sharecropped with Daddy. Sim farmed part time and did carpentry work part time. He had a humpback and walked with a limp. I think he fell off a mule once and hurt his back. It never healed right.

Bobby and Bryce rode home with me on the school bus the next day. They were excited to be going on a coon hunt. Neither one had ever been on one. Mama fixed us an extra special supper of fried chicken and sweet potatoes. She packed some of the leftover chicken in syrup buckets for us to take with us. We could hardly wait for dark.

The other men arrived about eight thirty, and Daddy loaded the dogs into the kennels on the back of our truck. Him and Red climbed in while the rest of us piled into Cousin Sim's old Ford. Daddy took off toward Red Rock. We were going to hunt on the Apperson plantation. The plantation covered over five thousand acres in the western part of the county not far south of Mercer's Mill. Over half of the land was woods and swamp, and it was stocked with all sorts of game. Mr. Apperson went on big hunting trips out west and to Africa. I heard that he had a lot of animal heads hanging on the walls in his house. He let us hunt on his property in exchange for some of the work Daddy did for him.

The narrow road from the highway into the woods petered out and became a winding, rutted, trail with weeds growing down the middle. I could hear them slapping at the floorboards. It ended at a log gate. Beyond the gate there was just a walking path through the fenced off game preserve.

Red opened the gate so he could drive the dogs through. Cousin Sim parked his car outside. By the time we caught up with the truck, Red was opening the cages so the dogs could get out. We had six coonhounds now that Bugle Ann and Sparky had joined the pack. They were moaning, and baying, and they were anxious to get started. The animal smells in those

woods must have been overwhelming to their keen noses. Red handed a
leash to all three boys and the two cousins. He kept the one for Biscuit.
Biscuit was the only Red Bone hound we had. He stood twenty-seven
inches tall at the shoulders and weighed sixty-five pounds. He was fast and
lean and could clear a five-foot fence. He had the best nose in the county.
The rest of the pack was made up of Blue Tick hounds. In addition to Bugle
Ann and Sparky there were, Lady, Ike and Panther. We walked about a
mile into the woods until we came to the edge of the swamp.

"Let's stop here," Daddy said. "We'll build a fire while Red gets the
dogs started."

While the grownups hacked out a clearing, the boys gathered up
firewood. I found a turpentine cup full of resin on a pine tree. It was
left over from the days before Mr. Apperson bought the property, a time
when the naval stores business was booming. I pried it off the tree with my
hunting knife and took it back to the clearing.

"That'll start a good fire, Derek," Cousin Sim said.

He placed the cup on the ground, picked up a fat lighter stick, and
flipped open his Zippo. Two rolls of the wheel and the lighter flared in the
dark. He lit the stick and dropped it into the resin. Within a few seconds,
the thick pitch caught and flared up. We piled more limbs and branches
on top and soon had a small bonfire going.

We could hear the sounds off to the north as Red looked for a coon
scent trail. Each dog had a distinctive voice. Each bark was as recognizable
as that of any human being. Biscuit's deep bass howl came first. He had
found the fresh track of a coon. Then Ike, Panther, and Lady chimed in.
Their baying harmonized with Biscuit's and sounded like music on the
night air. Finally, two new voices were heard. First Sparky, in a high-
pitched wail and then the soft sweet notes of Bugle Ann.

"There she is," I said. "Isn't she beautiful? I've never heard a mouth
like that." A chill ran up my spine as she continued to bugle into the
clear night air. I understood then what Mr. Kantor was trying to express
on those dull, gray, typewritten, pages. No one could ever fully capture
such beauty in mere words. I leaned back against a tree and closed my
eyes. The same God that had let Gobbler die on that muddy road had

also created that beautiful voice. How could I ever come to terms with that?

The trail of sound surged through the woods, first to the right of us, then circling back toward the south. That's when we heard the unmistakable keening in Biscuit's voice that said he had run the coon to ground. The six-voiced chorus got louder and louder as the others joined Biscuit at the base of the cypress tree where the coon had taken refuge. The dogs were in a frenzy. They were leaping up the trunk as far as they could hoping to gain footing to go after their prey.

"Let's go, boys," Daddy said. "Sounds like they've treed 'im. Bobby, throw a few more sticks on that fire to hold it until we get back."

The entire hunting party stormed off through the dark woods toward the sound of the dogs. Daddy was in the lead with his big, five-celled, flashlight. Sim and Marion trailed behind, each carrying a rifle. We boys brought up the rear. The woods were dense. Wild vines and briars clawed at our heavy clothes. A branch slapped me in the face. I tasted blood. There was a cut on my upper lip, but I kept going. We came out of the woods into a clearing on the edge of a small pond. The dogs were up to their bellies in the water when we got there. They were rearing up on the cypress tree. Red sat on his haunches rolling a cigarette.

"Howdy, Boss. It looks like we treed a fat one. I caught sight of him just as he jumped for the tree. I 'spect he might weigh ten to fifteen pounds. Biscuit got close enough for that old coon to swipe him across the nose. I don't know if you could hear the yelp he let out. It sure took him by surprise though."

"How'd the new dogs do?" Daddy asked.

"Sparky's gonna make a fine coon hound. He was right behind Biscuit when they picked up the scent, and he began bugling right away. Biscuit had to put him in his place a time or two, but that dog's gonna make a good leader one day."

"What about Bugle Ann?" I asked. "How was she?"

"She gone need a few more hunts to get it down right. But she done pretty good. She still young. The pack didn't leave her far behind though. When we got him treed, she jumped right into the pond with the rest of 'em and started trying to get up that tree. Yassuh. She gone be all right."

Red was quiet for a minute. He finished licking the cigarette and twisted the end. He reached for a match. The match flared and the bright end of the cigarette glowed as he inhaled. He blew out a cloud of smoke. There was a faraway look in his eye.

"I ain't never heard a voice like she got. I been huntin' coon nigh onto thirty year, and I never heard nothing as sweet as her before. I think she may win you a prize someday, boy."

For a few minutes we didn't need flashlights. The glow on my face was bright enough to light up the night.

That cypress was probably eighty feet tall. The coon had retreated as far as it could go toward the top. Daddy's flashlight searched back and forth through the branches. The beam came to rest on a small masked face, its frantic eyes reflecting the light back to earth. Cousin Marion raised his rifle and squeezed off a round. The animal swung by one paw and then dropped, bouncing off the branches as it fell down the length of the tree. There was a loud plop as the coon hit the water. The dogs thrashed through the tannin colored pond toward it. Red waded out into the pond to pull them off and grab the coon before they tore it to bits. He held it high above his head while fending the dogs off with his free hand.

"Derek. You boys get some leashes on these dogs," he said.

We jumped in, wrestled the leaping dogs away from Red, and got the leashes on them. We yanked on them until the dogs finally began to quiet down.

"He's a fat one all right, Mr. Hiram. He'll make some mighty good eatin' with some sweet taters."

Red waded over and dropped the dead coon on the bank. He got out his knife to bleed the animal and remove the musk glands from the legs so the meat wouldn't be tainted. He threw the carcass into a croaker sack and handed it to Bryce.

"Here boy, take this back to the fire."

"You gonna go after another coon now, Red?" I asked.

"I reckon so," Red said. "I don't think we oughta come way out here for just one. Might as well get enough to feed some of the folks back in Antioch."

"Can I stay out here with Red, Daddy? I want to see how Bugle Ann looks when she's on the scent."

"I guess so," he said. "Bobby, do you and Bryce want to stay?"

Both nodded yes. The men took the sack with the coon and headed back toward the fire while Red headed out with the dogs in search of a fresh scent. Bryce, Bobby and me tagged along behind. I figured that the men might have brought along some whiskey for medicinal purposes. Our being gone gave them a chance to test its effectiveness in the case of a snake bite or some other such emergency.

We'd gone no more than a couple of hundred yards when Panther struck another scent. We heard his cry. His throaty growl turned into a high-pitched wail as the other dogs gave chase. Biscuit surged to the front of the pack and took the lead. Sparky nosed out Ike and Lady for third place in line. Bugle Ann brought up the rear. Her voice rose above the chorus like a solo in a church choir—clear, distinct, thrilling.

We could see the beam from Red's light as he took up the chase. He cut across the neck of a pond. We could hear him splashing through the water. As we got closer, I veered off to the right to avoid the deeper water. It was too dark to see the crude wooden sign tacked to a cypress, "Danger – Quicksand Ahead." I sank to my knees in the water and I couldn't pull my foot out. I struggled to move my other leg, and it sank further. I began to panic.

"Bobby! Bryce! Help! I'm stuck!" I remembered something Bill told me once when we passed a quicksand bog out fishing.

"If you ever get caught in quicksand, don't struggle. Try to lay back, and create as much body surface as possible."

I stopped trying to move my legs. I lay back on the surface of the bog. I could hear the boys crashing back through the woods toward me.

"Stay back! If you get too close you'll get caught too. Call Red. He'll know what to do."

"I'll go for Red," Bryce said. "See if you can get something to reach him, Bobby."

Bobby found a clump of elders and broke off a long limb. He spread himself as far as he could without getting into the sand and reached it out to me. I grabbed the end and tried to pull myself out. It was no use. The more I pulled the deeper I sank.

""Derek," Bobby said. "Run the stick under your arms, so it'll hold you up a little bit. I'll go get some more."

He ran off. I could hear him chopping more limbs. The cold was seeping into my bones. My teeth started to chatter. I saw a light running through the trees. Red was back.

"You stay still, boy. The more you move the deeper you'll sink."

Red had a length of plow line. It was what he used to tie up the dogs at the end of the hunt to keep them from straying off. He tied a loop in the end of the rope.

"Derek, I'm gonna throw this rope to you. Put the loop over your head and under your arms."

It took all my energy to lift my arms. I finally caught the rope, and after a struggle I was able to get it under my arms. By the time I finished, I was up to my chest in the sucking sand.

"All right, boys. We're gonna have to pull like all git out to break him free. It's gone feel like he weighs a ton. The secret's to jest keep a steady pressure. Derek, you lay back as much as you can, and don't move. This rope's gonna cut into your chest, but they ain't nothing we can do 'bout that. You boys ready? Jest start pulling, slow and easy."

The rope tightened. I could feel it cutting into my skin. At first, nothing happened. Then I could feel movement. Slowly my upper body began to rise. The sucking noise told me that the wet sand was breaking loose. I started to slide across the surface until my feet broke free. In a few minutes, I felt the solid ground under me. I tried to stand up, but my knees buckled under me. My emotions overcame me. I started to cry.

"It's all right, boy. Crying don't mean you are a sissy or nothing. It's the good Lord's way of helping us to handle things in life. Come on. Let's git you back to the fire and git you outten them wet clothes. You boys head back with Derek while I round up the dogs."

Red disappeared into the darkness toward the bell-like voice of Bugle

Ann while we went back to the camp. Cousin Sim was wiping his mouth on his sleeve and putting the flask away when we edged into the light.

"What happened to you, Derek?" Daddy asked. "How'd you get so wet and dirty? Did you fall in the pond?"

"No sir. I ran into a patch of quicksand. I almost died. Bryce and Bobby kept my head above the water until Red could get there with his rope. They were able to pull me out. I thought I was a goner for sure."

"Come over here by the fire," he said. "Get out of those wet clothes."

I shucked off my overalls and shirt and hung them by the fire. Daddy handed me his jacket. It came to my knees. I sat down by the fire and shivered until the warmth started to seep into me. I dozed off, waking to something wet against my leg. Bugle Ann was back. She was licking me. Everything was all right now.

"Put out that fire and let's get home," Daddy said. "We've had enough excitement for one night."

The time-honored method for coon hunters to douse a turpentine fire was to pee on it. That was a strange sight. Two grown men and three boys, standing in a circle, peeing into a cup together. But it did put the fire out.

We got back home at midnight. When Mama heard what had happened, she grabbed me in a bear hug. I'd never seen her so upset. She tried not to show favoritism, but I was her last child. Most of her brood had left the nest, and she was trying to hang on to me as long as she could.

Mama filled a washtub with hot water, and she made me sit in it for a long time. The warm water felt good. By the time I got out and dried off, Bobby and Bryce were already asleep. I crawled into bed and was asleep in seconds. Mama shook me awake at six o'clock. It was time to set the fires and get ready for school.

Chapter 10

After the excitement of the last few days, I was ready for the routine of the classroom. It was not to be. It's strange how things seem to have a way of happening in threes. When I got home the next day, there was a note taped to the refrigerator. Mama knew that was the first place I'd go.

"I'm over at your Uncle Gordon's house. He took sick last night, and the doctor is real worried. He's running a high fever. Come on over if you want to. I'll probably be here all night with your Aunt Annie."

When I got over to the Paul house, Uncle Gordon had taken a turn for the worse. Mama called Dr. Sumner to come right away. They had moved a bed into the front room for him where there was more light. Aunt Annie was bathing Uncle Gordon's face with cold water. The sweat just kept pouring off him. He was a small man in the first place and very thin. Now he looked more gaunt than ever. He opened his eyes when I touched his hand.

"Hey, Derek," he said. "It sure is good to see you. Your ma was telling me about your little coon hunting scare. I'm sure glad you're all right." Talking weakened him. He closed his eyes again. His hand was on fire.

"Uncle Gordon, I'm praying for you," I said. I didn't know what else to say. He was the favorite of all my relatives. I didn't want him to die.

"You'd best leave him alone for now, Derek," Mama said. "He's mighty weak. He needs to rest."

I left the room as Aunt Annie came back in. She was crying. She sat down by the bed and laid her head on Uncle Gordon's hand. She stroked his face.

"Don't leave me, Gordon. I don't know what I'll do without you."

The last words I ever heard him say were, "Don't you worry Annie. The good Lord will look after you, and I'll be waiting for you on the other side."

He closed his eyes again. The air kind of went out of him. Death had come calling on me for the second time in three weeks. It seemed like my world was turning upside down. Our community, our church, and the whole county had lost one of its most respected and beloved citizens.

"I'm sorry, Annie, but there's nothing more to be done," Dr. Sumner said. "In his weakened condition, the fever was just too much for him." He took her hand and put his arm around her. "Do you want me to call Alston?"

Alston Banks owned Shiloh's only funeral home. If you died in Wyatt Count, chances were the last place you'd ever visit would be his funeral parlor.

Through choked back tears Aunt Annie said yes, she'd appreciate it if he'd take care of it for her. Mama took her back to the parlor where there was a daybed and got her to lie down. Then Mama got on the phone to all the children to let them know. She had to call the Red Cross to get word to Truett. He was a sailor on a navy ship, and no one knew how to get hold of him.

They scheduled the funeral for Sunday at the Antioch Baptist Church. When my family arrived for the services we were escorted down front to the pews reserved for relatives. Family members took up almost half the seating in the small church. Truett got in at two o'clock that morning. He'd caught a hop on a navy transport plane out of San Diego. They dropped him off at Turner Field in Albany. Friends and local officials filled the rest of the pews. The crowd overflowed into the churchyard, and the windows were thrown open so those outside could hear.

Reverend Jordan was nearly overcome as he told of all the wonderful things Uncle Gordon had done for the community and all he had achieved in life despite his humble beginnings. When the choir finished singing "In the Sweet Bye and Bye" everyone in earshot was weeping. It took half an hour to transfer all the floral offerings to the cemetery and for the funeral procession to wend its way past our house and up the hill to the cemetery. Two of my brothers and several other nephews acted as pallbearers.

When the pastor had finished his graveside message and said a prayer, a group of Negroes stepped from behind nearby gravestones. They lined up behind Uncle Gordon's casket and began singing all his favorite hymns and spirituals. They were songs he had heard over the years from his front porch across the woods from their little church: "Swing Low Sweet Chariot", "Go down Moses", and "There is a Balm in Gilead." Uncle Gordon was as beloved in the Negro community as he was in the white. No one could count the many kindnesses he had done for them, most of which went unspoken. Janey, who had worked for the Paul's for years, was overcome with grief and had to be helped from the cemetery. Red came over and put his hand on my shoulder.

"He was a good man, Derek. He sho helped me out of a mess or two." It was one of the saddest days of my life.

Life slowly returned to normal. School, work, and spelling practice filled my days. Every once in a while something would remind me of Uncle Gordon: seeing his name on a Sunday school bulletin, smelling the blossoms on his favorite fruit trees as the bus passed his house, hearing Aunt Annie on the phone with Mama. Eventually, as with Gobbler, life overcame death, and the days filled up with other things. I guess God does that to help us dull the pain. Otherwise, it would be hard to go on living.

When I went back to my homeroom the next morning, Miss Daniel was waiting for me with an armload of papers. More study words. I was becoming a walking vocabulary; eating, sleeping and dreaming words. I didn't know there were so many words in the entire English language.

"Derek, these are the last words I'll be giving you before we go to Macon. I know time is short, but cover as many of them as you can, and I'll go over them with you on the drive up.

" Oh, by the way. I spoke with Mr. Tyler this morning. He said we would have to leave before six to make it to Macon by nine o'clock. He suggested that you might want to stay with him Sunday night. That way you won't have to get up quite so early. Do you think that will be all right with your parents? Would you like for me to call them?"

"No, Ma'am. It'll be all right. I'll have Daddy drop me off when he makes the last mail run on Sunday. What time do you think we'll get back? So I can meet him at the depot."

"I imagine we'll be back by five o'clock. The contest starts at nine and should be over by two. If you miss your ride it'll probably be all right to stay over with Mr. Tyler on Monday night as well."

"I guess that'll be okay," I said.

I was excited about the trip to Macon. I was also a little scared. The only time I had been that far away from home was once when we visited my half-brother Elton in Gadsden, Alabama.

Macon was a much bigger stage than Albany, and the competition was bound to be a lot tougher. Miss Daniel was real excited. She had never had a student get this far in the competition. It would be a feather in her cap to take one to Atlanta. I was afraid of letting her down. She had worked almost as hard as I had to prepare for the contests.

I didn't have a suit to wear. Saturday morning Daddy took me down to the Empire Mercantile Company. We found a nice tweed suit that cost seventeen dollars. Daddy said it was fine with him, but I should try to get Mr. Edwards to knock some off the price. He had to go down the street to the bank before it closed. Heck, I didn't know anything about bargaining over prices. I just wanted the suit. As soon as Daddy disappeared out the door, I told Mr. Edwards I would take it. He put it in a suit bag and charged it to my daddy's account.

Daddy bought all his farm supplies from the Empire. They stocked everything from horse collars to fertilizer. I was real proud of that suit.

"Good luck in Macon," Mr. Edwards said as I left.

"Thank you, sir." I guess I looked surprised. I didn't know he even knew about the contest.

"I read about it in the *Local*," he said, seeing my surprise. "Marian Overton wrote a nice piece about it. The whole town is rooting for you."

I threw the suit bag over my shoulder and ran up the street to the *Shiloh Local* office. It was next to the burned out ruins of the old jail. I just had to get a copy of the Thursday edition of the paper. The only other time I had ever seen my name in print was that birth notice in Uncle Gordon's vault. The one that had the story about Will Rogers getting killed in a plane crash in Alaska. I walked in and handed Marian my last nickel. The caption over the two-column story read:

"Local Student Headed to Macon Spelling Bee"

Derek Barton, having won the district event last month in Albany, is set to represent Wyatt County and the Southwest Georgia district in Macon next Monday. He will be accompanied by Miss Sara Daniel, Miss Frances Kuhn and Mr. Leonard Tyler. The entire community wishes Derek continued success on his journey to becoming the champion speller in the entire state of Georgia.

Wow! Now I certainly couldn't afford to fail. I didn't dare disappoint all the people of Wyatt County and Southwest Georgia who were pulling so hard for me. I could feel the sweat begin to pop out on my forehead. My hands were clammy.

I ran across the street to an old filling station on the corner of Kelly and Antioch, across from the burned out jail. My Uncle George, Mama's brother, had converted the empty building into a shop for his shoe repair business. Mama was there visiting. I showed her the article in the *Local*.

"Derek," she said, "I didn't know you were getting to be so famous. Don't you go getting the big head now."

My mother was not one to hand out many compliments. Both her and my father were sparing with their praise. That was just the way it was in those big southern families. It had something to do with their Irish/Scot/Welsh heritage. Once you started favoring one child the others would get their noses out of joint. I knew she loved me. At the same time, I knew not to expect much open affection from her—or my father.

She handed the paper to my aunt Carrie Mae. Like Uncle Gordon on my daddy's side of the family, she was my favorite on Mama's side.

"Derek, that's wonderful," she said. She gave me a big hug. "I sure hope you win in Macon. We haven't had a celebrity in the family since Cousin Frank came back from the First World War."

Cousin Frank was with Sergeant York when they captured all those Germans in the Argonne Forest. He's the only person I ever knew who got his own parade down Main Street.

Uncle George was standing at the big machine he used to sew, trim and polish shoes. It was another of those Rube Goldberg contraptions that spewed the sweet smell of fresh cut leather into the air. He turned off the machine and pushed his half-glasses up on his nose as he took the paper.

"Well, boy. Looks like the Grimes' smarts rubbed off on you. Your granddaddy, Bill Grimes, didn't have a lot of book learning, but he was as smart as a whip. We're all proud of you."

Mama was right. She did have to worry about me getting the big head.

Chapter 11

It turned stormy when we got home that Saturday afternoon. Ominous clouds rolled in from the west. The skies got very dark. Mama asked me to take some eggs down to my two old maid cousins, Mattie Lou and Thelma. They lived alone in the big white house that Uncle Tommy left them. It was beyond the church. They relied on their brothers and other relatives to help them, although Thelma worked part time at the Coats and Clark thread mill in Albany.

I was on the way back home when the wind really kicked in. The skies got darker and darker. All kinds of things started flying through the air: Brush, limbs, washtubs, shingles. I was scared. I ran into the Garner's back yard just as the twister hit. By the time I walked from the back door to the living room, it had torn the entire roof off the house and dropped it right where I had been walking minutes before. I guess the good Lord was looking out for me. There wasn't a scratch on me, but the Garner house was a wreck, and everything inside was getting soaked.

Anza came out of her bedroom at the back of the house. She was as white as a sheet. It took a lot to scare her, but let me tell you she was shaking and crying. We stood there in front of their old pump organ in the living room looking up through the skeleton of rafters and wondering what had just happened. Miss Lola came in with an oilcloth and threw it over the organ.

"I guess we can't save much, but I can salvage my mother's old organ," she said. She had seen lots of tragedy in her life. This was just one more hurdle to get over.

"Are you okay, Derek?" she asked. I guess she could see how the two of us were shaking. She had seen me coming in just as the tornado struck the house.

"Yes ma'am. I'm just shook up a little. That thing sounded like a freight train coming. The sky turned green and stuff started flying around. I figured I needed to head for shelter. Thank goodness your house was here. Another minute either way and I'd be flying through the air; or that roof would be on top of me. I'd better get on home. I know Mama will be calling all over to see where I am. I'll come back to help you clean up as soon as this blows over.

Red was standing under the overhang of the store looking at a big pecan tree that was lying across the lane. Daddy let me have the pecans from those two trees every year. I'd pick up fifty-to-a-hundred pounds and sell them to Newlin's seed store. The five or ten dollars I got was my biggest payday of the year. It looked like my paydays would be smaller now.

"You all right, Derek?" Red said. "I saw you come by with them eggs a while ago. Didn't know if you'd come back already."

"I'm okay. I ducked into the Garner's house. They got hit pretty bad. I'm going back to help after I let Mama know I'm okay."

"I'll go on over and give them a hand," he said.

Mama was on the phone to Thelma when I walked in the door. She looked like she had seen a ghost. She just knew I had been killed by the tornado. She grabbed me and hugged me tight. Something she didn't do every day. Like I said. I knew she loved me; she just had a hard time showing it.

"You had me worried to death, Derek. Where were you? What did you do?"

"I ran into the Garner's house. I hadn't got to the front room good when the twister hit. It took the roof clean off the house. Just dropped it right in the back yard. Never saw anything like that in my life. Nearly scared me to death. It sounded like a freight train was coming it was so loud. Everything in the house is getting soaked. I told Miss Lola I'd come back and help them clean up as soon as you knew I was all right. Red's already gone over."

"You go on back and help. I'll get Hiram to come over with some tarpaulins and sheets. Tell Lola if she wants to send some things down here to dry out to just let me know. And tell'em they're welcome to stay here tonight if they need to."

It was dark before everything was covered, moved, or dried. Anza's daddy was going to have to spend the next few days re-roofing his house. He was a master carpenter by trade. He got laid off from Turner Field after the war, so he farmed and worked odd jobs around town now.

I had a hard time getting to sleep that night. The excitement of the tornado and the damage to the Garner house had the whole neighborhood shook up. I was also thinking about the contest and spending the night with Mr. Tyler the next day. I felt a little funny about that. I didn't really know Mr. Tyler all that well. He seemed like a nice enough man. He had been very helpful in getting me ready to spell once Jimmie Earle was eliminated. The one thing I didn't like about him was that unlit cigar butt that was always dangling from his mouth. He never seemed to light it. Just chewed on it and spit out the juice. Several of my kinfolk chewed tobacco or dipped snuff. I thought it was a disgusting habit. If the taste was as foul as the smell, I didn't understand why anyone would use tobacco. My daddy smoked unfiltered Camels. I'd go to the store every night to buy him a pack. Twenty cents. I could think of a lot better uses for that money.

Sleep finally came about ten o'clock. The next sound I remember hearing was the whistle from the five o'clock train as it pulled out of the station in Shiloh. It had dropped the mail in a lockbox at the depot and then headed for Albany. It would drop Acree's mail along the way. The tracks were almost three miles south of Antioch, but in the middle of the night the piercing shriek of its whistle carried forever. It had to be the most mournful sound in the world. Every time the engineer yanked on that cord, it seemed that all the sadness and loneliness in the world just boiled up in the night. It was a world that was struggling to recover from the twin nightmares of the Depression and World War II and the hundred million souls that had perished.

The last of the cloud cover lifted before dawn, and the sun came up as bright as I had ever seen it. Daddy let me sleep in that Sunday. He built the fires and did my chores for me.

It was close to eight when I heard the pans banging in the kitchen. About once a month, on Sunday morning, Daddy would treat Mama and me to his famous steak breakfast. On Saturday he had gone by the freezer locker and gotten a package of steaks. We didn't own our own freezer. We rented a couple of drawers in Mr. Overton's big freezer locker building on West Kelly Street across from the icehouse.

Daddy would start by making biscuits and then putting on a pot of grits before he scrubbed the eyes of the stove. When the grits began gurgling, and the biscuits started rising, he would pull the steaks out of the refrigerator and slap them on the stove in a puddle of butter and garlic. It didn't take long for me to get dressed when I smelled that. Before he finished cooking, I was seated on the long bench along the wall behind the dining table. The last step was frying the eggs. I liked mine over easy. Those Sunday breakfasts are some of the most cherished memories of my childhood.

Daddy told me to clear the table and wash the dishes. He said he had to get ready for the "big meeting" at Mt. Pisgah. That was the church near Gordy that my mother's family attended. Daddy first met her there. Before they were even introduced he told a friend he was going to marry her. Another member from Providence was going to come by and pick him up at ten o'clock.

Every three months one of the churches in the association of Primitive Baptist Churches would host what they called a "big meeting." It went on for three days. This month was Mt. Pisgah's turn. There would be sermons all day before some association business would be conducted and then there would be a huge dinner spread on the tables under the trees outside.

Daddy washed up and combed his hair. Mama came out on the porch to see if he needed any help.

"Hiram, what's that white stuff on your hair?" she asked.

Daddy whipped around and looked in the mirror. All our toiletries were stored in a wooden apple box nailed to the wall. He picked up a bottle and read the label. Now my father didn't cuss a lot, but he let loose a few choice words that morning.

"I thought I was putting Wildroot on my hair. Look at this. It's white shoe polish." He spent the next fifteen minutes trying to wash the stuff out of his hair. He finished just as his ride showed up.

"Julia, tell Doc I'll be ready in a minute," he said. He scurried off to put on his shirt and tie. He called back to me.

"Derek, if I don't get back in time call Roger to meet the late train. He can drop you off at Willard's. I should be back, but you know Brother Barber. Once he starts one of his hellfire and damnation sermons, he has a hard time stopping. If I don't see you before you leave, I hope you have a good time in Macon. You make us proud, you hear."

That was as close as Hiram Jefferson Barton could come to offering praise to one of his boys. I took it as the greatest compliment I had ever had.

Four o'clock came, and Daddy wasn't back. Roger lived around the corner right behind the Powells and the jail.

"Roger, Daddy's not back from Gordy yet. He told me to call you to get the mail if he wasn't back. I need a ride into town. I'm staying with Mr. Tyler tonight, so that I don't have to get up so early in the morning to go to Macon."

"Oh yeah," he said. "I forgot all about that. I'll be by to get you in a few minutes. Get your stuff packed."

We didn't have any suitcases, so Mama put some underwear and an extra shirt in a paper bag for me.

"You be good now, Derek. Mind your manners. Here's a dollar in case you need it. I expect they'll feed you up there, but I don't know. Call me tomorrow when you get back. If you don't make it in time for the mail run Miss Daniel said you could stay an extra night with Mr. Tyler. I hope you do good in that spelling bee. Me and your daddy's real proud of you."

Wow! Twice in the same day. Compliments from both my parents. What was the world coming to. I heard the tires on Roger's pickup crunching on the gravel as he came down the lane from the store. I picked up the bag of clothes, grabbed my suit, and ran out the door.

"Bye, Mama. I'll try my best. Thank you for the money."

I climbed into the front seat with Roger and we headed into town.

My life was about to change forever.

Chapter 12

The Willard Hotel sat at the corner of North Main and Front streets. Just across Front was the Sinclair service station, owned by Henry Hall Willard. His daddy owned the hotel. You could enter the hotel from either street, but the main entrance was on Front. The desk was across the lobby from that entrance. Two seating groups of well-worn, overstuffed, furniture were placed on either side of a big fireplace, dividing the elongated room in two. There were twelve rooms in the hotel, all upstairs. The stairwell behind the desk allowed the clerk to keep track of all the comings and goings.

All eight rooms off the long hallway at the top of the stairs were located over businesses on the east side of North Main: the Bon Ton florist, the Trailways bus depot, the Pastime Billiard Parlor and the City Café. Rooms 11 and 12 at the end of the hallway smelled of the fried onions and burnt grease seeping up through the floor from the café. The tenants in Rooms 9 and 10 listened to the steady click of billiard balls late into the night. The cries of small children marked the arrivals and departures of buses below Rooms 7 and 8. The quietest rooms were 5 and 6. They were over the florist shop. Mr. Tyler lived in Room 5.

I approached the man behind the desk. I had a strange feeling in the pit of my stomach. I hoped it was just the steak and eggs from this morning and not something more worrisome.

The hotel clerk turned when he heard my footsteps clacking across the wooden floor. I recognized him as Gary, the older son of Mr. Laird who owned The Ritz. He was Jerry's brother.

"Hey, Derek. What are you doing here?"

"I'm going to Macon tomorrow with Mr. Tyler. He asked me to spend the night with him so we wouldn't have to get up so early tomorrow. We have to be in Macon by nine. We're picking up Miss Daniel and Miss Kuhn on the way out of town."

"Oh, yeah," Gary Laird said. "I read about you in the *Local*. I reckon you must be excited about all this. I'll ring Mr. Tyler and let him know you are here."

Gary sat down at a small switchboard. He pulled a plug from the tray and inserted it into the jack labeled Room 5. There was a tattered, yellow note taped above the number. It read *Leonard Tyler*. He pressed a switch on the side of the board.

"Hello. Mr. Tyler? Derek Barton is down here in the lobby. Says he's spending the night with you. Do you want me to send him up?" Gary tugged at his ear as he listened to Mr. Tyler's reply.

"Okay, then. I'll ask him to have a seat until you get down here."

"He says he was just getting ready to go out for supper. He'll be right down. Looks like you're gonna get a free meal tonight. Just take a seat over by the fire. Gimme your stuff. I'll keep it behind the desk until you get back."

"Thank you," I said. I settled into one of the big chairs. The fire felt good. There was still a chill in the spring air.

"There you are, Derek," Mr. Tyler said as he stepped off the bottom tread of the stairs. "Are you hungry? I was going to get something to eat up at the City Café."

"Why, I guess so," I said. I hadn't thought much about food since that big breakfast, but a hamburger sounded good.

We went out the North Main door. A red and white Trailways bus wheeled around the corner and pulled to the curb. Its air brakes made an awful racket. The driver got out to raise the luggage compartment doors. We could see several white people moving down the aisle and stepping from the bus. They were followed by six or eight Negroes. The whites entered the station to await their luggage. The Negroes waited outside for theirs. We hurried to get past the crowded sidewalk.

The pool hall was closed on Sundays. The local blue laws didn't allow it to open even though they only sold beer. Most of the counties in Georgia were dry. Wyatt was among them. The only hard liquor to be had was dispensed from the trunks of dilapidated old cars in back alleys. The bottles of clear white liquid had probably been filtered through the copper coils of a backwoods still just yesterday. There was an awful stink last year when a moonshiner from the Bloody Ninth sold hooch that he ran through radiator coils. The lead poisoning killed five people. One of the Smoak boys was spending the next ten years out at the County Farm. Sheriff Hudson was normally lenient when it came to enforcing the liquor laws. As long as no one got killed.

Lenora Price ran the City Café. Her sister was a teacher at McPhaul Institute. I had her in the fifth grade. The café was one of the few businesses allowed to open on Sunday, despite the blue law prohibitions. I think they exempted the café because all the church folks in town liked to have some place to go for dinner on Sunday.

Mr. Tyler slid into a well-worn booth on the back wall of the café. I scooted in across from him. The tabletop was green Formica with a chrome band around the edge. I had never eaten there. My family didn't have that kind of money. *"Teachers must make a lot of money,"* I thought, as he pulled the menus from behind the ketchup bottle and handed one to me.

"The hamburgers are good," he said. "I'm kind of partial to the roast beef myself. Lenora does wonders with a tough cut of meat. She must cook it all night to get it that tender. It's served with mashed potatoes and green beans. Great gravy. Corn bread, too. See anything you like?"

The cheapest thing on the menu was a hamburger steak, served with French fries and tomato slices on lettuce with mayonnaise. It was fifty cents. That was more money than I saw most weeks unless there was work at the mill.

"I think I'll just have the hamburger steak," I said.

"Okay. What'll you have to drink?"

"Iced tea, please."

Mr. Tyler motioned to the waitress. She was leaning on the counter next to the cash register reading a magazine. Her upswept hairdo brushed the flypaper hanging over the counter as she stood up.

"Mary, this is Derek Barton. He's one of my students. You may have seen the story in the paper. We're going up to Macon tomorrow for the regional spelling bee. He's already won here and in Albany. We're all really proud of him."

"Naw, sir," she said. "I don't read the paper much. I do recollect Miss Lenora saying something about somebody winning some contest. I reckon it must have been you Derek."

"Well, you're going to hear a lot more about this young man," Mr. Tyler said. "He's going to put this little old town on the map. Nobody south of Macon has ever won the state spelling bee. I believe Derek's going to do that for us."

My face took on the shade of the ketchup bottle. All this praise was getting to be too much. I hadn't really done anything special, and now the whole town was expecting me to pull off a miracle. I began to think I should have said no to Miss Daniel.

"I'll have the roast beef with extra gravy on the potatoes. And I'll have iced tea to drink," Mr. Tyler said. "My young friend here will have the hamburger steak with French fries. Also, with iced tea."

Mary waddled toward the kitchen with our order. As she passed through the swinging doors they bounced off her broad backside. Her bosom spilled over the top of her white, gravy stained uniform. Little mounds of flesh oozed out between the overstressed buttons down the front. *"Mrs. Price must pay half of Mary's wages in mashed potatoes and gravy"*, I thought. The kitchen doors swung open again. Mary came back over to our booth.

"The cook wants to know how you want that steak done," she said, her pencil poised over the little green order pad. I had no idea what she was talking about. Mr. Tyler saw my confusion and stepped in.

"Do you like your meat well done, medium or rare?" he said.

"Oh, well done please." I didn't know you cooked meat any other way. The thought of serving bloody meat made my stomach flip. Mary took the order back to the kitchen and then resumed her station by the cash register. She picked up the magazine she had been reading when we came in. I could see the title, *Modern Romance*.

"Are you excited about tomorrow, Derek?" Mr. Tyler asked.

"Yes sir. But I'm scared too. I didn't know how much everyone was counting on me winning. When I was in The Empire, Mr. Edwards said there was a story in the *Local* about our trip to Macon. I bought a copy to show my folks. You know, that's a lot of pressure. I don't know if I'm up to it."

"Sure you are. You've just got a little stage fright. Besides, if you don't win it won't be the end of the world. You've already gone further than any other student from Shiloh. You can be proud of that. Any success from here is just icing on the cake. So don't worry about it. Just relax. Go out there, and give it your best. That's all anyone can ask of you."

"Thank you, Mr. Tyler. That means a lot coming from you."

Mary brought out our supper. The meat was good. The French fries were better. I doused them with ketchup and finished every one. I didn't realize how hungry I was. Mr. Tyler picked at his roast beef and potatoes. He ate only about half of his plate. His mind appeared to wander. Maybe he was thinking about tomorrow.

"Mary, will you bring our ticket please?" he said.

Mary heaved herself up from the barstool. She tossed the magazine on the counter and picked up the order pad. The fly strip resumed its swinging.

"You don't want no dessert tonight, Mr. Tyler? Got some good banana puddin' back there."

"None for me thank you. How about you, Derek? You got any room left?"

"No sir. That'll be fine," I said, even though the pudding sounded real good.

"Okay. Here's your ticket," Mary said as she moved back to the lunch counter.

Mr. Tyler pulled a quarter from his pocket and left it on the table. I didn't know what that was for. He walked over to the cash register and handed Mary two dollars. She handed him his change.

"Good night, Mary. I'll see you next week."

We walked out into the darkening night. A line of women was forming at the Ritz ticket window for that evening's showing of *Mom and Dad*. The theater had advertised the movie for weeks. Due to the nature of the movie they held separate screenings for men and women. There was an actual live birth on screen, and a doctor gave a lecture on sex and sex education. No one under eighteen was admitted. I wasn't sure I wanted to see a baby being born anyway.

"Have you seen that movie, Mr. Tyler?" I asked.

"No, and I don't plan to either. It's a big waste of time. A publicity stunt to separate the local yokels from their money. If we need more sex education, we ought to be teaching it in school. Most of these dumb hicks don't have a clue."

His hateful comments surprised me. I never knew he felt that way about the folks in Shiloh. We walked back to the hotel in silence. Mr. Tyler picked up his key at the desk. I retrieved my clothes.

"Good night, Gary. Please ask the night clerk to give me a wake-up call at five o'clock."

"Sure thing, Mr. Tyler. You and Derek have a good night, and good luck in Macon."

"Thanks, Gary."

The last time I had been upstairs at the Willard, I was ten. Elton stayed there for a couple of nights. He was a district manager for Warfarin Rat Poison. He held meetings with his distributors there. His oldest son came with him on this trip. Daddy and me picked Jerry up and took him to Antioch. Jerry was my half-nephew. He was actually a year older than me. They were staying in Room 12 on the alley. I remembered the smell and the noise. The quietness of Room 5 surprised me. Mr. Tyler slid the key into the lock and opened the door. He reached to his right and flipped a switch, flooding the room in light.

"You can hang your suit in the closet, Derek, and put your underwear in a drawer. Put your toiletries in the cabinet in the bathroom. I left a fresh tube of toothpaste for you."

There was a double bed on the wall to the right with a nightstand and lamp on each side. A chest of drawers was on the opposite wall. There was a framed mirror hanging above it. There was one straight back and one upholstered chair. The closet was next to the bathroom. The rose patterned wallpaper was peeling back in several places. The rug showed its years of wear.

"I'm going to listen to Gabriel Heatter if you don't mind," Mr. Tyler said.

A small, brown, Arvin radio sat on the chest of drawers. He flipped it on. For many people, including my father, nine o'clock on Sunday nights was reserved for Gabriel Heatter. Through the darkest hours of the war he always signed on with, "Good evening everyone, there's good news tonight." That upbeat catch phrase boosted spirits on the home front through a long and trying war.

"*Noczema* and The Mutual Broadcasting Company proudly present Gabriel Heatter and the news," the resonant voice announced. Even though good news was often hard to come by, his upbeat words coming each Sunday night made him a national hero and a household name.

"There's good news tonight," blared from the radio. "We have just received spectacular new pictures from Admiral Richard Byrd's latest expedition to the South Pole...." The voice droned on for another fifteen minutes, detailing that story and other newsworthy events from around the world. After a while, the announcer interrupted with a final commercial.

"*Serutan*, nature's answer to irregularity..." Mr. Tyler turned the radio off.

"Well, I guess it's time to turn in Derek. Five o'clock will get here awfully early." He took off his suit and tie and hung them in the closet. "Do you want to brush your teeth before I go into the bathroom?"

"Yes, sir." I said. He had left a new tube of *Ipana* on the sink. There was a half-used one in the glass with his toothbrush. I guess he knew I didn't like the cigars. The *Ipana* had a strange, bitter taste to it. Not like the *Colgate* I normally used.

When I came out Mr. Tyler was in his undershirt and shorts. I stripped down to my shorts and started to get into bed.

"Do you always sleep in your shorts?" he asked.

"Yes, sir." I thought it was a strange question.

"Did you ever think about sleeping nude? It liberates the body. Helps you sleep better."

"I don't know," I said. "I think I'd feel kind of funny doing that."

"Suit yourself, but I sleep nude."

I couldn't understand anyone sleeping naked. My father slept in a nightshirt. My mother wore a flannel gown. All my brothers slept in their underwear. This declaration by Mr. Tyler was unsettling. I slipped into bed quickly. I lay as close to my side of the bed as I could.

"Good night, Derek. Sleep well," he said. My back was to him but I heard his underwear hit the floor. The bed jostled as he settled in. He reached for the lamp and the room went black.

Chapter 13

I felt him slide over toward me. He put his hand on my side and pulled me toward him.

"What are you doing?"

"Come on, Derek. You can't tell me you don't know about this stuff. I know you've spent the night with some of the other boys who do."

"What are you talking about?"

"You know. Boys playing with other boys."

I was totally confused. And scared. I didn't know what to say. I felt dizzy. I could taste the toothpaste. I tried to focus on what he was saying. It was difficult. The room was spinning.

"No, sir. I've never done that, and I don't know anyone else who has. That's wrong."

"Derek did you know that some of the most famous people in history were homosexuals? Socrates, Plato, Alexander the Great, Leonardo da Vinci, Michelangelo. All these great men were homosexuals. Now if they thought it was all right then it can't be all wrong."

"I don't understand. What's a homosexual? I've never heard that word before."

"You must be kidding me. How can anyone in today's world not know what homosexual means. It means what it says in Latin. Man sex. Up north where I come from just about every other man is a homosexual. There's any number of them right here in Shiloh. Homosexuality is a well-accepted fact-of-life. Do you know Mr. Pryor at the jewelry store? He's one. And

Richard, that clerk at the Famous Store. He's one. So are at least five boys you know at school."

My eyes wouldn't focus. I couldn't imagine anyone I knew doing such a thing although I did recall once when Everett Hill tried to get me and his nephew to kiss each other's privates. We were six or seven then. I wouldn't do it. Everett got real mad and stomped off. He's a senior now. Does that mean he is one of them?

"Have you heard the term *queer*?" he asked.

"I've heard some of the boys call Billy Kelly *queer*. I thought they just meant he was odd or different."

"They did. That's where the term comes from. Haven't you noticed the way Billy acts? Some people would call him a sissy. He's effeminate and he prances around like a girl."

"Why would he choose to be a—*queer*?"

"He didn't choose. He was born that way. Some do-gooders try to tell us that homosexuality is a choice. It's not. People are born that way. Others once they've tried it decide they like it. They are what we call bisexuals. You might say they enjoy the best of both worlds." He laughed at his private joke.

I didn't know what to think. I could smell the tobacco on his breath. I thought I was going to be sick. I felt his hand on my crotch. I flinched.

"Come on, Derek, don't you masturbate? I'm just going to help you."

"What's that?"

"You know. Jack off."

I could feel his hands on me. I tried to raise my arms. I couldn't. I knew what he was doing to me, but I was powerless to stop him. Why? Why was he doing this?

"See, that wasn't so bad. That didn't hurt anybody, now did it?"

I lay there bewildered. What had happened? I stared up at the shadows cast by the streetlights below. They danced about in crazy, colorful, patterns on the ceiling. Suddenly, I felt very dirty. How could a teacher do such a thing? I couldn't sleep. I was awake most of the night wondering what to expect next. I heard Mr. Tyler snoring. Mercifully, nothing else happened. The phone woke me at five. I had gone to sleep after all.

"Time to rise and shine, Derek," Mr. Tyler said. "We have an important date in Macon, remember."

Wait a minute. Was last night a dream? My mind was still woozy. If Mr. Tyler did what I think he did, he wouldn't be so casual about it. Would he? I must have dreamed it. Then I felt my shorts around my ankles. I knew it wasn't a dream.

"Do you want to use the bathroom first?" he said.

"No, sir. You go ahead."

My mind raced back to last night. *Queers. Homosexuals. Man sex. Masturbation.* I wasn't imagining those words. He had used them. Does that mean he's one of them too? He must be. But how can he be? He's a teacher. I had many more questions than I had answers.

I heard the shower running. I reckoned it would be a while before he was finished. I walked over to the window and looked out on a darkened Main Street. A garbage truck rumbled by. There was the shriek of a train whistle. The five o'clock pulled into the station right on time. The lights of the station shone through the open mail car. I saw the clerk throw the mailbags into the lockbox. Daddy would be coming to town in a couple of hours to pick them up. Should I go down to the station and wait for him? I didn't know what to do. I had to go to Macon. They're all counting on me. What would Miss Daniel say? What would I tell her, or anyone else, if I didn't show up? Mr. Tyler said what he did to me was normal. Maybe so in his world, but not in mine. Maybe I can just ignore what happened, and it will go away. If he doesn't say anything, I won't. I'll act like it never happened.

The bathroom door opened. Steam poured out. He was drying his hair with a big towel. I couldn't see his face. Just as well.

"It's all yours, Derek. Nothing like a good hot shower in the morning to get the old circulation going."

I hurried into the bathroom, closed the door, and quietly turned the lock. I didn't want him to hear, but I also didn't want him coming in on me. The hot water felt good. Some of the dirtiness began to wash away. I would try to put what happened last night out of my mind. I knew I had to if I was going to get ready for the day ahead.

The chill of the morning air on my face as we stepped into the street reminded me that it was still spring. We walked across to the Sinclair station. Mr. Tyler kept his car parked behind the service bays. He unlocked the door for me to get in while he cleaned the dew off the windshield. I sat on the front seat beside him, as close to the door as I could manage. I felt the round knob of the window crank burrowing into my leg. I looked out the window as he drove up Main. He turned left on the Albany highway then right on Antioch Street. The five-block drive to Miss Daniel's crept by. I desperately wanted someone else in the car with us before I completely jumped out of my skin. We were finally there. Miss Kuhn had walked down from her house and was waiting on the Cone's porch. Miss Daniel came down when she saw the lights turn into the driveway.

"Good morning, ladies," Mr. Tyler said. "Looks like we'll have good weather for the drive today."

He acted like nothing had happened. I couldn't believe how calm he was. He acted like last night was an everyday occurrence for him. I began to think it might be. How did he know about the other *homosexuals* in Shiloh? Obviously I wasn't the first boy he had messed with. How many others? I tried to think back. When did he have the opportunity? Then it hit me. Charles. Thomasville. The Ritz. The night of the jail fire. I wondered if Lillith knew.

"Good morning," Miss Daniel answered. She was wearing a green dress with a pleated skirt. She sported a fox stole around her shoulders. This was a big moment in her life, and she dressed for the occasion. Miss Kuhn, on the other hand, was wearing one of the frumpy numbers she wore to school. Even the latest fashions from Roddenberry's in Albany wouldn't do much for her lumpy body, but what she lacked in physical beauty was more than made up by her cheerful spirit.

"Good morning, Leonard," Miss Kuhn said. She wore a smile from ear to ear. "Isn't it exciting? Just imagine. Our own Derek competing in Macon." She could hardly contain her excitement.

"Derek, why don't you sit in back with me?" Miss Daniel said, "That way we can go over a few last minute instructions I received Friday. I also have a few more words. They were used in Alabama last week. Can't hurt to know them. One never knows."

I was relieved that I didn't have to sit by Mr. Tyler all the way to Macon. Those three additional feet of space made me feel a lot better. Now, if I could just get my mind back on the contest.

Georgia highway 33 was a straight shot north to Cordele where we would pick up US41 to Macon. The first glimmer of dawn broke as we pulled onto the highway. Lights came on in Mrs. Lundy's house as we passed the turnoff to Antioch. More lights dotted the countryside where the farmers were getting an early start on their morning chores. We had traveled only ten miles when the brilliant morning sun burst over the tops of the pecan groves. The trees were fully leafed. A fine dusting of pollen swirled in the wake of the car. Miss Kuhn flipped the visor down and rotated it to shield her eyes. Shortly after six-thirty, we rolled through downtown Cordele.

"Anybody hungry?" Mr. Tyler asked. "There's a little cafe just north of downtown."

"Maybe we should stop," Miss Kuhn said. "I don't know what time they'll break for lunch."

"Okay. Breakfast in Cordele it is," Mr. Tyler decreed.

Shiloh claimed to be the peanut capital of the world. For Cordele, it was watermelons. On hot August afternoons, truckloads of Cuban Queens and Charleston Grays covered the loading docks of the farmer's market. The rest of the year Cordele was a sleepy stopover on the main tourist route from the Midwest to Florida. Myrtle's Main Street Café was a favorite of locals and travelers alike. Myrtle's blueberry pancakes had developed a following from Muskegon to Miami.

The gravel crunched as Mr. Tyler turned into the parking lot. He came around to open the door for Miss Kuhn. I followed his lead and scurried around to open Miss Daniel's door. A few truck drivers and early rising storeowners were seated along the counter. The drivers nursed steaming cups of coffee in a futile attempt to dispel the drowsiness of a long night on the road. The two shopkeepers were engrossed in the morning edition of the *Cordele Dispatch*. Mable was pouring refills for the truck drivers.

"You folks take a seat, and I'll be right with you." The order-up bell clanged behind her. She grabbed the steaming plate of eggs, bacon, and grits and set it in front of one of the locals.

"Here you go Joe. Your usual. Toast'll be ready in a sec."

Mr. Tyler steered us to a booth next to the front. Miss Daniel slid in by the window. I sat down next to her. She picked up menus from the little wire stand holding the salt and pepper shakers. Last night flashed through my mind. Menus behind the ketchup bottle. Hamburger steak. Mary's bosom. Mr. Tyler's hand. I closed my eyes. The visions wouldn't go away.

"You folks know what you want, or do you need a few more minutes with the menu?" Myrtle asked as she sloshed coffee into our cups.

"I know what I want," Miss Kuhn said. "Everybody in Shiloh just raves about your blueberry pancakes. That's what I'm going to have. I understand you grow your own berries and freeze them."

"Yes, ma'am. Been doing it for twenty years. First year I put up about ten gallons. They were gone before Christmas. Now I freeze over two hundred gallons every year. I have my own section down at the freezer locker. It costs me a little more, and I have to charge a little more, but everybody says it is worth it. How 'bout the rest of ya'll? You ready?"

"I'll have the same," Miss Daniel said. "What about you, Derek?"

"That sounds good to me," I said.

"Well, I'm going to be different," Mr. Tyler said. "I'll have two eggs over easy with country ham and hash browns. I never have gotten used to your grits down here. And I'll have rye toast please." Most local restaurants in rural Georgia didn't serve hash browns *or* rye toast, but Mable's clientele was such that those items were standard.

More patrons were streaming into the restaurant when we left. The town was coming to life. Mr. Tyler paid the bill, explaining that the principal had given him twenty dollars from petty cash to cover our expenses for the day.

Across the street were several stores that took advantage of the tourist trade drawn in by Myrtles. A sign in the window of a curio shop caught my eye. One of the words was misspelled. *Souveneirs* it said. I knew from the unending list of words I had studied that it should be spelled *souvenirs*.

"Look, Miss Daniel. Isn't *souvenirs* spelled wrong in that sign?"

"Why, yes it is, Derek. I think that's a good omen for the day. I believe you are going to do very well in Macon."

A few miles north of Cordele a sign proclaimed "Vienna, Georgia. Proud Home of Senator Walter F. George." The senator was the subject of one of my research projects in Mr. Tyler's civics class. I pictured this giant of American politics as he was surrounded by other powerful men in our nation's capital. It was inspiring to see the greatness he had achieved from these humble beginnings. Maybe there was a chance for me after all.

Chapter 14

Signs at the Macon city limits directed us to the Mercer University campus. Mercer had a strong reputation in the arts and humanities. We found the auditorium off Adams Street near the center of the Campus. Cars from Muscogee, Glynn, Candler, McDuffie and Fulton counties were already in the parking lot.

"It looks like we are the last to arrive," Mr. Tyler said. "I thought we made good time. I guess we enjoyed those pancakes a little too long." He chuckled at his joke before gathering up his hat and briefcase to head into the auditorium. A tall, gray haired man, wearing a tweed jacket with leather elbow patches, met us at the door.

"You must be the delegation from Shiloh," he said. "Please allow me to introduce myself. I am Bertrand Warren. I represent the *Atlanta Journal*. It is a distinct pleasure to welcome you to the semi-finals of this year's contest." He reached for my hand.

"This must be Derek Barton. Congratulations, young man. I understand you bested some fine spellers down in southwest Georgia to make it here."

"Thank you, sir." I stammered. "It is an honor for me to represent my school and the district."

Mr. Tyler introduced himself and the women. "My name is Leonard Tyler. This is Miss Sara Daniel and Miss Frances Kuhn. Miss Daniel is Derek's chief advisor. She has worked mighty hard to get young Derek ready for this."

"It is a pleasure to meet all of you. Now if you will follow me, we'll join the others."

Mr. Warren took us through a side door into a large conference room off the main auditorium. There was a raised stage and seating in the audience for forty or so. Mr. Warren took the stage.

"Welcome to the semi-finals of the *Atlanta Journal's* annual spelling bee. We are pleased to have all of you here. I believe we have an exciting day before us, and I wish all our contestants the very best.

"With two exceptions we will operate under the same rules as the district contests. I believe you are all familiar with those. We employ a double elimination format at this level. By that I mean each contestant is allowed one incorrect misspelling without being eliminated. However, on the second misspelling that contestant is disqualified. The second exception; the two finalists will move on to Atlanta.

"Mr. Andrew Gibbs and Miss Winifred Sutherby from the *Journal* editorial department will act as judges. They will be the sole arbiters of the rules." He nodded toward the couple seated at stage left. They stood to acknowledge his introduction. Mr. Warren walked to the edge of the stage.

"I will ask each delegation to stand as I introduce your contestant."

"Mr. Randall Pryor from Columbus High School, Muscogee County." A gangly, pimple-faced, redheaded boy rose.

"Miss Hattie Barnes from Brunswick High School, Glynn County." Hattie wore a blue and white, polka dot dress, and she had very prominent braces on her teeth. She seemed extremely ill at ease.

"Mr. Derek Barton, Shiloh High School, Wyatt County." I was surprised that we were the only delegation with three advisors.

"Miss Hortense Chestnut, Thomson High School, McDuffie County." Hortense was much prettier than her first name, and her hair was the same color as her last.

"Miss Melanie Kitchens, Metter High School, Candler County." Melanie was a beautiful, petite, blond with the whitest teeth I had ever seen.

"Now my executive assistant, Miss Tess Harper, will escort the contestants to the waiting room, and we will get this show on the road."

The first four words took over an hour to complete. Miss Harper called me to spell the fifth word. All five contestants were still in the waiting room.

"Derek, the next word is *paradigm*. A *paradigm* is a philosophical or theoretical network. I will use it in a sentence. With Galileo's discoveries, the cosmic *paradigm* shifted."

I had seen the word on at least two of Miss Daniel's lists. I remember thinking what a very strange word it was, and how it was not spelled anything like it sounded.

"*Paradigm. P-a-r-a-d-i-g-m. Paradigm.*"

"That is correct," Mr. Warren said. "Well done, Derek."

I was the third contestant for that word. The pimply-faced redhead was the fourth. He did not return. After three more rounds, we broke for lunch. There were three of us left: Melanie, Hortense, and me.

"It's been a very exciting morning hasn't it?" Mr. Warren said. "I'm sorry that Ronald and Hattie didn't make it, but they can be very proud of their accomplishments. With any luck we may see them back here again next year.

"Now you all are invited to join the staff for lunch in the university dining hall one block over on Edgewood Avenue. They have a special section reserved for us. All of the delegations are welcome to join us for lunch. We will meet back here at one thirty. Enjoy your lunch."

We stepped out into the brilliant sunshine of a middle Georgia spring day. Students bustled along the streets heading to their next class, to the library, or to lunch. They assumed a head down, no nonsense posture, paying scant attention to a group of gawking students and their teachers.

The cafeteria fare was a cut above what I had come to expect at the high school back home. I chose fried chicken, mashed potatoes, and green beans with pecan pie for dessert. By now I had used up most of the energy from my pancake breakfast. Mr. Tyler loaded his plate. The women were more prudent. They had salads.

The three remaining contestants sat at their own table, a bit away from the others. Mr. Warren said he thought it would be good for us to become better acquainted, and that it might help relieve the tension. We sat down to an awkward silence. None of us knew quite how to break the ice. A thought came to me, and I jumped in.

"Don't you think it's strange that the three of us who are left all come from small towns in rural areas? I figured the schools in Columbus and Brunswick would be so much better."

"I think," Hortense said, "that it proves that one's success in life is more dependent on individual character than on one's environment. We've been studying the "Nature-versus-Nurture" debate at Thomson, and most of us come down on the side of nature. Nurture certainly plays a role in a child's development, but inherited traits are much more determinative."

Wow! Did that blow me away! I had no idea there were girls in the world who could talk like that. We had some fairly bright ones in Shiloh, but I never heard anything like what Hortense just said coming from any of them. I was about to display my ignorance with a comment when Melanie chimed in.

"I tend to agree with you, Hortense. In our church we believe in predestination. That pretty much says that our path in life is set before we are ever born. So, if God ordains that one person will have more success in life than another then there's not an awful lot we can do about it."

I could tell I was way out of my league with these two, so I kept my mouth shut. They continued to discuss the merits of each position, and I ate my lunch. I was saved from further embarrassment by Miss Daniel. She came over to say that the group was going to take a stroll around the campus and asked if we'd like to come.

Mercer had a beautiful campus. The streets were lined with stately, red, brick buildings. Manicured lawns and parks filled the spaces in between. The library was topped by a clock tower that announced class changes on the hour. For such a small school, Mercer offered a wide range of studies: law, medicine, nursing, theology, education, mathematics, science. The school was privately endowed and affiliated with the Southern Baptist Convention. I dreamed of some day being able to attend a school like this.

We all headed back toward the auditorium at one twenty. There was great tension as the next round of words began. At the end of the day, we knew that one of us would be eliminated.

"Hortense, Melanie," I said when we were seated, "no matter how this turns out I just want to say how much I've enjoyed meeting you. I must tell you your conversation at lunch was way over my head. It's too bad we can't all go to Atlanta. I think it would be great fun." Thoughts from the night before receded further from my mind.

"Mr. Barton, alphabetically you have the honor of going first this afternoon," Miss Harper announced. Hortense will go next, to be followed by Melanie. Good luck to you all." I nervously knocked over my chair as I got up.

All three of us were still in the running when two thirty came. We had gone through *chartreuse, masochistic, entrepreneur, pompadour* and *ambidextrous.* I had one misstep. *Abstemious.* I didn't know how Hortense and Melanie stood. Miss Harper came and asked us to come back onto the stage.

"We'll take twenty minutes for everyone to freshen up and get a soda," Mr. Warren said. "We'll start back at three."

I went to the restroom. Miss Daniel had a Coke waiting for me when I got back.

"I am not allowed to tell you how the others stand, Derek, but I can say that you have as good a chance as anyone. Just go back in there, and do your best. I'm really proud of you."

We went through six more words before we were called back to the stage.

"It's a shame that all of you can't represent us in Atlanta," Mr. Warren said. "You've all been such wonderful contestants. However, Miss Chestnut misspelled *antediluvian,* and according to the rules she must be disqualified. Therefore, Miss Kitchens and Mr. Barton will be the South Georgia representatives next month in Atlanta. Congratulations to all of you for a well fought contest. In the past five years I can't remember a more competitive group than the three of you. Those folks in north Georgia had better be ready. They'll be facing two very worthy opponents."

We said our goodbyes to the other delegations. I was sorry that Hortense wouldn't be in Atlanta. I enjoyed my time with her. Perhaps our paths would cross again someday. Melanie lingered at the curb. It was obvious that she didn't want to leave without wishing me a personal goodbye.

"Derek, I think it's so exciting that the two of us are going to Atlanta. I have to confess that when Mr. Warren said that two contestants would go I secretly hoped it would be you. I look forward to it. You take care now, and I'll see you next month."

I mumbled some lame response as she walked away. My heart was in my throat. I couldn't believe she had taken such an interest in me. It was past four when the Macon city limits slipped into the rearview mirror.

"I don't think we'll make it back in time to meet your dad at five," Miss Daniel said. "Do you mind spending another night with Mr. Tyler?"

She had no idea how much I minded, but I couldn't think of any excuse to give her that wouldn't cause more trouble than agreeing to stay. I prayed that last night was a bad dream and that tonight Mr. Tyler would leave me alone.

Chapter 15

"Derek, I am really excited for you," Miss Daniel said. "I'm amazed that you were able to spell all those words. There were some that even I was not certain of."

"Thank you. I owe it to all those books you encouraged me to read and all those lists you gave me to study. I must admit there were a couple of the words that I just took a wild stab at. I guess it pays to be lucky."

Silence settled over the car. The drone of the tires on the asphalt lulled me to sleep. We were past Perry when Mr. Tyler spoke up.

"We're not going to get back before seven or so. Do ya'll want to stop for a bite somewhere?"

"I'd just as soon do that," Miss Kuhn said. "I don't think I have a thing to eat in the Lattimer's refrigerator. I've got to go shopping tomorrow. I've been so busy with preparations for this trip that I haven't taken care of any of my chores."

We pulled into a roadside diner south of Perry. Their sign said "Best Hamburgers South of Atlanta." We each ordered a hamburger with French fries.

"I think I'll order a big basket of onion rings for the table to celebrate Derek's win today," Mr. Tyler said.

"Derek, if you win at state, I understand there's a thousand dollar scholarship," Miss Kuhn said between bites of hamburger. "Have you thought about what you would do with it?"

"My oldest brother Bill is a veterinarian. I think I'd like to be one too and maybe join him in his practice."

"That would be wonderful," Miss Daniel added. "You might want to talk to Miss Deariso about what subjects you should take. She has a lot of information on various school curriculums and the prerequisites needed for various courses of study. Certainly you'll need biology and chemistry."

"Bill went to school on the GI Bill," I said. "His wife worked for the telephone company at night while Bill looked after their daughter, Ann. Between the two of them they got by. I used to go over to Auburn to stay with Evelyn in the summers while Bill was doing his internships in Valdosta. Ann stayed with her grandparents, the Woodfins. I don't think my folks will be able to send me to college. If not, I'll just join the navy and go to school on the GI Bill when I get out."

"Well at least you have a plan," Miss Kuhn said. I wish I could say that for all my students. Most of them have no idea what they will do after school. I expect they'll stay on the farm or take a job at the Marine base in Albany. That's a shame, since this country will need doctors, lawyers, engineers and a whole host of other skills to get us past the depression and the war."

I could see Miss Kuhn's head start to bobble as sleep overtook her. Miss Daniel took a book from her briefcase and began reading. I nodded off. We rode on in silence.

"Here we are," Mr. Tyler said as he pulled into the Cone's driveway. "I don't know about the rest of you, but I'm plumb tuckered out."

I hoped that meant he would turn in early tonight and not bother me. The two women exited the car. Miss Kuhn said goodbye and headed across Antioch Street to the Lassiter's house.

"Derek, I'll see you tomorrow," Miss Daniel said. "We'll go over the preparations for the finals in Atlanta. The date will be here before we know it. It's only a few weeks away. Good night, Mr. Tyler."

"Good night, Sara. See you tomorrow."

I dreaded the thought of returning to the Willard with Mr. Tyler. I thought of calling Daddy or Roger to come down and pick me up. Then I thought better of it. I didn't want to have to explain why. I was too ashamed.

"Hi, Gary," Mr. Tyler called as we breezed through the lobby.

"Hi, Mr. Tyler. Derek. How'd it go in Macon?"

"Our young hero here was one of the two finalists. He'll be going on to Atlanta soon. You should have seen some of the words he had to spell. Unbelievable. I can only imagine what they'll throw at him in the finals. Oughta be a lot of fun though. Gary, can I get a couple of cold Cokes? Just put them on my bill." Mr. Tyler took the drinks and moved toward the stairs.

"Come on Derek. Let's have a little refreshment before we go to bed. I've got a couple of Twinkies that I squirreled away last week."

I climbed the stairs behind him, my panic rising as we reached the top, and he opened the door. Oh, God, please don't let it happen tonight.

"Come on in Derek. Take your suit off and get comfortable. I'll get us a couple of glasses."

He went into the bathroom. I could hear the clatter as he took the glasses down from the glass tray by the medicine cabinet. I heard the door to the cabinet open, and I wondered why.

"Here you go," he said as he poured my Coke. "If you're as keyed up as I am you can use a little calming influence. This is something Dr. Mullis over at the drugstore gave me. It's good for jangled nerves. Helps me sleep after a day of dealing with some of those goons at school."

He stripped the end off a cellophane packet and poured a white powder into my glass.

"It's kind of a Goody's headache powder with a little more kick. Here, drink up."

"Aren't you having some too?" I asked. I was hesitant to drink it.

"Yeah. I poured mine in the bathroom."

The Coke had a slightly bitter taste.

"When you finish your Coke and Twinkie, brush your teeth, and we'll go to bed."

When I came out of the bathroom, Mr. Tyler was already in bed. I took off my clothes down to my undershorts and got in as quietly as I could.

"Goodnight, Derek," I heard from the other side. Suddenly I was very sleepy.

"I don't know what time it was when I awoke. I had a burning sensation. I was on my stomach. There was a heavy weight on my back. In a fog, I realized Mr. Tyler was on top of me. I tried to move.

"Just lay still, Derek. I'm not going to hurt you. I gave you pleasure last night. I just wanted a little for myself tonight."

I tried to protest, but my words came out garbled. My head was spinning. I couldn't pull myself up from the bad dream I was having. I fell back to sleep. When I awoke, the sun was bouncing off the windows across Main Street. I could hear water running in the shower. My shorts were lying on the floor by the bed. My head ached. I threw the covers back and sat up. There was a red spot on the sheet. There was a jar of Vaseline on the nightstand.

When Mr. Tyler emerged from the bathroom, I couldn't look him in the face. I still didn't understand what had happened to me. I was ashamed. I knew it had to do with the talk last night. About *queers* and *homosexuals* and *man sex*. I figured Mr. Tyler must be one. Was I one?"

"Derek, what happened the last couple of nights is just between you and me. You don't tell anybody, and I won't. It would be very embarrassing for you as well as for me. You don't want your buddies at school to start calling you *queer* do you, like they do to Billy Kelly?"

"No, sir, but I'm not a *queer*."

"You may not think so, but you are now. We've had *man sex*. Twice. That makes you a *queer*. So the less said the better. If you go blabbing, something bad might happen to you or maybe even your family. Some *queers* get beat up. Even killed. We don't want that to happen to you now do we?"

"No, sir." My head hurt real bad. I was confused.

He went to his bureau. He reached into the bottom drawer and pulled out a pistol. It had black grips and a short, nickel-plated barrel. He spun the chamber and held the gun up to the light as he sighted down the barrel.

"I've never had to use this before, but I do know how. You understand? Just remember, if the police come after me there are others watching. And they are very loyal to me. You have no idea who they are. If anything happens to me, they won't forget. You might get to meet them some day if you keep your mouth shut."

Chapter 16

The next day was the longest day of my life. I wanted to scream at the top of my lungs. I wanted to tell my folks what that man had done to me. But I knew I couldn't. Not without putting their lives in danger. I couldn't even tell Red about it for fear he might tell them. I knew he was the one person in the world who could help me, and I couldn't tell him. That was the morning Minnie found the blood.

When the other kids at the bus stop looked at me, I just knew they could tell I had done something wrong. I felt such guilt. Surely, it must show on my face.

"Hi, Derek," Anza said. I waited for her question. What would I say?

"Mama made me another peanut butter and jelly sandwich. You want to swap?"

"Sure," I said. I was relieved that it wasn't the other question. "I think I may have a ham sandwich today. I'd much rather have peanut butter and jelly." I pried off the lid to my bucket and handed her the sandwich. She took hers out of her Red Ryder lunch box and gave it to me.

"What were you and Willie talking about when I came up?" I asked Gene Williams. "Did I hear you say you might go fishing when you get home?"

"Naw. Willie said his brother went fishing up at Sheep Hole Creek yesterday, and he caught a two-pound bluegill. I've never seen a bluegill that big."

I figured he made that up to keep me from going with them. That was okay. Red and me were planning on shooting rats anyway. We had lots of wharf rats in the corncrib. Red had a single shot, 22-gauge, rifle. I had a pellet gun. Mama wouldn't let me shoot a regular gun. We would lay on the ground real quiet, and when the rats came out, we'd pick 'em off. One day we killed 22 rats.

That day Miss Daniel sent a note to my homeroom teacher. She wanted to see me right after lunch. That was study period, and she knew I could get off. Henry and I walked back from the lunchroom. He stopped off for his study hall. I continued on to the library. I figured Miss Daniel wanted to talk about the finals. I stood in the door waiting for her to look up from her desk.

"Come in, Derek," she said when she saw me. "The whole school is buzzing about your performance in Macon. Mr. Gear wanted to have another assembly to honor you, but I told him how embarrassed you were before, and that you would prefer that he not do it. He said, 'Okay this time, but if Derek wins at state we're having a celebration.' He even talked about a ceremony with the mayor and town council."

I didn't see Mr. Tyler until I was almost at her desk. He was standing behind a bookcase. I felt my heart race. I turned white.

"What's the matter, Derek?" Miss Daniel said. "You look like you've seen a ghost."

"It's nothing," I said. "I didn't see Mr. Tyler there. When he moved it scared me a little." Mr. Tyler's eyes narrowed. He was behind Miss Daniel. He reached inside his coat. When he took his hand out, he had shaped it like a gun. I got the message.

"Derek, Mr. Tyler has volunteered to put in some extra time to help us get ready for Atlanta. I think that's very generous of him considering his workload. He's offered to let you study with him after school at his hotel. He'll even take you home when you're finished."

"What do you say, Derek?" Mr. Tyler said. "You're going to need a lot of preparation if you expect to go up against those kids from Atlanta."

I didn't know what to say. I did not want to be alone with this man anymore. I knew I was not a *queer* no matter what he said. How clever he was to make the offer in front of Miss Daniel. If I said no, she would think I was not grateful or not serious enough about winning. If I said yes, I knew what would happen.

"I'll have to check with my parents. If they say it's okay, then I'll do it." I left the library trembling. How was I going to get out of this?"

I got off the bus and went straight to Red's room. I prayed that he would be off early from the mill. He wasn't there. I walked down the lane to our house, still searching for a way out. Mama and Minnie were on the back porch shelling peas. It was canning season. Our garden, located between the house and the abandoned store where Red lived, had produced a bumper crop this spring. Mama canned as much as she could at home then she took the rest down to the canning plant that was located in the agriculture building near the high school. Mr. Tom Graham ran the canning plant and taught agriculture. His wife taught home economics. I had an idea.

"Mama, Miss Daniel wants me to study with Mr. Tyler after school at his hotel. What do you think?"

"Why at his hotel? Do you want to do that?" she asked.

"Not really," I said. "I've spent so much time away already, and I know you and Daddy need me to pick up the slack during canning season. Suppose I tell them that you're going to be canning every afternoon for the next two or three weeks, and you need me to help. That way I won't hurt Miss Daniel's feelings."

"Well, I can certainly use the help. Minnie and I have been going fast and furious for the last week, and we can't keep up with that garden. The purple hull peas are just coming into season. I want to preserve as many cans as possible. Your daddy said he's adding more people at the mill. That'll mean more mouths to feed next winter when the fresh vegetables are gone. Why don't you come down to the canning plant after school lets out? There'll be plenty for you to do."

"Okay, Mama. That's what I'll tell Miss Daniel. By the way, have you seen Red today? I have a question I want to ask him."

"He came up to the house for dinner about one o'clock. I think he went back to the mill. I understand they're trying to finish up the Strangward cut this week."

I went to the living room and lay down on the sofa. I thought that maybe the Lone Ranger, the Green Hornet, and Superman might take my mind off my troubles. I fell asleep during Kato's Kung Fu attack on the bad guys. I woke to a tug on my foot. Red was standing at the foot of the sofa, one hand on my toe.

"Your mama said you wuz looking for me," he said.

"Yeah. Are you going back to your place now?"

"After I finish with the livestock. Be about a half-hour."

"Okay. I'll come up to your place."

The lingering odor of tobacco mingled with the smell of grease. Red was frying pork chops on his wood stove.

"You didn't eat at the house tonight?" I asked.

"Naw. I had a hankering for some pork chops. Miss Julia gave me some peas and turnips to go with 'em. They're about done. You want some?"

"No. I already ate."

Pee Wee crawled from under a pile of tobacco sticks that were stacked against the wall. They were left over from last fall after we finished grading the tobacco. I suddenly remembered that Daddy had told me to take them back down to the barn. I'd better do that before he finds out I didn't. Tomorrow maybe. I scratched Pee Wee's ears. He flipped onto his back. Red reached over to scratch his stomach.

"Red. Do you remember when we went up to Mercer's Mill and stopped at Cousin Lester's for the night."

"Yeah, I remember. What about it?" He picked up a pork chop and took a bite. He put it back on his plate and licked his fingers.

"You remember when I asked Bobby about *queers*? He didn't seem to want to talk about it very much. What do you know about *queers*, Red?"

"The question is what do *you* know about *queers*?"

"Well. There's this kid at school. Billy Kelly. Some of the other boys call him *queer*."

"Tell me about Billy."

"He's kinda small and thin. He doesn't hang around with the boys, and he doesn't play football with the rest of us. He's kinda prissy and stays mostly with the girls."

"What's wrong with that?" Red said. "We're all cut from different cloth. Just because some of us do one thing and some another, don't mean we're *queer*. It just means we're different."

"Then why do the boys call him *queer*?"

"You know that old chicken that lost most of its feathers? The one your mama called a *frizzled* chicken."

"Yeah. Mama wound up serving that chicken to the preacher last Sunday. The other chickens nearly pecked it to death."

"See! That's what I mean. That *frizzled* chicken won't no different than any of the other chickens once you got beneath the feathers, but the others pecked at him all the time. They's something in nature that won't abide different. Look at you and me. 'Neath our skin, we're the same. You cut me, I gone bleed red. Cut you, you gone bleed red. Same as that *frizzled* chicken.

"Billy Kelly ain't like them other boys, so they pick on him. For something he cain't help. It ain't fair, but it a fact of life. My grand pappy, he didn't want to be no slave, but he didn't have no choice. Them slave traders snatched him outten his home in Africa and brung him over here to work the land. Now that Mr. Lincoln done set us free, almost a hunnert years ago, you think black folks ain't still different? We still does all the work. What we got to show for it? I don't know no black man what works his own land. I don't know if I'll ever see that change in my lifetime. They's good white folks, like yo pa. They treats us good and everything, but if push comes to shove, they's still white and we's still black."

He leaned back as if to catch his breath. I had never seen Red like this. It was a little scary.

Seeing my reaction he said, "I didn't mean to preach no sermon, boy. It's just that sometimes it kinda biles over in me. Jest like it's gonna bile over in Billy Kelly one day. When it do, I don't wanna be one of them boys what's picking on him.

"What do you really wanna know about *queers*?" Red said.

"I've heard that they have sex with other men. I don't understand it. Why? God made men and women to lie down with each other and to have children. Men can't do that with other men."

"Derek, some men just ain't taken to women. I don't know why God would make 'em like that, but he did. Or, somebody did. And some women too. I knew some folks down in Cairo, black and white, who were that way. They sneaked around in the back alleys. They met down by the river. They thought no one knew. Everybody knew. As long as they didn't bother the straight folks they wuz left alone."

"What if someone isn't *queer* and is forced to have sex with a man. Does that make him *queer* then?"

"Naw. You either born *queer* or you ain't. Why you asking these questions, Derek? Has somebody been messing with you?"

I heard a noise behind me. Someone was standing in the door. I couldn't see who it was. The light was in my eyes.

"Derek, Mama says for you to come on home." It was Roger. "I was walking home, and she asked me to stop and tell you. You go on home now." Roger left. Red stared at me.

"Boy, if somebody's messing with you, you tell me. You hear?"

"Yeah. I will."

I kicked at the rocks in the lane as I walked back home thinking I wasn't sure I knew any more about *queers* now than I did before. One thing though. I was glad Red said I wasn't *queer* even though Mr. Tyler did what he did.

Chapter 17

"Miss Daniel, I won't be able to study with Mr. Tyler." It was after noon before I had a chance to go by the library to tell her. "I have to help Mamma with the canning. She'll be coming to the canning plant every afternoon for a while, and she wants me to come down there after school lets out. She needs someone stronger to move the big baskets around and put them in the steam bath."

"That's too bad. I was hoping you could get in some extra time, but I understand. I'll put together some more lists for you. Please go by Mr. Tyler's office on the way back to your room, and let him know. Thank you, Derek."

I really didn't want to face Mr. Tyler. What he had done to me was too fresh in my mind. I wanted to avoid him if I could. Now I had no choice but to see him.

"Come in Derek." He was sitting at his desk going over some papers. "How are you today?" He had a smirk on his face.

"I just came by to tell you that I can't study with you. I have to help my mother. It's canning season, and she needs me down at the canning plant every afternoon."

"I'm sorry to hear that. I was looking forward to working with you. You need a lot of practice to get ready for Atlanta. Maybe we can find some other way to work in some study time. I'll give it some thought."

As soon as he stopped talking, I hurried out of his room. I knew I was not a *queer*. I knew now that he was. I didn't want to be around him.

"See you later, Derek," he called out to me. "We have some unfinished business."

I shuddered. I knew what kind of business he meant.

Miss Daniel loaded me up with words. I took them to the canning plant every afternoon. When there was a lull in the work, I would hop up on a table and memorize them.

"Here, Derek." I looked up from the list I was studying. It was my mother. She handed me a bottle of Coca-Cola. The squat red machine sitting in the corner kept the bottles ice cold. The drink tasted especially good in the heat of the boiler room. "You've been a big help this week."

"Thanks, Mama. I know how hard you and Minnie work. I'm just glad to help out." She didn't know the other reason I was there. I hoped she never would.

I was hunched over my desk in the library. It was study period. Miss Daniel was grading papers. Bryce and Charles were in the same study hall.

"Psst!" I looked up to see Bryce signaling to me. He motioned for me to join him in the book stacks. I waited until Miss Daniel turned her back then I slid out of my seat.

"What's up?" I asked.

"Some of the boys are going to grab Billy Kelly on the way home from school. They're going to take off all his clothes and tie him to a tree then paint *QUEER* on his chest in big red letters. You want to come with us."

"No!" I said louder than I intended. "Why in the world would you want to do that? He hasn't hurt anybody."

"Aw, come on. We're just gonna have a little fun with him. We ain't gonna hurt him or nothing like that. It's been boring around here. We haven't had any excitement since Jimmie Earle ran into that tombstone."

"I can't even if I wanted to. I'm still helping Mama with the canning every afternoon after school."

"Okay, but you're gonna miss out on the fun."

I sneaked back to my desk praying that Miss Daniel hadn't heard us. She was still poring over the test papers. I said a silent prayer for Billy.

Wednesday afternoon we were finishing up with the tomatoes when Mr. Graham came down the steps from his office. He was carrying a copy of the *Shiloh Local*.

"Did you hear about Billy Kelly?" he asked my mother.

"No. What about him?" He handed her the paper. She started to read it and she turned pale.

"What's wrong Mama?" I reached for the paper. She snatched it away.

"It's not something you should see," she said. "It looks like some of the boys played a prank on Billy Kelly, and it kind of backfired."

I didn't pursue the matter any further. I knew what the article would say. I had hoped the boys wouldn't go through with it, but obviously they did. I looked for Bryce the next morning.

"What happened?" I asked him. "Were you there?"

"No. After I talked to you, I decided I wouldn't go. I heard Daddy talking to Mama last night after I went to bed. They thought I was asleep. He said that the rope around Billy was so tight that it cut off his breathing, and he almost died. When the police found him, he had a sack over his head. They rushed him to the hospital. The doctors had to put him on some kind of machine to help him breathe. They don't know if he'll be all right or not. His folks are real upset. They said if they found out who did this there would be hell to pay. They painted *queer* on him in big red letters. Sheriff Hudson is trying to find fingerprints on the paintbrush and paint can. Billy said he didn't see who it was before they put the sack over his head. Boy, I'm sure glad I didn't go."

"Who did it, Bryce?"

"I can't tell you. They made me promise I wouldn't tell anybody, or they'd beat the living crap out of me. You can guess who it was. They were all on the football team."

I knew that Koy Horton was probably the ringleader. He was the fullback on Shiloh's football team. He was a bully. He was always taunting Billy. He picked on everybody. He picked on me a time or two. I figured I knew some of the others who helped him.

The only subject on anyone's tongue at school was Billy Kelly. When we saw the sheriff's car drive up, we all ran to the window. He went into principal Gear's office. He emerged a few minutes later with Mr. Gear. They walked down the hall to Mr. Harrington's classroom. Five minutes later, they came back with Koy Horton in tow. The sheriff drove off with Koy handcuffed in the back seat. That night I went over to the jailhouse. Mike Cantrell was the deputy on duty.

"Hey, Mike," I said. "You got Koy in there?"

"Yep. I got him locked up tighter than a tick."

"Can I talk to him?"

"No. Sheriff Hudson said I was to hold him *incumando* or some big word like that. He doesn't want Koy talking to anyone until he finds out who else was involved."

There was a light in a cell on the second floor. I figured that must be Koy. I figured he was plenty scared by now. His daddy always got him out of his other scrapes. This one was different.

Red's lights were out when I went by. I wanted to ask him if he'd heard about Billy Kelly. It was odd that we were just talking about him. Life takes some strange twists at times.

I awoke to sirens. The clock by my bed read two thirty. I got up and ran to the window facing the courthouse. I could see flashing red lights, and there was a spotlight shining on the second floor of the jail. Daddy was already up. I jumped into my pants and joined him on the porch.

"What's going on?"

"I don't know," Daddy said. "Looks like some trouble at the jail. I think I'll walk over there and check it out. You can tag along if you'll promise to stay back out of the way."

A small crowd had gathered by the courthouse in the area where the minstrel show always set up. Nick Reynolds was there. He owned the store at the crossroads that was catty-cornered from where Red lived. The Powell boys and some of the other neighbors were already there. Mr. Garner was walking across from his house as we came up.

"What's going on Nick?" Daddy asked.

"I'm not quite sure, Hiram. It looks like somebody conked Mike Cantrell on the head and broke into the jail. I couldn't make out who it was. Kinda funny though. Most times people are trying to break out of jail, not in." He laughed.

Sheriff Hudson stood off to the side of the jail near the road. He had something in his hand. He held it up to his mouth.

"Whoever's in there, come on out. We've got the place surrounded. You can't get away." He put the bullhorn down and waited for a response. The crowd shuffled closer for a better look.

A shadow crossed the window. It stood to one side making for less of a target.

"I'll come out when I finish what I came here to do," the voice said. "You stay back, and nobody else will get hurt."

"What do you mean nobody else?" Sheriff Hudson asked.

"Just wait a minute, and you'll see." The shadow moved back across the window. It was carrying a shotgun.

"You men stay back. He's got a gun. Come on boys," he yelled to the two deputies standing by the front door. The door was locked from the inside. Burly Jonas Cook threw his 250 pound bulk into the door, and it splintered. After all, it was over a hundred years old. The three men charged up the stairs. There was a scream and a loud explosion.

"Okay, Mr. Kelly, put the gun down. There's three pistols aimed at your heart. You can't get all of us."

"I ain't got no quarrel with you sheriff. Just with this boy here. He done nearly killed my boy, and he said all those dirty things about him. He didn't have no right to do that. Billy wasn't hurtin' nobody. He's a good boy. He takes care of his Ma. She cain't get around much since she had the infantile paralysis."

Buster Kelly dropped the shotgun down the stairwell. The clatter echoed across the square. Footsteps ran up the stairs. A few minutes later, a cell door slammed shut. The sheriff came downstairs. By this time, everybody had rushed toward the jail. We could hear the sheriff through the open window as he cranked the phone.

"Hey, Mary Lou. I see they've got you on the night shift again. I know it's late, but would you ring up Dr. Sumner for me." A few seconds passed. The sheriff closed his eyes. He ran his hand across his face like he was trying to wipe something from his memory. "Doc? This is Sheriff Hudson. I know it's awful late, but I'm gone need you to come out to the Antioch jail. There's been a shooting, and since you are the acting county coroner, I need you to rule on it. Okay. See you in half an hour." Sheriff Hudson came out to address the crowd.

"You folks need to go on back home now. There's been an awful thing happen here tonight. Buster Kelly has shot Koy Horton. It's all about that incident with his boy Billy. I think he just went crazy. I don't want anyone going up there until Doc Sumner gets here and checks out the situation and we get the place cleaned up. Jonas, you keep everybody out. A double barrel, twelve-gauge, shotgun from ten feet away don't leave much that's recognizable. I've got Buster locked up. The county attorney will have to deal with him tomorrow. I reckon Buster felt like he was doing the right thing by his boy, but he's just brought a whole lot more misery to a family that's had enough already.

Daddy and me walked back to the house. Red was standing on the front steps of the store. In the dim light, I could see him lick the rolled up paper and twist the end. He closed the lid on the Prince Albert can and dropped it in his shirt pocket. The flare of a match lit up his stubbly face.

"Boss man, what's going on over there? That gunshot woke me up out of a dead sleep."

"Looks like Buster Kelly was looking to get even for what they did to his boy Billy. He shot Koy Horton at point blank range with a twelve-gauge shotgun. The sheriff said there wasn't much left of the boy that's recognizable. It's a sad, sad, situation. Buster's probably going to jail for a long time. That is, if he's not sent to the electric chair. His wife's laid up with polio. I don't know what will happen to her and Billy." Red shook his head. We continued on home.

"Good night, Red," I said. "I'll see you tomorrow."

"Good night, Derek."

I knew he was thinking the same thing I was thinking. We both thought it would have been Billy that did it.

The next day Mr. Gear called a special assembly of the entire high school. The bell rang at nine o'clock, and students poured into the hallways headed for the auditorium. The mood was somber, not the normal raucous carryings on. There were not enough seats for everyone. Many stood around the edge of the room leaning against the walls. Mr. Gear and Sheriff Hudson were seated on the stage. Mr. Gear got up to address the assembly. He was only about five and a half feet tall. He adjusted the microphone to his height and tapped it to ensure it was on. The *woof-woof* echo confirmed that it was.

"I'm sure by now all of you have heard about the terrible tragedies that occurred this week. What happened to Billy Kelly was shocking and totally out of keeping with this school and this community. I believe, when it's all said and done, that there will be very few implicated in the attack on Billy. Just a few troublemakers who chose not to conform to our civilized norms. However, what started out as a schoolboy prank has led to the humiliation of one student, the death of another, and the ruination of two families. The Hortons have lost their son, and the Kellys are going to lose their father and husband for a long, long time. Maybe forever." He paused to let the impact of his words sink in to the stunned audience.

"It didn't have to be this way. In our churches, in our homes, and in our schools, we teach that we should show tolerance for others. To be forgiving of their differences. To walk in their shoes before we condemn them for their actions. Well, these three institutions, collectively, have failed us this week. Koy knew better yet he let his prejudices overrule his good sense, and he committed a heinous crime. Those who aided and abetted him knew better too, and they will be brought to the bar of justice. Thankfully, they will not have to pay the ultimate price for their folly that Koy did. I pray that they will learn from this mistake and return from their punishment to become law abiding, productive citizens of our society.

"Local church leaders from throughout the community will be available today for any of you who feel a need to share your feelings with someone. As a community, we need to grieve for Koy and for Billy but especially for Mr. Kelly. He did what all loving parents are taught to do. He sought to protect his child. He just went about it in the wrong way, and now he and his family will pay a terrible price for that.

"I ask each of you to welcome Billy back in the coming weeks, and make him feel more a part of this school. He's going to need that. We're all going to need each other to get through this and to come out the other side a stronger community.

"Over the next few weeks, we will be working with each home room teacher to develop a program that will help us instill the values and sensitivities we need to make sure that nothing like this ever happens again.

"Now, I'd like to turn the floor over to Sheriff Hudson."

"Thank you, Mr. Gear. I couldn't agree more with your comments here this morning. I don't believe in my twenty-some years as your sheriff that I've seen anything that has torn this community apart more than what's happened this past week. We must see that nothing like this ever happens again.

"Now, we know there were three other boys with Koy when he jumped out of the bushes and put that bag over Billy's head. We have a good idea who they were, and we're processing several sets of fingerprints from the scene. Billy didn't see who jumped him, but he recognized their voices. My advice to the three of you is for you to come on down to my office and turn yourselves in. It'll make the law go a little easier on you. It'll also let you get a head start on putting this terrible episode behind you. I expect to see you there."

Tyler Melton, Glen Cunningham, and Harley Holt turned themselves in to Sheriff Hudson that afternoon. He booked them, and then released them to their parents with the understanding they would report back to court on Monday.

The lingering effects of the week echoed through everything that happened at school. The furor over Billy Kelly's attack caused Mr. Tyler to pull in his horns. I guess it struck too close to home. I didn't know if Billy figured into any of the situations he described, but he appeared somewhat chastened. He didn't pursue the *study* situation for the rest of the week. I avoided all contact with him by escaping to the safe confines of the library. I didn't think that she or Miss Kuhn had any inkling of Mr. Tyler's true nature. If either had, I couldn't imagine that they wouldn't have gone immediately to Mr. Gear. No, he was very clever in camouflaging himself and his intentions. Who would ever suspect him to be a homosexual? He kept company with two women and appeared to show a romantic interest in one of them.

We finished the canning at the end of the second week. The garden was still producing, but Mama didn't have any more room in her pantry or in the smokehouse, and we still had the summer crop to think about. She decided to rent a drawer for vegetables at the freezer locker.

I was anxious to see whether Mr. Tyler would bring up the subject of studying at the Willard again. He didn't, and I was grateful.

"Derek, we're driving up to Atlanta early next Monday morning," Miss Daniel announced. "We'll have to leave even earlier. Will you stay with Mr. Tyler again?"

"No, ma'am," I was quick to answer. "We have a special program at church next Sunday evening, and I have to be there for that. Daddy said he'll drop me off at the hotel. He'll come in early for his morning mail run."

That was a bald-faced lie, but I was not going to subject myself to Mr. Tyler again.

The week flew by. Following Koy's funeral on Saturday, the remnants of the Kelly/Horton saga slowly faded. Life at school returned to normal. Daddy took me to the basketball game on Tuesday night. It was the last game of the season. We beat Tifton 58 to 56. It had been six years since we last beat them. The *Shell*, our old, weather beaten, unpainted gymnasium was located across from the agriculture building. It was also used as a dressing room for football practice. Musty shoulder pads and grass stained pants hung from the rafters above the top row of seats. Only necking couples ventured up into those dark, smelly, recesses. Mr. Tyler was there. He was seated with several students, mostly boys. He motioned for me to join them. I declined.

Miss Daniel handed her final group of words to me on Thursday. She had winnowed through lists from every state contest that would provide them. She selected what she considered the one hundred toughest words. If there was *any* word, on *any* list, from *any* state, for the past ten years that she did not have, I would be surprised. I knew what I'd be doing for the next three days.

"Derek, don't forget to pick up your suit from Sterling's cleaners Saturday," Mama said as I came in the door that afternoon. "You don't want to go to Atlanta without it. I've already washed and ironed your dress shirt. It's hanging in the chifforobe in the hall with your tie. I left it tied so you can just slip it over your head and tighten the knot. I know you have trouble tying it."

"Thanks, Mama. I'm going to get my chores out of the way so that I can study tonight. I have some homework, and Miss Daniel gave me a new list of words. I took a quick glance at them, and boy, are they hard. I don't know if I'm good enough for this level of competition."

"Now don't you go losing faith in yourself. You're just as good as anybody else who'll be up there. You stay calm, take your time, and you'll be just fine. I believe in you. I wouldn't want any of the other boys to hear me say this, but I think you're my smartest. I know that whatever you choose to do in life you will be successful." I needed that reassurance, especially from Mama.

After I fed and groomed my show cattle, I collected the eggs and checked on the biddies. Daddy had built a chicken coop in a large fenced area beyond the toilet. He installed an electric incubator at one end and ordered biddies from Sears Roebuck. They arrived in small, cardboard boxes with air holes. Their *cheeping* sounds filled the mail car. My job was to make sure they always had fresh water and food. I filled their troughs each morning with cracked corn, millet, and grit. I cleaned out the droppings once a week and put down fresh sawdust. Laying nests filled the spaces above the chicken roosts. I often helped my cousin, Ruth McCrary, prepare for the Saturday farmer's market in Albany. Daddy let me take our surplus eggs to sell. I got to keep half of what they brought. Red took care of the other cows, the pigs, and the mules. He was coming up the path from the barn as I returned with a basketful of eggs. He stamped his feet to knock off the mud and manure. Pee Wee ran along the fence by the dog run snuffling at the hounds. Bugle Ann came over and stuck her nose through the wire to whisper in his ear. I think she was inviting Pee Wee to the next coon hunt.

"Ever since your daddy switched from the Rhode Island Reds to them White Leghorns you been gittin' a bunch more eggs. I still like the brown eggs from the Reds better. They seems to have more taste to 'em, and they makes better fried chicken."

Daddy was coming across the yard. Saturday was the date for Daddy's yearly fishing trip to Fargo. He asked Red if he wanted to go this year. Red loved to fish.

Fargo was on the western edge of the Okefenokee Swamp. Lem Griffis ran a fish camp near there on Billy's Lake way back in the swamp. He was a Primitive Baptist like Daddy, and they got along real well. He and his son Billy—the lake was named for him— would take us deep into the swamp in their pole boats, and we'd go home with a ton of fish. Lem always had a new batch of tall tales for us every year.

"Hiram, did I tell you about my honey business?" he asked.

"I don't believe you did Lem, but I did notice a heap of honey on the shelf at your store."

"Yessiree. I been making more honey than anybody else in the swamp. Both Tupelo and Gallberry. You see, I figgered out how to mix my honeybees with lightning bugs, so they can see at night. That way I get two crops a year."

Daddy laughed so hard I thought he was going to fall overboard. Cousin Marion, who was sitting with his bare feet dangling in the water, nearly split his side.

"Marion, I don't reckon you oughtta be doing that," Lem said. "They's some gators in here that can smell your feet from a mile off." Marion jumped up like he'd been shot. His feet were already turning red from too much sun. He would be in misery going home that night.

We left Fargo with two five-gallon lard cans full of bream and bass for the annual fish-fry to be held on the courthouse square Sunday afternoon. It was always put on by the Ladies Missionary Society. All the fish, hushpuppies, and slaw you could eat for fifty cents. Thelma and Mattie Lou would drop those fish and hushpuppies into the wash pots full of boiling oil, and when they floated to the top, they were done. Half of the money went for the Lottie Moon Missionary Fund. On the way home, I took a plate to Red.

"I guess tomorrow's your big day Derek?" Red said as he sat down to his fish supper. Pee Wee sat up on his hind legs until Red gave him a hushpuppy.

"Yeah, I'll be glad when it's all over. I never knew so many people cared about a silly old spelling bee. You'd think it was the second coming or something."

"I hope you does good, Derek. I reckon your folks'll be proud. I heard your daddy say he didn't know you wuz so smart, and how he was praying for you." I was humbled that my father was proud of me. I prayed that I wouldn't disappoint him.

Chapter 18

The rain was coming down in buckets. Daddy drove as close as he could to the front door of the Willard.

"Good luck, Derek. We'll be pulling for you."

"Thanks, Daddy. I'll be back late tonight or tomorrow. If by any chance I should win, I think we might have to stay over, so don't worry. I'll call you when I get back."

I jumped out with my bag of clothes. The truck splashed off in the glare of a towering bolt of lightning. I ran for cover. Mr. Tyler was sitting in the lobby having a cup of coffee.

"You want a cup of coffee before we go, Derek?"

"No, sir. I'm fine. You go ahead and finish up. I'll dry off over here by the fire." Gary Laird was behind the counter. He was reading the *Albany Herald* sports section.

"Looks like the boys are gonna make it to the regionals this year. They just have to beat Camilla and Bainbridge. It's been three years since we made the tournament. Delbert Combs has done turned into one helluva player since he grew so tall. Him and Jimmy Hobby are the heart of the team this year."

Mr. Tyler glared at Gary over the rim of his cup. He couldn't care less. He wasn't into sports and stuff. I wondered if that went along with being *queer*.

Few lights were on along Antioch Street at that early hour. Only the ones on the second floor of the Cone's and the Lattimer's. Both ladies were up and about. Mr. Tyler pulled into the Lattimer's drive. Miss Kuhn came down the steps. We picked up Miss Daniel a short block later.

"Good morning everyone," she said, sliding into the back seat. "What a glorious day. I feel it in my bones, Derek. You are going to bring that prize back to Shiloh and put it in the case next to all those athletic trophies. We'll show them that Shiloh High is about more than just football and basketball."

I had never seen Miss Daniel so excited. She was very proud of the academic spirit she brought to her literature classes, but it had been hard for her to demonstrate her success in any concrete way. Most of the parents were illiterate or poorly educated at best. That their children were enrolled in school at all was a major triumph. Most were dragged away for weeks in the spring and fall to work in the fields. Still, progress was being made even if it was maddeningly slow.

"Well, aren't you the chipper one this morning," Frances Kuhn said. "I hope you are right. It would be a real feather in our caps if Derek could win. But we musn't put too much pressure on him. Lord knows there's enough already what with the whole town talking about it."

We stopped again for pancakes in Cordele. Myrtle was rolling up the green and white awning as we pulled to the curb. There was a lone figure seated at the counter. He was absorbed in his newspaper.

"Penny for your thoughts, Derek?" Miss Daniel said. "You look like you're a thousand miles away."

I wished that I could talk to her about my thoughts, but they were too dark and upsetting to discuss with anyone. Out of the corner of my eye, I thought I saw Mr. Tyler grin. I'm sure he knew what I was thinking.

"Oh, it's nothing. Some of the words I studied this weekend on the way to Fargo keep running through my head. I hope I have them memorized.

"Miss Daniel, do people really use these words in everyday conversation?"

"Yes, Derek, they do. Obviously not so many and not so often, but civilized, educated, people do speak using powerful words. Sometimes ordinary, everyday words don't suffice. They don't fully express what we're trying to say."

"I've noticed that when I try to use some of the words I've learned the other boys make fun of me."

"Derek, you're going to find throughout your life that small minds close themselves off to learning, and they resent those who do try to improve themselves. They don't have the ambition for themselves, yet they resent it when others do. You can't allow that to keep you from expanding your own horizons. If you seek out kindred spirits, those who understand you, they will encourage you."

"I know, but it's so hard when you want to fit in. It's like Billy Kelly." I watched for Mr. Tyler's reaction. "He wanted to fit in too, but the other boys wouldn't let him, so he hung out with the girls." Mr. Tyler flinched and squinted into the sun as he rotated the unlit cigar in his mouth. He looked uncomfortable. Good. He made me uncomfortable.

The pecan groves and peach orchards slid by. We fell into silence. Macon came and went. Jonesboro loomed in the distance. Billboards touting Tara and *Gone with the Wind* littered the roadsides. We eased past the Quonset style hangars at Candler Field, Atlanta's municipal airport. A four-engine plane swooped across the roadway in front of us. I thought it would take our roof off as it floated in to land. It was the largest plane I had ever seen. I was used to the small, yellow, bi-plane crop-dusters over the fields of Wyatt County.

We drove through Five Points, the heart of downtown Atlanta, where the original terminus of the railroad marked the founding of the city. We passed Loew's theater, site of the *Gone with the Wind* premier in 1939 and past the large department stores on Peachtree Street. Mr. Tyler was looking for the Fox Theater at the intersection of Peachtree and Ponce de Leon. I stared in amazement as it came into view. Nothing quite so grand existed in my world. It was a vision straight out of *The Arabian Nights*. Minarets, domes, and crenellated parapets dominated an entire city block. I couldn't believe this elegant building could be the site of the finals for the *Journal* spelling bee. But it was. Not in the 5,000 seat main theater, but in the smaller hall of the Yaarab Temple. Mr. Tyler parked on Ponce de Leon, and we entered the building from that side. Mr. Warren of the *Journal* staff greeted us.

"Welcome to Atlanta, and welcome to the fabulous Fox. It's so good to see you again. I trust your trip in from Shiloh was without incident." He led us into the theater.

"The contest will be held in the Yaarab Shrine meeting hall. However, if you'd like a tour of the main theater I'll be happy to oblige." We all nodded in unison. "Follow me," he said.

He led us through a maze of tunnels and stairwells until we emerged at the top of the balcony. I looked down onto a grand stage flanked on the right by a huge pipe organ. The ranks of chrome cylinders above it seemed to go on forever. Clouds appeared to float by overhead. Stars winked at us. Bedouin tents and striped awnings shifted in the breeze. I had to pinch myself to realize this was all illusion. *The Arabian Nights* came alive before my eyes. I was awestruck.

"This amazing building was erected by Mr. William Fox in collaboration with the Yaarab Shrine Temple. It is a monument to both the Shriners and to Hollywood," Mr. Warren said. "A portion of the proceeds from the theater goes to support the Shriner's burn centers and children's hospitals. They have been extremely gracious in allowing us the use of these facilities for our contests."

He took us down to the main level and then backstage where preparations were underway for the upcoming spring tour of the Metropolitan Opera. The opera was returning to Atlanta following its absence during the war years. Afterwards, he led us down the long entry corridor opening off Peachtree Street where elevators whisked us up to the meeting hall. The elaborate, decorative theme of the main theater carried over into the hall. Gilded frescoes and colorful tapestries covered every surface. Any minute I expected to see Ali Baba and his forty thieves come charging around a corner.

Melanie Kitchens sat in the second row with the teachers from Metter. She smiled as she caught sight of me. She rose to meet us. I was as smitten with her now as I had been in Macon. If anything, she was even more beautiful in a blue and gold dress with lace at her neck. I took her hand feeling the flush in my cheeks.

"Hi, Melanie. It's so good to see you again. That's a beautiful dress."

"Thank you, Derek. It's good to see you too. I've really been looking forward to this. Both the bee *and* seeing you again," she said impishly. I turned an even deeper shade of red.

"I want you to know that however this turns out I hope we can keep in touch with each other," she said.

"Me, too. Be sure you give me your address," I stammered. "I'll write mine down for you."

"Okay, I will."

Mr. Warren had mounted the stage and was testing the microphone. It squealed.

"Ladies and gentlemen, if you will all be seated we'll get started." There was rustling and shuffling as the small knots of people disengaged and took their seats.

"I can't tell you how thrilled I am to finally be presiding over the finals of this year's statewide spelling contest. It has been a wonderfully rewarding experience for me to visit all across this great state. I continue to be amazed at the depth of talent we have uncovered. For all those who lament the state of our educational system, I invite them to meet the many wonderful students and educators whom I have met these last few months. All of you are to be congratulated for your hard work. I wish that each of you could leave here as the winner today. Rest assured however, that you are all winners in my book. It is a fantastic achievement for you to have made it here to the finals. So, when we leave here today every one of you can feel justifiably proud of your accomplishment.

"Now I'd like to introduce our contestants. First, representing the southern half of the state we have Miss Melanie Kitchens from Metter, Georgia. Her advisors are Miss Kathy Strunk and Miss Cora Johnson. If you ladies will please stand." There was polite applause.

"From Shiloh, Georgia we have Mr. Derek Barton with his advisors, Miss Sara Daniel, Miss Frances Kuhn and Mr. Leonard Tyler." We stood.

"From the northern region of the state we have Miss Sandra Ellis from Roosevelt High here in Atlanta. Many of you will know this school as the old Girl's High that was recently renamed in honor of the late president. Miss Ellis' advisors are Miss Bunny Cline and Mr. Samuel Briscoe."

"Lastly, we have Mr. James McIver from Tech High. Also here in Atlanta. Next year Tech High and Boy's High are merging to become Henry Grady High. This honor being bestowed on the late Mr. Grady is especially poignant for those of us in the newspaper business. He was one of the most illustrious editors of the *Constitution,* our sister publication. Mr. McIver's advisors are Miss Catherine Winship and Mr. Carlos Castleberry." He motioned for their contingent to stand.

"I would also like to introduce our special, honored guests for the day. From the office of Mayor Hartsfield, we have Miss Ethel Burgess, Administrator for Cultural Affairs. From Georgia Tech we welcome Mr. Avery Winston, head of the English department. From Emory University, we are honored to have their chairman of the Humanities, Mr. Bertram Langford and from Agnes Scott College, Miss Millicent Dewbury, distinguished chair of their education department. Others are here from the press, radio, television and the academic community. Welcome one and all."

"The same rules and procedures that were followed in the semifinals will obtain here today as well. The only difference being there will be a single winner. If everyone will please take their seats, we'll get started.

"Miss Jane Arbuckle from Marietta and Miss Audrey Callen from Decatur will read the words for us today. Good luck to you all. Mr. Phillips, will you please lead the contestants to the waiting room?"

The anteroom where we waited featured a large painting depicting Arabian warriors. They were on charging steeds battling for control of Mecca. I was drawn to the beauty of the horses and the splendid costumes of the fighters. The few paintings in our library back home paled by comparison. Mr. Phillips had to call twice to break my concentration.

"Mr. Barton, you are next," he said.

He led me back down the corridor to the meeting hall. I was the second contestant to spell.

"*Raconteur,*" Miss Callen intoned. "A storyteller or good conversationalist. *Raconteur.*"

"*Raconteur. R-a-c-o-n-t-e-u-r. Raconteur,*" I said. The word was on the list I took to Fargo.

"Thank you, Mr. Barton. That is correct," Miss Callen said. Sandra Ellis stood as I re-entered the waiting room. She was next. She returned in a few minutes, smiling. James McIver followed her. We were on the seventh word before a contestant failed to return. Sandra Ellis faltered on *catafalque*. Three remained when we were called back to the hall.

"It's almost noon," Mr. Warren said. "A lovely buffet is awaiting us in the dining hall. Everyone is invited. We will reconvene at one thirty. *Bon appétit.*"

I hurried to claim a seat at Melanie's table. I sat directly across from her. I was too nervous to eat much. I took one piece of chicken and some squash casserole. I don't remember how they tasted.

"What will you be doing this summer?" I asked, trying to make conversation without seeming too eager.

"I think my mother and I are going down to Florida to visit my grandparents. I usually spend several weeks with them. What about you?"

"Oh, I guess I'll be working with my father at the sawmill. I'll probably spend some time helping my brother Bill. He has a veterinary clinic in Adel."

"How interesting," she said. "That's one of the fields I'm considering when I go to college. Maybe I'll get a chance to meet him sometime."

"I tell you what. You let me know when you'll be driving down to Florida this summer, and I'll try to meet you when you go through Adel."

"That would be wonderful," Melanie said. "I'll make sure we go when you are there. You don't think your brother will mind do you?"

"No. He loves what he's doing, and he's always encouraging others who are interested. He'll be happy to talk to you."

"What do you plan to do when you finish high school, Derek?" Melanie asked.

"I'd like to be a veterinarian too, but I don't know if my folks will be able to afford college for me. If not, I'll probably go into the service to get the G.I. Bill. Then I'll go to college when I get out."

"Great! It would be fun if we could go to college together."

"That would be wonderful," I said. In my heart, I knew that I would never be able to go to college right out of high school.

"You kids want to walk around before we start again?" Miss Strunk said.

"Sure," Melanie said. I quickly added my agreement.

The sunlight beaming down on Peachtree Street at noon was blinding. I shielded my eyes and squinted at the building across the street. The sign read, Georgian Terrace Hotel. We walked across to get a closer look. The ten floor, beige brick, structure was very imposing. It faced both Peachtree and Ponce de Leon. The two facades were joined at the corner by a cylindrical tower. There was a plaque in the lobby attesting to its famous guests: Enrico Caruso, Lily Pons, Artur Rubinstein, Clark Gable, Vivien Leigh, the list went on. Names I had only read about. Now I was standing in the very spot where they had stood.

"It must be really nice to stay in a hotel like this," Miss Strunk said. "We don't have anything to compare with this where we come from."

"Neither do we," I said. "The Willard in Shiloh has twelve rooms, a lobby, and a staircase. The most famous person that has ever stayed there is probably Fuzzy Q. St. John." Miss Strunk had a blank look. Melanie laughed.

"He's in cowboy movies," she explained. "Saturday afternoons."

"Oh," Miss Strunk said. "I don't see too many of those. We'd better head back. The afternoon session will start soon."

Miss Daniel smiled as we took our seats. She knew I liked Melanie. She had asked how I felt about competing against her. I said I hadn't given it much thought, but I was sure each of us would give it our best and wish the other well.

"Ladies and gentlemen, I trust you enjoyed your lunch and are now ready for the conclusion of the contest. I must say I was surprised that three contestants made it through that barrage of difficult words this morning. I told you they were smart. This afternoon we'll ratchet up the difficulty a little bit more. Now, if Mr. Phillips will escort our three stars to the waiting room we'll get started." Alphabetically, I went first.

"*Fenestration*," Miss Arbuckle said. "*Fenestration* is the design and placing of windows in a building. *Fenestration.*"

"*Fenestration. F-e-n-e-s-t-r-a-t-i-o-n. Fenestration.*"

"Correct, Derek," Miss Callen said. "You may return, and please send Miss Kitchens out."

Melanie returned, and she was followed by James McIver. He did not return. Melanie and I were called back to the stage.

"Congratulations," Mr. Warren said. "You two are now our finalists. When the first of you misses a word, we will call the other back. If that person spells it correctly, he or she will be the winner. If both of you misspell the word, you will be sent back, and we'll start again. Mr. Barton will go first." Melanie returned to wait.

"*Onomatopoeia*," Miss Arbuckle said. "*Onomatopoeia* is the formation or use of words that imitate the sound associated with something. For example, words like *hiss* or *buzz*. *Onomatopoeia*."

I knew the word had its derivation in the Greek language, and I knew most of the root suffixes in Greek used compound vowels, or diphthongs.

"*Onomatopoeia. O-n-o-m-a-t-o-p-o-e-i-a. Onomatopoeia.*"

There was an audible release of breath from the second row. Miss Kuhn seemed about to burst.

"Derek, you are amazing," Miss Arbuckle said. "I doubt one in a thousand people could spell that word. Please return and ask Melanie to come out."

Two minutes later, I heard a burst of applause from the hall, and I knew Melanie was just as amazing. Seconds later, she was back.

"Okay, Derek. Here you go again."

"Thanks, Melanie. I just stabbed at that last word. A person could live a lifetime and never see *onomatopoeia* in print. Wish me luck."

"Good luck, Derek." I knew she meant it.

"You, too," I said as I headed to the stage.

"*Pterodactyl*. An extinct flying reptile from the Jurassic period. *Pterodactyl*."

My reading interests took me to Sherlock Holmes and to other books by Arthur Conan Doyle. One of the most fascinating stories he ever wrote was *The Lost World*. Among the creatures inhabiting that imaginary Brazilian rain forest were *pterodactyls*." I doubt there's any other way I could have known the word or how to spell it.

"*Pterodactyl. P-t-e-r-o-d-a-c-t-y-l. Pterodactyl.*

"Amazing. Simply amazing. Derek please send Miss Kitchens out," Mr. Warren said. He was shaking his head as I left the stage.

Melanie left, and I waited. Several minutes passed. I waited for the applause. It never came. Mr. Phillips came for me. When I returned, Melanie was smiling at me through her tears.

"Congratulations, Derek," she said. "You deserve it. You'll be a great champion." She hugged me. At that moment, I wished I had failed.

"Derek. Melanie. That was a bravura performance, worthy of the magnificent operas performed in this famous theater." He paused to catch his breath. "It is now my distinct honor to bestow upon you the medals you have worked so hard to achieve.

"Melanie. What can I say?" he did say. "Hundreds of contestants started down this road with you six months ago. Only two still stand. You and Derek. This silver medallion and the five hundred dollar scholarship that accompanies it represent all the hard work and dedication you have given to this effort. Congratulations from the bottom of my heart." Mr. Phillips placed the red, white, and blue ribbon around Melanie's neck. Light from the overhead spots glinted off the bright silver medal. "Would you like to say a few words, Melanie?"

"Thank you, Mr. Warren. To all of you at the *Journal* who have made this possible, it has been a marvelous experience. I've met so many wonderful people. I dreamed of winning the top prize, but if I couldn't win it, I'm glad Derek did. He will represent us very well. Congratulations, Derek." She brushed away a tear and went back to her seat.

"Derek. Words fail me. This has been the most spirited contest I can remember, and I've been associated with these events for twenty years. The competition was keener and the words harder. At this rate, they're going to have to create some new words for future contestants. I don't think we have any left in our lexicon tougher than the ones you spelled today, and, as I said to Melanie, I don't think we could ask for two more personable and refreshing students as you." He picked up an ornate, green velvet case from the table and flipped it open. "Derek, this gold medallion is emblematic of the finest speller the school systems of Georgia can produce.

You have faced the best from all corners of the state and emerged victorious. Congratulations." He placed the medallion around my neck and shook my hand heartily. "As Melanie said, I know you will represent the state of Georgia well in the coming year as its champion speller, and this thousand dollar scholarship will come in handy as you go off to college."

The audience rose in applause. I bowed stiffly, holding the medal out in front of me and staring at it. It was all like a dream. I looked into Melanie's eyes. I knew her tears were for my joy. At that moment, my world was complete.

"That concludes the contest for this year," Mr. Warren said. "I hope to see many of you back here again next year. Drive carefully going home. I would like the Shiloh delegation to stay after everyone else has left. Thank you."

It was mid-afternoon. I had hoped we could get back on the road and get home before dark. Now, we were going to stay over.

"Derek, I am speechless," Miss Daniel said, as I made my way through the crowd. Everyone reached to shake my hand. Several photographers snapped photos as each dignitary congratulated me. I figured I would make the *Journal,* the *Herald* and the *Local* this week.

"Well done," Miss Kuhn said. "I'm so proud of you. I can't wait until the news gets back to Shiloh."

"Nice going, Derek," Mr. Tyler said. He pumped my arm several times. I couldn't look him in the eye. By now, the crowd had thinned out, and Mr. Warren was addressing us.

"Miss Daniel, I don't know if you were told, but it's customary for the winner to stay over for interviews by the press and television. We've reserved two rooms at the Georgian Terrace across the street. Dinner and breakfast will be complimentary for all of you in their dining room. My assistant, Miss Rogers, has a schedule for you. Derek will be pretty busy from now until dinnertime. The interviews will take place at the hotel after you've checked in and had a chance to freshen up a bit. I'll see you over there later this afternoon. Here's Miss Rogers."

A petite, young blond, probably no more than two years out of the University of Georgia School of Journalism, opened her notebook and began to tick off the names and organizations that would be interviewing me: the *Journal,* the *Constitution,* the *Macon Telegraph,* WSB-TV and WAGA-TV. Mr. Warren was right. I would be very busy. The only problem I could see was that at the end of all this I had to go to bed with Mr. Tyler.

Chapter 19

The cameraman from WSB put down his camera and turned off the bright lights. They were blinding me. Rivulets of sweat coursed through the powder that Miss Rogers' assistant had applied to my face.

"That's to keep your face from looking shiny," she had said. "It gets real hot from all the lights."

WSB was the last interview. It was almost sundown, and I was getting tired.

"Derek, why don't you go up to your room and freshen up?" Miss Daniel said. She sat through all the interviews and helped me respond to several of the questions. I think she was enjoying the limelight more than I was. I just wanted to get through it. "Miss Kuhn and Mr. Tyler have already gone upstairs. We agreed to meet at seven for supper."

The elevator in the hall behind registration took me to the eighth floor. Room 816 was located at the intersection of the two facades. I knocked. I could hear a door closing inside the room and a drawer sliding shut. The door opened slowly. It stopped at the end of the safety chain. When Mr. Tyler saw that it was me, he unhooked the chain to let me in.

"Well, Derek. Is all the excitement over? Has the Shiloh Whiz Kid had his moment in the sun?" His voice dripped with sarcasm. I didn't know why he was so upset. I tried to ignore it.

"Yes, sir. They've all gone. I think that if I'd known I had to go through all this, I'd have stayed home. They all asked the same silly questions. I guess it's just their job. I'm glad it's over."

Mr. Tyler didn't respond. He went to the dresser where one drawer remained ajar as if in his haste he'd failed to close it. I saw a glint of silver as he slid it closed. He had brought the gun. The hair stood up on my neck.

"Derek, I'm going to take a little nap before supper. You might want to do the same. It's been a tiring day, and I don't want to go to sleep in my soup."

"Yes, sir. I think I will. After I go to the bathroom."

When I returned, Mr. Tyler was stretched out on the bed in his underwear.

"Didn't want to mess up my clothes," he offered by way of explanation. "I suggest you do the same."

I slipped my tie off careful not to lose the knot. I hung my shirt and pants on a chair. I was leery of what Mr. Tyler might try. Surely, he wouldn't bother me now. Supper was just over an hour away. I lay on the bed tensed for any move he might make. After a few minutes, his steady breathing said he was asleep. I drifted off.

When I awoke, dusk had settled in. The neon marquee of the Fox flashed gold and red on the window. Mr. Tyler was on his stomach next to me, his left arm draped across my chest. He was still asleep. I eased myself from under his arm trying not to wake him. He grunted and rolled away. I went to the bathroom, brushed my teeth, and washed my face. He was still asleep when I came back. I slipped quietly into my clothes, before I shook him awake.

"Mr. Tyler, it's nearly supper time. I think I'll go on down to the lobby. I'll see you there." He roused himself, groggy from his nap.

"Okay, Derek. I'll be down directly," he said with a half-smile. I didn't like the look. I hurried out the door and ran to the elevator. I couldn't get away from him fast enough.

Miss Daniel and Miss Kuhn were seated on the terrace facing the Fox. Each had a small glass of amber liquid in front of them.

"Derek," Miss Daniel said. She seemed surprised. "Frances and I were having a little celebration in your honor. You must promise not to tell anyone back home that we had a glass of champagne. There are some who might disapprove." She blushed like a schoolgirl caught in her first kiss.

"Don't worry, ma'am. Your secret is safe with me."

"Would you like a Coke, Derek?" she asked.

"Yes, ma'am, that would be great."

She motioned to a tuxedoed waiter. He came over to take my order. When he returned, he had my Coke and three small dishes of nuts.

"For your pre-dinner enjoyment," he said with a flourish.

"My, my," Miss Kuhn said. "Aren't we living in high cotton?" She was very pleased with herself.

"Where is Mr. Tyler?" she asked.

"He took a nap and wasn't quite ready when I left. He said he'd be along directly."

We sat there enjoying our drinks and watching the limousines as they deposited their passengers at the Fox. Tuxedoed and gowned patrons were arriving for the pre-opera gala in the grand ballroom. I felt like Dorothy in the *Wizard of Oz*. We were definitely not in Shiloh anymore.

"There you are," a voice boomed from over my shoulder. Mr. Tyler pulled out the fourth chair and sat down. "I see you ladies have a head start on me." He called the waiter over again. "I believe I'll have a beer if you don't mind. I wouldn't be a proper gentleman if I let these ladies drink alone."

"Yes, sir. Right away, sir."

The beer and another dish of nuts appeared. Mr. Tyler lifted his glass.

"I propose a toast to young Mr. Barton on his significant achievement today. Here's to you, Derek. May this be only the first of many more to come." He clinked his glass against the other three and took a sip of the beer. "I must say, this is a cut above Pop Gullet's rotgut brew."

"Why, Leonard. I didn't know you frequented that den of iniquity," Miss Kuhn said in mock surprise. "You stand to be tarred and feathered and ridden out of town on a rail."

"Now, Frances, you know that I and the other single male teachers need to let our hair down every once in a while. However, I assure you we are very discreet about it. We go and come only after dark when all the town fathers are tucked snugly into their beds. That is unless they are there as well." He slapped his knee and laughed. "I'll bet you that more moonshine deliveries are made to the eight blocks of North Antioch Street than the rest of Shiloh combined. You know what they say about the electorate of our fair county, don't you? In every referendum on the legalization of liquor it is said that they stagger to the polls and vote *NO*." He laughed even louder.

"Leonard, you should be ashamed of yourself," Miss Daniel said between spasms of laughter. "You'll get us all fired with your scandalous tales. Besides, you shouldn't assault the tender young ears of our star pupil with such colorful descriptions of our civic leaders."

"Derek?" he said. "You don't have to worry about him. He knows how to keep a secret. Don't you Derek?" His words of reassurance to the other two struck an entirely different chord in me. They couldn't know what he meant by that statement. I did.

The dining room of the Georgian Terrace occupied a large space in the atrium of the wing facing the Fox. Crystal chandeliers, suspended from forty-foot, fabric-covered chains, diffused their light across the room. White linen napkins lay folded on gold-rimmed plates that in turn sat atop starched white tablecloths. I had never seen such magnificence. I was afraid to touch anything. I took my cues from Miss Daniel. When she slipped her napkin from its ring and spread it across her lap, I followed suit. The waiter set a small salad plate on the larger plate in front of us. Miss Daniel chose the smallest fork to her right. So did I. We went through two forks, a spoon and a knife before dessert. When the pie with ice cream was served, she reached for the small fork above her plate. Now what was that last spoon for? The answer came when the coffee was served. The last remaining piece of silverware was a sugar spoon.

"It's almost nine o'clock," Mr. Tyler said as he looked at the fobbed watch from his vest pocket. "I don't know about the three of you, but I'm pooped. I think I'll turn in. You coming, Derek?"

"No!" my brain screamed, *"I'm not coming!"*

"I think I'll stay up a while longer if you don't mind."

He looked mildly annoyed.

"Then you'd better stop by the desk and get another key. I don't want to leave the door unlocked, and I may be asleep when you come up."

"All right, Mr. Tyler. I'll do that. Good night."

"Good night, Derek. And a fine good night to you lovely ladies." He bowed deeply, sweeping his arms out and bending his right leg behind him. "I'll see you tomorrow morning. Breakfast at seven thirty shall we say. I think we should leave by nine, after the traffic has cleared out."

"That will be fine, Leonard," Miss Daniel said. "Thank you again for driving us here. I don't know how we would have managed without you."

"My pleasure, dear lady."

"Good night, Leonard," Miss Kuhn said coyly.

He weaved his way between the tables and toward the front terrace. He pulled a fresh cigar from his vest pocket and ran it under his nose before biting off the end. He reached into a coat pocket for his lighter. It ignited after three clicks. The flare reflected off the glass doors as he exited.

It was after ten before the women called it an evening. I was still reluctant to go to the room. I fingered the key in my pocket. I wondered what would happen if I just curled up in a corner of the vast atrium and stayed there all night. I knew that would be hard to explain in the morning. I rose slowly from the chair and made my way toward the elevator. At that moment, I knew something of what a death row prisoner must feel before he walks the last mile.

I slipped the key into the door as quietly as I could. I prayed he was already asleep. I pushed the door open slowly listening for his snore. My eyes slowly adjusted to the darkness. A red glow flared from across the room. He was sitting in a chair with cigar smoke wreathing his face as it rose to the ceiling. He was naked.

"Derek. What took you so long? I've been waiting. I have your drink ready for you. It's on the counter in the bathroom."

My first thought was to run, but where would I go? Before I could move, he was across the room bolting the door.

"Don't make this any more difficult than it has to be, Derek. Besides, now that you are a *queer,* you need to learn to enjoy it. It can be a very pleasurable experience. Now go ahead into the bathroom."

The path to the bathroom loomed before me the distance becoming longer with each step. My legs were leaden. I had to force them to move. God, don't let this happen to me. I closed the door behind me. The glass of opaque liquid sat there like a Lorelei, luring me to my destruction. I picked it up and started to drink it. My hand stopped halfway. I turned and went out into the bedroom. I walked over to Mr. Tyler and threw the drink in his face. His cigar sputtered out.

"No!" I shouted. "I will not do this! I am not a *queer*!"

He glared at me as the liquid dripped from his nose. His member was fully erect. His eyes burned with lust.

"Damn you, boy! You're going to do this whether you like it or not."

He grabbed me by the arm and threw me across the bed. I bounced off the other side and backed into the corner by the dresser. He came around the end of the bed, cornering me. He pulled the bottom drawer open. He reached in for the pistol.

"Are you going to do this peaceably, or do I have to beat the crap out of you?"

He pulled me from the corner and struck me across the face with the back of his hand. I tasted blood. He grabbed me around the neck and held the gun to my head.

"Take your clothes off and get on the bed, or I'll make it worse this time." He drew the gun back as if to hit me. I disrobed and crawled onto the bed.

"Now. Up on your all fours."

I kneeled on the bed. I heard the rasp of a jar top as it was unscrewed. I felt the cold, oily substance on my ass. He pulled me to the edge. I jerked away and lunged across the bed. I grabbed the gun from the nightstand. Before I could turn on him, he had me in an arm lock around the neck. He wrestled the gun from my hand and slammed it against my head. I blacked out. I awoke to a searing pain.

"What did you do to me?"

"Shut up! Go into the bathroom, and get cleaned up. If you're a good kid, I won't bother you any more tonight. We'll save the next pleasure for another time."

He followed me into the bathroom. He wet a washcloth and cleaned himself. I got into the shower. I tried to wash the last hour from my life. The filth wouldn't wash off. I held my face up to the flowing water. I cried.

"Come on back to bed, Derek. I won't bother you anymore. He sounded contrite. I didn't trust him. I wasn't sure I would ever trust anyone again. I sat alone in the dark.

"I'll be there in a minute," I said.

When I heard him snoring, I went back to the bedroom. I walked over to the corner window and looked out onto a city going to sleep. The marquee of the Fox went dark. There were few headlights on Peachtree. In the distance, a large, round, Coca-Cola sign blinked on and off. My life, which had been complete that afternoon, died that night in Room 816.

Chapter 20

"What happened to your face?" Miss Daniel asked. My left cheek was red and puffy. My lip was split. There was swelling behind my ear.

"Derek was a little clumsy this morning," Mr. Tyler said. "He slipped on the wet tile in the bathroom and hit his face on the sink. I checked him out pretty good. I don't think he has any broken bones."

The man could lie with the best of them. His explanation was so plausible that neither woman brought up the subject again. My face ached. I sat gingerly on the edge of the hard breakfast chair. My butt hurt. I couldn't tell them about that wound. I ate my breakfast in silence happy to have an excuse for not talking. I wanted to go home. I wanted to put as much distance as possible between Atlanta and me and the ugly memories I would carry from here for the rest of my life. I wanted to go back to being an unknown farm boy who couldn't spell *cat*. I wanted my life back. I sat in back with Miss Daniel. She brought copies of both the *Journal* and the *Constitution*. The headline on the "Arts and Education" section of the *Journal* said:

"Young Super Speller Flies Away with First Prize"

Young Derek Barton of Shiloh, Georgia, flew away with the first prize in yesterday's finals of the *Journal* spelling bee. *Pterodactyl,* a flying dinosaur, was the key to victory for the young wordsmith from South Georgia. When asked how he knew such a word, he gave credit to his teacher, Miss Sara Daniel. He said she had instilled in him a love for reading. One of his favorite authors is Arthur Conan Doyle of Sherlock Holmes fame. It turns out Mr. Doyle also penned *The Lost World* which Mr. Barton read and that happens to be populated with, what else, *pterodactyls*.

"Isn't that a wonderful article?" she said. "I can't believe that young lady got everything so accurate. Usually, there are several errors in most newspaper articles. Let me see how the *Constitution* did. She read their article. It took a different tack in its play on words. They spelled my name Derrick. Oh well. You can't win them all.

The return trip was quiet. I scrunched up in my corner of the back seat and went to sleep. The less I had to talk the better I felt. I was in no mood for conversation. Whenever the adults veered into a subject that needed my input, I snored a little louder. We reached the Willard at three.

"Derek, do you want to come into the hotel until your father gets here?" Mr. Tyler asked. I glared at him. "Remember. What happened last night is our secret. You don't want to hurt anyone with malicious rumors. Besides, my word carries lots more weight than yours does."

"No! I'll wait for him at the depot," I said. "He'll be there soon."

I got out of the car and slammed the door. I walked across the tracks without looking back. Mr. Cameron was tapping away with his telegraph key as the door to the depot slammed behind me. He looked up and nodded. When he finished sending his message, he spun around in his wheeled chair.

"Derek. You're back from Atlanta. Your daddy said you were going up there yesterday. How'd it go?"

I didn't really want to talk about it. I didn't want to talk about anything or to anybody. I grunted a response.

"It went okay I guess."

"Did you do all right with the spelling?"

"Yes, sir. I reckon so. I won the thing."

"Hey! That's mighty good. I know your ma and pa will be pleased. I never was very good at spelling myself. I still keep a dictionary here on the table by my key. I have to break it open nearly every day. Spelling's a real talent. It oughta carry you far."

The familiar blue pickup rolled down the path between the tracks and the depot. Daddy got out and came inside.

"Hey, Jesse. How's it going with you today?"

"I can't complain, Hiram. Nobody'd listen anyhow. How 'bout you?"

"Same here. I saw a bad wreck coming into town. It was on the big curve where the Shingler road pulls off from the Cordele highway. I feared for a minute that it might be Derek and the teachers coming back from Atlanta. Thank goodness it wasn't. One car was from Florida. I didn't recognize the other people. Nobody was hurt bad." He turned my way. "Derek, I'm glad to see you made it back all right. How did it go?" I turned so that my left side was to him. His eyes got wide. "What happened to your face, boy?"

"I slipped in the bathroom and hit my head on the sink. It looks worse than it is. I'll be all right. I won Daddy". I was too full of emotion to say anything more. If I opened my mouth again, I knew I would cry. He'd want to know why, and I wouldn't be able to tell him.

"That's great, boy. I'm real proud of you. I guess they'll make a big fuss over you at school tomorrow?"

I waited a few seconds to answer. I needed time to regain control.

"Miss Daniel said there'll be some kind of ceremony. I think it will be next week. The mayor will be invited. I think Mr. Gear will ask you and Mama to come."

"Well, that's good. At least we have one smart one in the family. Right, Jesse?"

"Yeah, Hiram. I was just telling Derek. My spelling's so bad I have to keep a dictionary on my desk. I seem to recollect William being pretty smart too."

"Yeah. He's doing all right. Him and Evelyn are over in Adel now. He's a veterinarian. The first and the last of Julia's boys," he mused while rubbing his chin. "One at both ends. Not too bad. Come on, Derek. I hear the whistle." The four o'clock rolled in right on time, all steam and squealing wheels.

"Howdy, Mr. Barton," the clerk called down. "We got several bags of money for Shiloh Banking Company. Be careful. We had a robbery down in Waycross last week. They got away with over 20,000 dollars. The FBI caught up with the robbers in Florida. They got most of the money back."

Most people were unaware of the large amounts of currency and coin transported openly by the railroad. Daddy had a shotgun slung across the back window of the pickup. I didn't think anybody was going to take him on. I rode in back the two blocks to the post office. Just in case. You could never be too careful.

Daddy parked under the big pecan tree in the side yard. I saw Mama standing on the porch. She wouldn't let on, but I knew she was nervous about my going to Atlanta. Especially, if we had to stay overnight.

"Hey, Derek. Welcome home. Did everything go all right?" Then she saw my swollen face. She put her hand to her mouth. "What happened to you?" I recreated the lie again, hating myself more each time I told it

"I won the bee, Mama," I said, hoping to change the subject.

"That's good, son. I knew you could do it." It was gratifying to see the pride in her eyes. "Thank you, Mama. I'm real tired, and my face hurts a little. I think I'll go to bed early tonight."

"I made pork chops and crowder peas for supper. They'll be ready in a few minutes. You can eat and go on to bed."

"Thanks, Ma. I think I will."

I went to my bedroom and threw my clothes bag in the corner. I would sort it out tomorrow. Red came up the steps as I passed on the way to the kitchen.

"Hey, Derek. When did you get back?" He noticed my swollen face. "What happened to you?"

"Oh, it's nothing. I fell in the bathroom at the hotel. It throbs a little. I'm going to eat early and go on to bed. I'm real tired."

"Okay, boy. I'll catch up with you tomorrow."

Mama brought Red's plate out to the porch.

"Did Derek tell you he won the whole thing in Atlanta?" she asked.

"Well, I'll be doggoned. I reckon that must have been something."

"Mama, I think I'll eat out here with Red if you don't mind. I don't want to eat alone."

"Suit yourself. I don't reckon Red will mind. He probably enjoys some company now and again, don't you Red?"

"Yes ma'am. I sho do. Derek can tell me all about his trip to the big city. I ain't never been to Atlanta. I hear tell it's quite a sight. Big tall buildings and neon signs all over the place. Someday, if I can save up enough money, I'd like to go up there. I have a cousin that lives in Cabbagetown. He works in the Fulton Bag mill. He said he'd put me up if I could get there."

I finished two pork chops, a big helping of peas, and two biscuits with butter and syrup. I was sopping up the last of the syrup when Red asked me a question.

"You seems a mite down for somebody that just won a big contest. What's the matter, boy?"

"It's nothing, Red. I'm just tired. I'll feel better about everything tomorrow. I'll talk to you after school."

I raked my scraps into the slop bucket. Red would feed them to the pigs later. I washed my hands and brushed my teeth. Red was still sitting at the table picking his teeth with a broom straw. I headed to my bedroom.

"Goodnight, Red. See you tomorrow."

I walked up the hall to my room and plopped on the bed. I wanted so much to tell Red what had happened, but I couldn't. I wasn't sure he wouldn't tell my folks. If he did all hell would break loose, and someone would get hurt. I had to sort this out for myself.

The sun was well up when I awoke. Mama was sorting through some clothes in my closet.

"I thought I'd let you sleep in this morning," she said. "Red took care of your chores."

"Thanks, Mama. I'll be up in a minute. The bus will be here soon."

She left the room for a second. I jumped up and grabbed the bag of clothes before she got to them. I pulled out the shorts I was wearing yesterday and stuffed them under the mattress. I planned to poke them down in the wash pot when Minnie's back was turned. I didn't want to do any more explaining to Mama. I washed my face and got dressed. I grabbed a biscuit and some fried streak-o-lean. Mama gave me a dime for lunch.

"Derek, I'm real proud that you won that spelling bee," she said as she handed me the dime. "We don't have much, but you've got a good mind, and I want to see you be able to use it. I'm hoping we can scrape up the money for you to go to college. William said if his practice does well he'll try to help out. You keep on working hard, you hear."

"Yes ma'am. Thank you, Mama. I really would like to be able to go to college. Maybe Bill can pay me something to help him in the summers, and I'll put that in the bank. Mr. Pollard at the Colonial Store said he needs grocery baggers. I applied last week. I may be able to work on Saturdays during school and all week during the summer."

My step was lighter than it might have been that morning. There was a glimmer of hope that I might be able to go on to college right out of high school. I really wanted to make something of myself.

Word spread like wildfire that I had won the state spelling bee. The kids at the bus stop kidded me mercilessly. Gene punched me on the shoulder. Anza said my swollen face made me look like I'd run into Joe Louis in Atlanta. I didn't care. I had achieved something nobody else had. I had a right to be proud, and I had a thousand dollar scholarship to prove it. Mr. Gear greeted me as I stepped off the bus.

"Young man, I've never been as proud of any of my students as I am of you." He shook my hand until my arm felt like it would come out of its socket. Miss Kuhn was there. She had explained my swollen face to him. "I've already cleared a space for that medal in our trophy case. Tifton and Albany can have their football statues. None of them have a state spelling champion." I turned red again. "Mrs. Overton is coming over this morning to take some pictures and get a story for the *Local.* I also understand someone will be over this afternoon from the *Herald* and from WALB-TV. You're going to be a celebrity all over this part of the state." Miss Daniel came into his office.

"There you are, Sara," Mr. Gear said. "Congratulations to you and your team. I believe this is the highest academic honor this school has ever received. I've had calls from all over creation. We've got folks coming in all day for interviews. I saw the stories in the *Journal* and *Constitution* this morning. What marvelous publicity this is for Shiloh." He paused to catch his breath. "The Chamber of Commerce should pay you for it. You couldn't buy publicity like this for a million dollars."

"Thank you, Mr. Gear, but all the credit must go to this young man. I just pointed him in the right direction, and he did the rest."

"Don't you believe that for a minute," I said. "I would never have had this opportunity if it hadn't been for Miss Daniel. It was her encouragement to read and study that got me up on that stage. I'll never forget what she did for me." Now it was her turn to blush.

"No matter," he said. "There's plenty of credit to go around. I'm going to call another assembly for tomorrow. I want the entire school to know and appreciate what you've achieved."

The rest of the school day was more of the same. Razzing and good-natured joking. Like Henry Tillman at Field Day, it was my turn to shine, and I tried to enjoy it, but the nagging memory of Room 816 kept intruding. It hovered like a dark cloud over a day that should have been the brightest of my life.

Chapter 21

I was changing classes from English to Science when I saw Mr. Tyler. He was walking straight toward me. He was talking to another student. He caught my eye then quickly looked away. I don't know if he was remorseful or just playing games. It didn't matter. I never wanted to be alone in his presence again.

The assembly at one o'clock the next day was a more energetic version of the one after Albany. Most of the kids were just grateful to be skipping their afternoon classes. That made me a hero more than winning the spelling bee did. Mr. Gear held up the medallion. As it turned in his hand, reflections bounced off the walls and curtains.

"This, ladies and gentlemen, is what one can achieve when one sets his mind to it and is willing to work hard. I want what Derek has done to be a challenge to the rest of you. Whatever your talent—language, mathematics, science, music—there are goals like this for you. Talk to your teachers. Ask them to help you and sponsor you. Next year I hope I can stand up here and announce another prize for one of you. Think about it."

The ceremony continued for a half hour. Miss Daniel spoke. Miss Kuhn spoke. Mr. Tyler was conspicuously absent. I wanted it to be over. I wanted to go home.

"Now we'll have a few words from Derek Barton, champion speller of the entire state of Georgia."

My mind was a jumble of thoughts as I moved to the rostrum: the degradation and shame I had experienced, the pride I took in winning, the confidence and love shown by my parents, the unswerving support of Miss Daniel. Above all was the realization that my life was now going to move in a different direction. I knew the events of the past few weeks would manifest themselves in ways that I could not begin to imagine, and the thought frightened me.

"I want to thank all of you for the support you have shown me during this entire contest. Every time I faced a new word, I would think of you, and know that I was not up there representing Derek Barton that I was up there representing all of you. I knew I couldn't let you down. I'm glad I didn't. Thank you.

After school, I went directly to my room. Mama had stripped my bed. The spread and comforter were draped across the wrought iron foot. I heard her on the back porch.

"Derek, is that you?"

"Yes, Mama."

"Come out here." I didn't like her tone.

"What is it, Mama?"

"I thought I told you to let me know if you had any more trouble with hemorrhoids." My mind flew back to the bed. Had she found the shorts when she stripped it?

"Yes ma'am, but I haven't. At least, I don't think so."

I was certain she had found the shorts.

"Then how do you explain this?"

She had my sheets lying on the porch table. She flipped the bottom sheet over and pointed to a dark blotch where my butt had laid. I hadn't noticed it when I got up. I reckon the blood soaked right through the shorts. Damn I was stupid.

"I'm sorry Mama. I didn't see it. It was dark when I got up."

"Well, I'm calling Gordon. We have to get to the bottom of this."

I was terrified. What if Dr. Sumner thought it was something other than hemorrhoids? What would he think? Did he have any experience with homosexuals? Had he seen other boys like me? My mind raced in a thousand different directions at once. Mama saw the fear in my eyes.

"Now, don't you worry, Derek. Both Tom and Roger had the same problem. Gordon took care of it, and they're as good as new. They had to spend a few days in the hospital and sit on a rubber cushion for a while, but they're none-the-worse for wear. You can ask Roger about it the next time you see him."

I knew what hemorrhoids were. I knew that was not what Dr. Sumner would find.

"Nellie? This is Julia Barton."

Nellie was Dr. Sumner's nurse. I saw her twice a year when she came to school to give shots.

"Is Gordon in today? Oh, I see. Will you ask him to call me when he gets back? Thank you."

"He's in Poulan," Mama said. "Mrs. Carruthers is having trouble. She lives next door to your cousin Cecil Carter, Lizzie's boy. Poor woman. She's already lost two children to the whooping cough, and she's had three stillborn. Bad luck seems to haunt some folks."

I hoped Mama would forget about it. I knew she wouldn't.

"Derek," Mama called as I came in from my chores. "I talked to Gordon. He'll be in his office tomorrow morning. He normally doesn't come in on Saturdays, but he said he had to catch up on some prescriptions he's ordered. He'll see us about nine o'clock. If everything's all right, you can stay in town and go on to the picture show."

Dr. Gordon Sumner's offices were upstairs over Newlin's Feed and Seed. The smell of fertilizer drifted up the stairwell. Dr. O'Sheild, our dentist, had offices right across the hall. They looked out on Liberty Street. He nearly killed me once while cutting out an impacted tooth. I haven't been to a dentist since.

"Come on in Julia," a voice from the back called. "I'll be right out."

Medicinal smells wafted across the waiting room. The door to his back room was open. He was pouring different colored liquids from large jars.

"Come on back, Derek. I'll show you what I do."

I tiptoed into his pharmacy. I was wary of breaking something.

"It's all right. You can't hurt anything. Most of the drugs I prescribe are available at the drug store, but sometimes I have to compound special ones myself."

Shelves lined the walls of the room. They were laden with containers and bottles filled with liquids and powders. A balance scale and multiple weights sat in the middle of a white, porcelain-enameled table. I watched as he tamped out a mound of white powder until the scale balanced. He poured the powder into a small jar and finished filling it with a yellow liquid. He shook it vigorously.

"This is for the Carruther's girl. She has a bad case of the croup." He screwed the cap on tight and dropped the bottle in his bag.

"I'm going back over there this afternoon. I think her mama's going to deliver today."

We went into the waiting room. Dr. Sumner gave Mama a big hug.

"How are you, Julia? I haven't seen you for a while. I understand your boy here has done us all proud."

"He has, Gordon. Between the Bartons and the Grimes we finally produced somebody with a few brains. I believe maybe the Thornhills had a little to do with it. Look at you. You're the first doctor in either of our families."

Dr. Sumner put his hand on my chin and tilted my face to the light.

"That's a nasty bruise, Derek."

"He fell while he was in Atlanta and hit his head," Mama said. "Do you think it'll be all right?"

He probed my face and looked into my mouth. I winced.

"I don't think anything is broken. You might want to put a warm poultice on him when he gets home. It'll take the swelling down some. Nellie said you had some other concerns about Derek. Hemorrhoids, I think she said."

"Yes," Mama said. "You remember both Tom and Roger had them. I reckon it runs in the Barton family. I hoped none of the other boys would be afflicted, but it looks like Derek might have them. He's had a couple of spells of bleeding, so I thought I'd get you to check him out."

"Come on back to the examining room, Derek, and let's have a look. Julia, why don't you wait out here? Young men of Derek's age like a little privacy in these matters." He laughed and led me out of the room.

"Just take off your dungarees and your shorts and lay down on your stomach on the table." He washed his hands and put on rubber gloves, while I slipped my clothes off.

"Now let me see," he said. "Have you been having much pain?" He probed around a bit.

"No, sir. A little the past month or so. Nothing to complain about."

"I want you to slide down with your knees on that shelf, and bend over the table."

He pulled up a stool. He placed a black band around his head. It was equipped with a mirror and a light. He poked about for a while. I winced again.

"Okay, Derek. I think I've seen enough. You can clean up in the bathroom, and put your clothes back on."

When I came out of the bathroom, I could hear them talking in the waiting room. The door was slightly ajar. I moved closer.

"Julia, Derek doesn't have hemorrhoids."

"Then what is it, Gordon?"

"I don't know how to tell you this any other way. He's been sodomized."

"What do you mean?"

"Just that. Something, or someone, has penetrated his anus and ruptured the blood vessels. That's what caused the bleeding."

Through the partially opened door, I could see Mama's face go white. I felt terrible. Now I had brought shame to her. I didn't know what to do.

"Julia, do you have any idea how this happened? Has he been experimenting with some of his friends? You know young boys do a lot of crazy things when they reach puberty and first discover sex."

"I don't think so. I can't remember him being alone with any of the other boys. He hasn't been on any sleepovers recently. Of course, I don't know what goes on at school. I'm just plumb flabbergasted. This is the last thing I would expect from him. He's such a good boy. He goes to church every Sunday." She began to cry.

"This doesn't have anything to do with being good or bad, Julia. Sex urges cause strange things to happen to young boys. Do you want me to talk to Derek?"

"Yes. I want to know how this happened, and to put a stop to it," she said angrily while wiping away her tears with a handkerchief. Dr. Sumner came toward the examining room. I quickly retreated to the bathroom.

"Derek, come on out here. There's something I want to talk to you about."

I knew what was coming, and I didn't know what I would say.

"Derek, I know that someone has been messing with you. The blood your mama found came from burst blood vessels in your anus. Those can only occur if some foreign object has forcefully penetrated you. Do you want to tell me about it?"

"I can't Dr. Sumner. It'll get people in trouble. They told me if I tell anyone they'll hurt me or my family. I just want it to go away. I'm not going to let it happen again."

"Do those bruises and cut lip have something to do with it?"

"No, sir. I told you I fell and hit my head on the bathtub."

"If you don't tell me who did this, Derek, you'll have to tell Sheriff Hudson. I'm bound by the law to report abuses like this."

"Can't I just go home now? I'm scared."

"Come with me." He led me back to the waiting room.

"What do you have to say for yourself, young man?" Mama blurted out as soon as I entered the room. "What have you been doing? What did he tell you, Gordon?"

"He's pretty upset by the whole thing, Julia. He doesn't want to talk about it. He's afraid of reprisals or of getting others in trouble. I told him I'll have to report this to the sheriff, and that he'll have his own questions."

"Have any of your friends or cousins been fooling with you?" Mama asked.

"No ma'am."

"Then who was it? You'd better tell me before we get home. Hiram will skin the hide off you. You know how he hates this sort of thing."

I couldn't look at her. I couldn't bear to see the hurt in her eyes. I walked over and stared out on Main Street. My eyes went to the window over the florist shop. I saw a slat in the venetian blind bend slightly and then pop back into place. He knew.

Chapter 22

"The boy won't talk to me," my father shouted from the front room. "I threatened to get my razor strop, but he didn't flinch. I've never known him to be so stubborn. I reckon he's embarrassed to high heaven, but he knows we're gonna get to the bottom of this. Who's he been alone with, Julia? Who had the chance to do this?"

"He hasn't been to stay with Bryce or Charles or any of the other boys in quite a spell. He's been playing with Gene and the Braswell boys, but I can't believe they could've done this."

"What about Jack Smith or some of the other Negro sharecropper boys on the place? Do you think they've been fooling around?"

"I don't think so," Mama said. "Somebody would have seen them. The only other men who've been alone with him lately, that I know of, are Red and that Mr. Tyler."

"Aww, Red wouldn't hurt the boy. He loves Derek like a son. I can't believe such a thing. As for Mr. Tyler, I don't know much about him. I assume the school board would've checked him out pretty good. Besides, he had them two lady teachers along. I'm sure they would've known if anything funny was going on." The phone rang.

"Hello. Yes Davis, this is Julia Barton. Sure. He's right here. Hiram, he wants to talk to you."

"Hello, Sheriff. Yeah. I'll be here all day. Sure, two o'clock will be fine." He sat the phone back in the cradle.

"Sheriff Hudson's coming out to talk to Derek this afternoon. I hope he has better luck with him than we did. I still don't believe he won't tell us who did this."

I stayed in my room all day. I couldn't face my parents. Promptly at two, Sheriff Hudson's black Dodge with the silver county shield on the door pulled into our driveway. Daddy called me to come to the front room.

"Derek, you know Sheriff Hudson. He has a few questions he wants to ask you."

"Derek, it would be better for everyone concerned if you'd come on out and tell us what happened. I know you told Dr. Sumner you are scared that someone will get in trouble, but that's gonna happen anyway. Sooner or later, the truth's gotta come out, and when it does, whoever did this is gonna have to answer to me."

"I can't, Sheriff. I just can't. Something terrible will happen if I do. You remember what happened to Koy Horton."

The questioning went on for an hour. I refused to tell them anything. I had never disobeyed my parents before. I felt awful, but this was something I just couldn't do. I knew that Mr. Tyler would use that gun if he got backed into a corner.

"Hiram, I want you and Julia to give me the names of anyone you know who has been in a position to do something like this. I'll go through the list and check them out and get back to you."

Ten minutes later the sheriff had a list of seven names: Gene Williams, Jack Smith, Bryce Hatcher, Charles Westbrook, Willie Braswell, Leonard Tyler and Red Crawford.

"These are all I can come up with Davis, but there isn't a person on this list that I believe could have done this."

"Maybe not Hiram, but the boy knew whoever it was. It wasn't a stranger. There are a few more folks around town I want to talk to as well," he said, while tucking the slip of paper into his shirt pocket. "I'll get back to you in a day or so."

The Dodge splashed through a big puddle, spattering red mud on the tires and fenders. It had been raining all day. Roger came in shortly after the sheriff left. I heard him whispering to Daddy on the back porch.

"Can't keep something like this a secret," he said. "One of the deputies over at the jail overheard the sheriff on the phone, and now it's all over town. Our family's name is being dragged through the mud. If I ever find out who did this…" his voice trailed off without finishing.

Roger was a big man. Six-foot two and over two hundred and twenty-five pounds. Now I had to worry about what he might do to Mr. Tyler if he found out and what the repercussions from that would be. Things were beginning to snowball.

I didn't go to church on Sunday. I couldn't face all the stares and the unspoken accusations. My life was spiraling downward, and I couldn't stop it. On Monday, I told Mama I didn't want to go to school. She wasn't having any of that.

"This isn't something you can run away from, Derek. Sooner or later, you're going to have to face up to it. I know you're scared and embarrassed, but once you deal with it you can get on with your life. It'll take a little while, but folks are pretty forgiving. I know you didn't do this without somebody forcing you into it. You're just not that kind of boy. That's why I can't figure out why you won't tell us who did it."

It was a miserable day. I sat alone at the back of the bus. I couldn't tell who had heard and who hadn't. Every glance and stare was like a knife slicing through me. I wanted to crawl into a hole and die.

Miss Daniel greeted me with her usual cheery smile. Either she hadn't heard, or she was putting up a front for my sake. Either way, I was thankful. A substitute teacher was in Mr. Tyler's class. He said Mr. Tyler had been unavoidably detained. I had visions of him down at the sheriff's office sweating under a bright light.

The day finally ended. I returned to the relative sanctuary of home. I had finished taking care of the chickens and cows when I saw the familiar Dodge pull into the driveway. Sheriff Hudson knocked on the door. Mama let him in. She brought him a glass of iced tea and said she would send someone for Daddy. He was at the mill. I crawled under the house and squeezed into the recess under the chimney. I heard a chair scrape as Sheriff Hudson got up to greet Daddy.

"Hiram, I've talked to everybody on that list but Red Crawford. I've pretty much cleared everybody but him and Leonard Tyler. I've sent a telegram to Tyler's old school district in New York and to the DA's office up there to see if there's something in his background we may not be aware of. I've also contacted the authorities in Grady County to see if they have a file on Red Crawford when he lived in Cairo. When I was talking to Tyler, he said Derek had made some comments about Red that were disturbing to him. He said Derek talked about a conversation he'd had with Red about *queers* and such. He said he didn't make much of it at the time, but in light of what I was telling him, it might mean something."

I knew Mr. Tyler was panicking. He was trying to shift the spotlight onto someone else and off himself. There was no way anyone could believe Red would do such a thing to me. Why he would die in my defense.

"Red is down at the mill right now," Daddy said. "Do you want me to fetch him for you?"

"No. I'm gonna wait for the report from Cairo first. If that turns up anything, I'll get back to you. Meantime, you and Julia need to be thinking if there may be somebody you overlooked, maybe a visiting relative, or somebody like that. I assume you've tried to get Derek to talk. Any luck?"

"Davis, that boy won't say a word. He's scared to death of something. I've never known him to be like this. His ma's about to go crazy. She dotes on that boy. He's her last you know. He's got a special place in her heart. It's killing her."

It was all I could do to keep from busting out crying. What had I done? There were small inverted cones in the dry sand under the house. They were ant lion traps. They would catch any unwary ants that might fall in. As I waited for the sheriff to drive off, I twirled a stick in one. An ant lion rose to the surface looking for its prey.

Later in the week, Daddy got a call from the sheriff's office. Sheriff Hudson wanted to know if he'd be home at three o'clock and if he'd bring Red Crawford to meet him at the old store. Daddy said sure. I certainly didn't like the sound of that. What could Red possibly have to say? I went to the store and hid in the bushes under the back window. I almost fell asleep waiting. A car drove up. It was the sheriff. A few minutes later, Daddy and Red arrived.

"Come on in, Hiram. Is this Red Crawford?"

"Yeah. Red has been working for me nigh onto four years. He works hard, and he helps out around the place. I never had any reason to complain about him."

"I'm sure that's true Hiram, but I have to cover all the bases. I just have a few questions for Red. I'm sure he'll have satisfactory answers for them."

"Red, how old are you?" The sheriff asked.

"I'll be 47 come October.'

"How long did you live in Cairo?"

"Born and bred there. My folks had a little place south of town. Little crossroads community called Midway. They lost the farm in the Depression."

"Were you ever in any trouble with the law down there?"

"They was once some folks tried to say I was involved in something that I didn't have nothing to do with. They called the law on me. Sheriff Pritchard put me in jail for a few days. He said he couldn't prove nothing on me so he let me go."

"What was it you were accused of?"

"They was two young boys that disappeared. White boys. The whole town was out looking for 'em. These folks said they saw them at the crossroads near Midway, and that I was with them. That was a plain lie. They may have been in Midway, but I didn't see them."

"What happened then?"

"One of the boys was found floating in the Ochlocknee River, 'bout two miles below Midway. The other boy showed up in Havana, Florida at his brother's house. Sheriff Pritchard went down there to question him and brought him back to the Cairo jail. Two days later, they found the boy hanging by his belt in his cell. The sheriff said the boy had told him that the two of 'em got in a fight over money, and he hit the other boy in the head with a brick. He said he threw the body in the river and kept on going. A while after that, the sheriff let me go."

"Is that the only run-in you had?"

Nawsuh. They was one other time. They was a cuttin' at a juke joint. It was a woman I had been sportin' around. I won't even in town that night."

"Sheriff Pritchard mentioned one other incident that you were involved in. He said the wife of a prominent farmer who lived near you claimed that you made inappropriate remarks to her while you were doing some work around the place. She told her husband, and him and some other men came down that night and dragged you out of your house. They threatened to string you up. The sheriff said he got an anonymous phone call and showed up in time to stop it."

"That woman was always saying crazy things. I never said nothing like that to her. They had problems, and she liked to stir him up. She didn't care if it got other folks in trouble. Sheriff Pritchard knew 'bout her. That's why he let me go. He told me that as long as that woman was around she was gonna cause me trouble. He said I oughta think about leaving town. That's when I came up here."

"And that's all, Red?"

"Yassuh. That's the truth, boss."

"Hiram, does Red know what this is all about?"

"No. I figured you'd tell him when you were ready."

The sheriff took a deep breath.

"Red, Derek has been sodomized. Do you know what that means?"

"Nawsuh. I ain't never heard that word befo'."

"It means somebody *buggered* him. You've heard that term I'm sure."

"Yassuh. I knows that word, but what's that got to do with me?"

"I'm just checking out everyone who had an opportunity to be alone with Derek in the last few weeks. Your name came up. That doesn't mean you're a suspect, it just means I have to check you out. Derek won't tell us who did this. He's scared to death. Whoever did it has threatened him and his family if he tells. I've tried to convince Derek that we can protect him, but he won't budge."

"Boss, they ain't no way I'd ever hurt that boy. Anybody that says so is lying."

"Has Derek ever said anything to you that would lead you to believe he was in trouble?"

Red thought for a moment.

"A little while back he asked me about *queers*. I told him what I know. I asked him why he was interested and he wouldn't say. I reckoned it was some talk going around at school. 'Specially after that thing with the Kelly boy."

"How long ago would you say?"

"I'd say it was near the time he went to Macon. Yassuh. That's about right."

"I want to thank you for your help, Red. In the meantime I'm afraid I'll need to hold you in protective custody."

"What's that mean?"

"It means that to make sure you stick around and that nothing happens to you, I'm going to hold you in jail. Just until we get this thing sorted out. Shouldn't be too long."

"Boss, I ain't done nothing wrong. Derek will tell you that. I been in jail befo', and it ain't no place for me."

"Don't worry, Red. Like I said, this'll be over real soon, and you can go on about your business."

I watched from the bushes as Sheriff Hudson walked Red across to the jail. What had I done? Mama was in tears. Daddy was mad as hell at me. Now Red was in jail. I ran back to the house and waited on the porch for Daddy.

"Daddy, why is the sheriff taking Red to jail? He didn't do anything."

"Then you'd better go over there and tell Davis who did. Cause he won't let Red go until he finds out. It's up to you now, boy."

I didn't know what to do. I wanted to be alone. I wanted to think. I went out to the chicken house. There, among the clucks and the peeps, I prayed.

"Dear Lord, tell me what to do. I don't want anything to happen to Red. He's my friend. I don't know what will happen if I tell Sheriff Hudson that it was Mr. Tyler. I've seen how crazy that man can get. I don't know if the sheriff can protect me *or* my family."

I thought about what happened to Koy. Supposedly, he was safely locked up in jail. That didn't protect *him*. I felt the welt above my ear. It was still tender. I thought about what Red had said. About the things that happened in Cairo. Did the sheriff think Red was capable of *buggering* young boys? I sat on the lowest roost and buried my head in my hands.

Roger was there when I went back to the house. He had seen Red walking to the jail in handcuffs. He sat down next to Daddy on the front porch.

"Why did they put Red in jail?"

"Davis doesn't think Red had anything to do with it, but he wants to make sure he doesn't run off while he's following up on his history in Cairo. There were several things that hadn't come to light before."

"Like what?"

"Oh, he'd been involved in a dust up about a white woman. She accused him of making advances toward her. Some of the men wanted to string Red up."

"What happened?"

"Turns out it wasn't the first time she'd made accusations like that. The sheriff let things cool off, and then he turned Red loose. He recommended that he leave town for his health. That's when Red moved up here."

"That doesn't sound like something Davis would connect with Derek's case."

"No, but there was another thing happened that piqued his interest. A few years back a couple of white boys disappeared. One of 'em turned up floating in the Ochlocknee near where Red lived. Someone said he saw Red with the boys in a nearby store earlier that day. They found the other boy in Florida two days later, and the sheriff brought him back to Cairo. It looked like an open and shut case of a fight that got out of hand. One boy hit the other with a brick so he said. Long story short, that boy hung himself in the jail. The sheriff had autopsies done on both boys. Turns out the one in the water had been *buggered*. The coroner couldn't tell about the other boy. Too much time had passed. The sheriff figured the second boy had jumped the first one, and that's what really caused the fight. He turned Red loose."

"What do you think?" Roger asked.

"I don't see any connection, myself. I think the sheriff made the right decision. It would have been mighty tough to make a case that Red could have had anything to do with it. Especially based on the testimony of the boy that hung himself."

"Even so," Roger said, "I've got an old army buddy who works for the highway patrol. He lives in Whigham, near Cairo. I think I'll give him a call. See if he can dig up anything."

Roger never did think much of Red. He thought he was a smelly old bum who spent too much time hanging around our house and around me. I figured that nothing good would come from that call.

It was the next afternoon when Roger came over again. I was lying on the sofa when I saw his truck pass the window. He parked behind the house. Daddy was sitting on the back steps. Mama was in the kitchen. I heard the car door slam. I slipped into the other bedroom that was just off the back porch. Through the screen door I saw Roger come over and sit down by Daddy.

"I talked to my buddy Claude today," he said quietly.

"He the state trooper in Cairo?"

"Yes, sir."

"What did he have to say?"

"He went down to the courthouse and pulled out all the reports on Red. Seems the sheriff wasn't so sure about Red not having something to do with that dead boy."

"Yeah, how's that?"

"When he got to nosing around he discovered there was a whole gang of *queers* in Cairo. Several of them were in high school. Some were in the boy scouts. A couple of scout leaders left town shortly after this all happened. It seems their favorite meeting place was this small park down by the river. The sheriff thinks there may have been some others there the day that boy died. He could never get the other kid to tell him. He asked him if Red Crawford was involved, and the boy got real quiet and wouldn't talk anymore. It was the next day when they found him dead. There was no way to link Red to the boys, so he had to let him go."

"Have you told this to Davis?" Daddy asked.

"I thought I'd see him tomorrow when he comes out to the jail. He probably knows all this anyway."

I didn't like the way this was going. It looked more and more like Red was going to get dragged into it. But what could I do about it short of telling them Mr. Tyler did it and opening up that can-of-worms? I had to figure out a way to help Red. I went back into the living room. I walked down the hall to the back porch. I picked up a bar of Lava soap and put it in my pocket. I walked past Daddy and Roger and headed toward the toilet, but I didn't stop there. As soon as I was out of sight, I cut across the chicken run and climbed the fence into the Powell's pecan grove. From there I crossed over to the jail. Jonas Cook had his feet up on the desk eating a hamburger.

"Hey, Derek. What are you doing here? Come to tell me who poked you?" He giggled. He was as crude as he was fat.

"No, Jonas. I just wanted to talk to Red."

"I don't know if I should allow that seeing as how he may be involved in this here case."

"It'll be okay. I just want to be sure he's all right. Has soap and stuff."

"I guess it'll be okay, but I can't let you in the cell. I'll need to be there to see you don't slip nothing to him."

"Okay, Jonas. I won't be long."

Jonas labored up the double flight of stairs ahead of me. It was like watching an elephant's behind in the circus parade.

"Here you are," he announced. He was puffing. "I'll be right over here. I need to be able to see your hands at all times."

"Hey, Red. How you holding up?"

"I'm doing tolerable well, but I sho don't like the inside of jails."

"Do you need anything?" I said in a voice that was louder than necessary. "Soap? Toothpaste?" Then, in a quieter voice, I said, "Red they're digging up all kinds of stuff from Cairo. Roger talked to an old army buddy of his from down there, and he said they thought you might have been hanging around with a gang of *queers*. I'm worried."

"They ain't no truth to that. You know that. But lotsa people won't believe a nigger, no matter what. They want to think the worst. Pretty soon lies is facts." The phone rang downstairs.

"You'll have to come down with me while I answer that," Jonas said. "Can't leave you alone with the prisoner."

I followed the deputy downstairs. He motioned me to a seat across the desk from him.

"Howdy, sheriff. Yes, sir. Everything's under control. Derek Barton came over to visit the prisoner. No, sir, I didn't leave him alone. Yes, sir, I'll be careful. What time you coming out? Derek's brother Roger dropped by earlier. Said he'd like to talk to you. Something about Cairo. Okay. I'll see you later then."

"Derek I been having the runs lately. You sit there while I go to the bathroom. I'll be right back."

As soon as I heard the door close and the hasp slide, I jumped up and lifted the ring of cellblock keys from the peg behind the desk. I un-wrapped the cover from the softened bar of Lava soap and pressed the master key into it. When I eased it out of the surface, it left a perfect imprint. I re-wrapped the soap and put it back into my pocket. I was careful to turn the impression away from my body. I wiped off the key and hung the ring back on the peg. When Jonas returned, I was sitting down.

"You need to talk to Red anymore?" he asked.

"I just want to say bye to him. That's all."

"Just go to the stairwell and holler up. I don't want to climb them stairs again."

I looked up the stairwell. Motes of dust floated down in the beams of fading sunlight.

"Bye, Red. I'll see you later. Keep your spirits up."

"Thank you, Derek. I 'preciate you coming over. You might bring my Prince Albert and some rolling paper when you come back."

"Okay. I'll be back tomorrow." I could feel Jonas' eyes following me out the door. Did he suspect anything? I didn't see how he could. He wasn't the sharpest tack in the drawer.

I excused myself from the table after supper.

"Mama, I'm going out to the tractor shed to work on my bicycle. The sprocket is bent, and the chain keeps slipping off."

"Don't you be out there too late. You have school tomorrow."

"No, ma'am. I won't be long."

Skeleton keys collect around a farm like flies around honey. A boxful sat on a shelf above the grinding wheel. I emptied the contents onto the workbench. There were twelve or so keys in the jumbled pile. I lined them up in a row and compared them with the imprint. There were only three likely candidates. I tried all three in the mold. One fit almost perfectly. I clamped it in a vise and filed it until it would drop into the mold with ease. I re-wrapped the soap, sealing it with a dab of mucilage. I said a little prayer that the key would work. I would find out tomorrow.

The commotion over my *incident* died down. Most of the kids didn't understand what had happened anyway. Words like *homosexual, sodomy* and *buggering* were foreign to the average school kid in the God-fearing, isolated, world of Wyatt County. They were sheltered from such things, just as I had been before Leonard Tyler came along.

The day dragged. I couldn't concentrate. I was too absorbed with thoughts about tonight and my next visit to Red. I had it all planned out. How I was going to take Red his tobacco and some soap, all innocent and above board. I crossed my fingers that Jonas would be on guard duty. It would be easier with him than with some of the other deputies. I would go over after supper, just before dark. I was nervous.

"Mama, Red asked me if I'd bring him his tobacco. I think I'll run over there and do it now before it gets too dark."

"Don't you be gone long. You've got some chores left. With Red in jail there's more to do around here. I didn't realize how much of the slack he had taken up. I'll be glad when this all gets straightened out and things get back to normal."

I started to leave. Mama put a hand on my shoulder.

"Derek, I know you didn't bring all this on yourself, and I know you think you're doing the right thing. But I sure wish you'd just tell us what happened. Your daddy and the sheriff aren't going to let anything happen to you or to any of us."

"I wish I could believe that Mama, but I can't. I know what he's capable of. The minute he thinks I've told, he'll know. And others will know. I don't think God himself can stop him if he wants to hurt somebody."

Jonas had just come on duty at six o'clock. He was hanging up his jacket as I walked in.

"Hey, Derek. You back again?"

"Yeah. Red wanted his tobacco and some soap. Is it all right if I take them up to him?"

"I'll have to go with you. Sheriff's orders."

I followed the elephant up the stairs again.

"Red, Derek's here. He's got some stuff for you."

"Let me see that can, Derek."

He flipped the top open and peered in. He shook it to see if it rattled. He tipped the can, and a pack of Bugler rolling paper fell out.

"You got anything else?"

"Just this bar of soap."

He looked at the soap. He saw that it was still in its wrapper.

"Okay. You can give them to him. I'll be over in the corner. Don't take long."

"Okay."

"Hope you enjoy the tobacco," I said. "Mama said I should bring you this bar of soap. She didn't know if they had any over here." I lowered my voice. "Be careful when you un-wrap the soap." I winked. He ran a finger across the wrapper. His eyes flashed, and he smiled.

"Thank you, Derek. I sho do need a smoke. And this soap is a whole heap better than what they has in here.

"You doin' all right?" he said. "They giving you a hard time 'bout not telling them who it was?"

"Yeah, but it's all right. I know I'm doing the right thing. Everything's gonna work out. You'll see."

"Okay, Derek, time's up," Jonas said.

"I'll see you tomorrow, Red. Anything else you need?"

"Maybe some more Prince Albert. I'll go through this by tomorrow night."

"I'll bring you another can. Good night, Red."

"So long, Derek." The tone of his voice bespoke more than a simple parting.

Chapter 23

I sat on the back porch late into the night. Weariness overcame me. I dozed in the chair until the deep throated baying of bloodhounds woke me. The key had worked. Red was gone. Lights came on all around the square. The swirling red lights atop police cars bounced off the courthouse walls. Cars and pickups streamed in from all directions. I ran across the garden to the jail and hid behind the oleanders at the edge of the Powell's yard. In the commotion, no one paid any attention to me.

"I swear to you sheriff, when I did a bed-check at ten o'clock he was laying on his cot," Jonas pleaded. "They ain't no way he coulda got outta that cell."

"Well, Jonas, he obviously did." The sheriff was visibly upset. "He's not there. Come on. I want to check his cell."

The lighter footfalls of the sheriff flew up the stairs ahead of those of the ponderous deputy. I could hear Jonas' panting from my hiding place.

"Look at that. He took some clothes and a pillow to make it look like he was under the blanket. When is the last time you are certain you saw him?"

"Musta been when I picked up the supper dishes. 'Bout seven I reckon."

"And did you have the keys with you at all times?"

"Yes sir! I snapped them on my belt when I picked up the dishes. I needed both hands to take them down the stairs."

"Were you at the desk at all times after that?"

"I shore was, Sheriff. The only time I wadn't was when I went to the john."

"What time was that?"

"Musta been about eight o'clock or so."

"And nobody was in the jail but you last night?"

"No sir. I expected Derek Barton to bring over some more tobacco for Red, but he never showed up."

"Why do you say that?"

"He brought over some last night along with a bar of soap. Red said he'd probably need some more tobacco today."

"Did you check the tobacco and soap?"

"I sure did, Sheriff. They wasn't nothing in that can of Prince Albert but some Bugler rolling paper. And the soap was still in its wrapper."

"Somehow or other Red got hold of a key. He was waiting for you to go to the bathroom, and then he took off. That means he left here about eight. It's two now, so he has a six hour head start on us."

Sheriff Hudson emerged from the jail and walked over to the knot of bystanders.

"Hiram Barton, are you out here?"

"Here, Davis." Daddy stepped out from behind the blue pickup.

"Jonas tells me Derek came over to see Red last night. He brought him some tobacco and soap. You know anything about that?"

"I knew he came over to bring the tobacco. I didn't know about the soap."

"One way or another Red got hold of a key, and the only person to see him other than my deputies was Derek. I'd like for you to bring him over here."

"Okay, Davis, but I don't know where Derek would have got a key to your jail."

I began to sweat. I had to get back to the house ahead of Daddy. I sneaked behind the jail and ran as fast as I could through the pecan trees and the chicken yard. I hadn't been in my bed more than a couple of minutes when Daddy shook me."

"Derek, wake up."

"What is it? What time is it?"

"It's almost three o'clock. Red has escaped. The sheriff wants to talk to you."

"Why me?"

"He says you're the last person to talk to Red apart from his men. He thinks someone slipped Red a key."

Where does he think I'd get a key to his jail?"

"I don't know, but you'd better have a good answer for him."

What was I going to say? Lies were compounding on top of lies. Oh how I wished this had never started.

"Derek, I believe somebody slipped a duplicate key to Red," the sheriff said. "You are the only person that visited him in the last two days. Jonas says he had the cell keys in his control at all times. Now can you explain how he might have gotten a key?"

"All I did was bring him a can of tobacco and a bar of soap. Jonas checked both of them. He was there the whole time I talked to Red. Ask him."

"That's the same story Jonas gave me. I think you wanted to protect Red, and somehow you got that key to him. I guess it's too late to worry about that now. There was no reason for Red to run if he wasn't guilty. I told him we'd have this whole situation cleared up in a few days, and then he'd be free to go. Maybe what Roger found out from Cairo carried more water than I thought." The sheriff returned to the crowd.

"All right men. I have three deputies and Herman Teeter with his two blood hounds. We're going to start tracking Red from here. Any of you who want to volunteer can come along. I'll swear you in as special deputies. We're probably going to be running the creeks and swamps north of here. That's where the scent seems to be headed. According to Hiram, Red has some relatives up in Atlanta. I figure he's headed there. He'll try to hitch a ride or hop a freight. He'll have a hard time getting anyone to stop in the dark of night, so my best guess is he's still on foot somewhere between here and Warwick. All right, Herman, let's go."

Herman Teeter dropped a pair of Red's pants on the ground in front of the dogs. He rubbed them over their faces and gave the order to track. They lunged toward the square almost pulling Teeter off his feet. They crossed to the store and turned up the road toward Doles forcing their owner to run to keep up. I knew the dogs had the stamina for a long chase. I didn't know about Herman Teeter. We'd gone about a mile when the sheriff called a halt.

"It's pretty plain he's taken the road. We'll kill ourselves and the dogs at this rate. Put 'em in the truck. We'll stop every few hundred yards and check for Red's scent. As long as he stays on the road, we'll keep doing that."

The trail repeated itself for four miles. We were near the turnoff to Providence Church.

"Lost it here boss. Seems he turned off toward the church. Something must have spooked him. He probably ain't familiar with this part of the county. Them woods back in there is mighty dangerous. I hope he knows what he's doing."

Daddy, Roger, and me were right behind the Sheriff. My heart sank. I'd been fishing in these woods with Bill; all along Abram's Creek. Cypress swamps covered the bottoms.

The dogs crashed through the cemetery and crossed the churchyard. They dragged Teeter down the slope toward the creek. He fell and slid across the swath of magnolia trees. He regained his feet at the bottom of the hill. Everyone scrambled out of their vehicles and followed.

The trail took us past the swimming hole where Bill shot the big moccasin. The dogs stopped at the edge of the creek, baying. Herman waded across a narrow section, and the dogs followed. They ran in circles on the opposite bank. Flashlight beams danced all over.

"Looks like he took to the water, Sheriff."

"Okay. You take Bess and go up that side. I'll take Adam and run this bank. A couple of you boys go with Herman." Daddy and I stayed with the Sheriff. Roger crossed over.

The undergrowth along the creek banks was almost impenetrable. We had to hack our way through tangles of briers and wild grape. As dawn approached, light began to filter through the canopy of trees. Bess cried out.

"He came out over here," Herman shouted. "He's headed west, toward Oakfield."

"Herman, take Bess and four or five men, and keep after him. I'll take a few men and head over toward Oakfield. We'll scout up and down the Albany highway to see if he's been along there. We'll meet up with you at the Oakfield-Egypt crossroads."

Daddy and I went with the sheriff. It took forever to get back to the churchyard. The sun was well up before we passed through Doles and turned west. We went down the Albany highway for two or three miles before the sheriff made a u-turn.

"All right, Buford. Turn Adam loose, and let's see what he can find."

The black and tan hound snuffled back and forth across the highway before taking off north. I couldn't tell if he had picked up a scent or was just searching. We followed him back northward. Above Egypt Road, Adam suddenly became frenzied.

"Looks like he's picked up something," Buford Ellington said. He was holding on to Adam's leash for dear life. Red had obviously crossed from the fields onto the roadway here. Adam had picked up his scent.

"Raymond, you go back and intercept Herman when he comes out of the woods. Bring him with you and catch up to us."

Buford stood on the running board of the sheriff's car. He gave Adam his head. We proceeded toward Oakfield at a fast clip. A mile up the road Adam began running in circles then turned into the churchyard of Friendship Church. He ran up the front steps and scratched on the door, baying all the time.

"Looks like he heard us coming and holed up in the church," Buford said.

"Okay, men," the sheriff said. "Spread out around the church. I'm going in."

He tried all the doors and found them locked. On the south wall there was a storm cellar leading to the church basement. Someone had pried off the flimsy lock.

"It looks like he went in through the storm door. Hiram, you and Derek come with me. Maybe you can talk him into giving himself up."

I figured with the big head start Red had that he might make it to Atlanta. I was wrong. He was just too unfamiliar with the territory.

Cobwebs brushed my face. Musty odors from decades of dampness and decay burned my nostrils. Poor Red. After all this, to be brought to bay in this old church. I wondered what would happen to him now.

Sheriff Hudson pushed open the door at the top of the stairs. Sunbeams filtered through the stained glass windows projecting their colorful images onto the pews and floors.

"Hiram, check the rooms at the front of the church. I'll check the choir loft and the rooms behind the pulpit." The sheriff came down from the choir loft as we made our way back toward him.

"He's not back there," he said. "Did you see anything?"

"Nope. No sign he's been here at all."

"We know he came in here, what with the busted lock and Adam's baying at the door. The only other place to look is the steeple. You wait here."

The door to the bell tower was off a narrow passageway behind the choir loft. The creaking hinges attested to the infrequent usage of the stairs. The sound of his feet on the treads retreated above us. The faraway sound of more rusty hinges greeted us as the sheriff pushed open the trap door to the bell tower.

"Okay, Red, come on out. I know you're in here. You've caused enough lost sleep and aggravation for one day. Now it's time to end it."

The clatter of loose boards and old boxes betrayed Red's hiding place. He climbed down from the corner of the tower behind the bell. There was no mistaking the sharp click of handcuffs. Red came down the stairs first, the sheriff holding him by the belt from behind.

"Mornin' Boss," he said. "I's sorry I got you and Derek into this mess. I just couldn't take it no more in that jail. I's seen too many bad things happen to black folks for no good reason."

"Running away just makes things worse, Red," Daddy said. "Whether you did anything or not it makes it look like you're guilty of something."

"Mr. Hiram, as soon as they put me in that jail I was guilty. I know how white folks thinks about niggers. 'Specially the po' white trash that picks on us all the time. They don't need no excuse, but this sho gives 'em one."

"Red, how'd you get out of that cell?" the sheriff asked.

"Oh, I just picked the lock." He lied for my sake. "That old lock was so rusted that it didn't take much to jimmy it loose."

"Damn! I guess I'm gonna have to replace them all now. The new jail won't be ready for months. Come on. Let's get you back."

Herman Teeter and Bess were waiting at the crossroads. Buford Ellington had gone back to Providence to get the other vehicles. We met him in Doles. The whole crowd headed to Antioch. No one was happier to see Red back in jail than Jonas Cook. He didn't want any more of the sheriff's wrath coming down on him.

"Did he say how he did it, Sheriff?" Jonas asked, even before he could get Red back to a cell.

"Said he picked the lock. Seems they're so old and rusted that it wasn't too difficult."

Jonas was visibly relieved to have that burden removed from his shoulders.

"Sheriff, I'll get some chains and padlocks to use until we can get some new locks installed. I don't want nothing like this happening again."

"Good idea, Jonas. Check with Mary in my office. She can get you enough petty cash to cover it."

"Sheriff, they was a lawyer called here this morning. Said he was from Atlanta representing something called the NAACP. He said he was contacted by Percy Tipton. Ain't he that nigger that's been stirring up trouble in town?"

"Jonas, I don't like that word. Percy Tipton is a Negro. He is head of the local chapter of the NAACP. That's the National Association for the Advancement of Colored People. Sometimes their Legal Defense Fund takes on high profile cases. They get a lot of donations from up north. Sounds like someone thinks Red's case warrants their involvement. What did you tell him?"

"I told him that Red had broken out of jail and was on the loose. He asked me to call him whenever we knew something."

"You better give him a call then. We don't want to be accused of interfering with a lawyer and his client if Red winds up in court."

With Red safely back behind bars, the crowd dispersed. Everyone headed home to clean up and get some rest. Mama filled the washtub on the screened porch for me. The hot, soapy, water stung the scratches on my arms and legs. It felt good to get clean.

"Did you talk to Red?" Mama asked.

"I was there when the sheriff found him. I heard what they said. He said the old lock was so rusty it was easy to pick."

"Well did he say why he ran?"

"He said he couldn't stand being in jail, especially since he hadn't done anything wrong. He said the white trash wouldn't believe a nigger in any case. He figured he didn't stand much of a chance in a white man's court room, so he'd take his chances on getting away."

"It's not going to make it go any easier on him. Those who didn't think he messed with you will now assume he did. I don't think they would even believe *you* now if you said it was someone else. Finish up and get some rest. You've got some studying to catch up on before school tomorrow."

Chapter 24

A shiny, black, Mercury sedan pulled up in front of the jail. Several of us kids were roller-skating in the old courtroom upstairs in the abandoned courthouse.

"Who do you think that is?" Anza asked.

"I don't know, but the license plate is from Fulton County. That's Atlanta. I'll ask Jonas when he leaves."

An hour later, I was sitting across from Jonas Cook.

"Who was that in the Mercury, Jonas?"

"Some highfalutin' lawyer from Atlanta. He's been sent down here by some big nigger organization to represent Red. I don't know why they don't just stay up there and mind their own business. We can take care of our own selves. Don't need someone coming in here to tell us how to run things."

"What did he say to Red?"

"He told him not to worry. That without your testimony they ain't got no real evidence against him. He said he thinks he can get Red off without a trial."

"I sure hope so. Red didn't hurt me, and everybody knows that. I don't know why the sheriff had to arrest him in the first place."

"Ain't everybody thinks you and Red is telling the truth. I heard one of the Lavender boys talking down at Pop Gullet's place. He said he thinks Red's got you cowed so you won't spill the beans on him. Thinks Red's holding something over your head so you won't dare say nothing."

"That's not true! Red didn't do anything!"

"If you feel real strong about it you better square yourself away with the law."

"I can't, Jonas. I can't say why, but I just can't."

The black Mercury returned to the jail several times during the next two weeks. There was to be some kind of hearing at the courthouse the following Wednesday.

"What are they going to do next week, Jonas? Is that gonna be a trial?"

"Naw. Best I understand it the sheriff and the county attorney have to show Judge Forehand a good reason to keep Red in jail. Something he called *habeas corpus*. That's some fancy Latin word. I don't got no idea what it means. I just know it's got a whole bunch of folks all riled up. Louis Lavender said if that slick lawyer gits Red off, they's gone be hell to pay around here."

"What do you think he meant by that?"

"I ain't sure, but the last time a nigger was in jail in Shiloh, for messing with a white woman, he got turnt loose on some legal loophole. Two days later, they found him dangling from a tree in the churchyard of the First Abyssinian Baptist Church in Poulan. That was near ten year ago. Ain't had no trouble like that since. Not till this mess with you showed up."

"Dawsey Matthews called this morning," Mama said when I got home from school. Dawsey Matthews was the county attorney for Wyatt County. "He says you'll have to be at the courthouse next Wednesday at one o'clock."

"What for?" I said.

"There's to be some kind of hearing for Red. Dawsey said you might be called to testify. That lawyer from Atlanta's trying to get Judge Forehand to turn Red loose. He says there is not enough evidence to hold him."

"What will I have to do?"

"Best I can remember from the time I had to serve on a jury either Red's lawyer or Dawsey Matthews can call you to testify. You'll go up and sit near the judge, and they'll swear you in. That means whatever you say has got to be true, or you can be charged with lying to the court. That's called perjury, and you can go to jail for it."

Not only had I got my parents mad at me, my friends wondering about me, and Red in deep trouble, but I was going to be forced to tell on Mr. Tyler. I knew that if he found out about the hearing he'd have someone there to tell him everything that I said. I could see no way out.

"Roger will take you," Mama said. "Hiram has to go to Albany after he meets the train. I'll send a note to Miss Daniel explaining why you'll be out of school Wednesday." I was sick to my stomach. I thought I might throw up.

News of the hearing didn't spread like most gossip in Shiloh. Judge Forehand imposed what's called a gag order on everyone associated with the case. That meant no one could even talk about it without getting into trouble with the court. He said emotions were running too high in the community because of the resentment over the NAACP and their lawyer, and he was just trying to tamp the fires down a little.

I went to see Red on Saturday. Buford Ellington was on duty.

"Hey, Buford. Can I see Red?"

"I reckon so, Derek, but Sheriff Hudson said we had to limit visitors to five minutes. I'll have to search you."

Buford patted me down. He satisfied himself that I wasn't smuggling anything in to Red. He led me up the stairs and took a seat on the chair in the corner. There was a shiny new chain snaking through the bars with a big padlock.

"Hi ya, Red." I tried to sound as unconcerned about the coming week as I could. "How you doing?"

"Hey, Derek. I'm doing okay. I sho hope that lawyer can get me outta here next Wednesday. He said they's a good chance the judge will dismiss the case since they ain't no hard evidence against me."

"You know they've said I have to testify don't you?"

"Yeah, Mr. Pearson said he wanted you to tell the judge what you told the sheriff. That I didn't do nothing to you."

"I know, but when I'm sworn in Mama says I have to answer all the questions, and if I lie I can go to jail. That means I'll have to tell them who did it. If I do he'll find out, and me and my family will be in danger."

"Derek, you gotta tell sooner or later. Soon's you do the sheriff will arrest the man, and he won't be able to hurt you."

"You don't understand, Red. It's not just him. He's got friends. He told me that if the police come after him some of his buddies will take care of me, or they'll hurt my family. I don't know what to do."

"In the end I reckon you just hafta do what you thinks is best, Derek. Don't worry. You're a good boy. Everything will be okay."

"I sure hope so, Red. I want things to be like they used to be. When we could work at the mill, or run the hounds, and we didn't have to worry about sheriffs and judges and lawyers. I want my old life back."

"You'll get it back, boy. In God's good time. We all has to go through trials and tribulations. Some of us more'n others. Keep your chin up."

"Time's up, Derek," Buford said from his dark corner.

"Okay, Buford. I'll see you next week then, Red. I hope they let you go."

"Me, too, Derek. Me too."

I followed Buford Ellington down the rickety stairs. Little did I know it would be my last trip to the jail.

Chapter 25

Mama said I should wear my spelling bee suit to the courthouse as a way of showing respect to the court. Roger and me arrived at twelve forty five and went directly to the second floor courtroom. It was located just beneath the clock tower. A court official asked our names then escorted us to seats down front right behind a banister that separated the spectators from the proceedings. The clock above struck one.

A deputy brought Red in from a side door. He sat down at a table next to the man in the black Mercury. Dawsey Matthews and a clerk sat at the other table.

"All rise," the bailiff said. Roger and I stood with everyone else. There were only a handful of people in the courtroom. It looked like the judge had limited the folks allowed in. Judge Forehand entered through a door behind his bench. He wore a long black robe and looked real imposing sitting high above the rest of us.

"Be seated," he said.

"Dawsey, are you prepared to make your case for holding Mr. Crawford?"

"I am your honor. It is my intention to show that there is sufficient evidence to warrant holding the defendant pending a grand jury indictment."

"Proceed," the judge said.

"I call Mr. Derek Barton to the stand."

Roger nudged me, and I got up slowly and went to the gate in the banister. It creaked as I pushed it open and walked to the witness chair. A man held up a bible and told me to place my left hand on it.

"Do you swear to tell the truth, the whole truth, and nothing but the truth, so help you God."

Boy. They sure had all the bases covered. There wasn't any wiggle room in that oath.

"I do."

"You may be seated."

"Is there anyone here to represent Mr. Barton?" the judge asked.

"I believe he is without counsel, Judge," Mr. Matthews said. I had no idea what that meant.

"Derek, since you are not represented by a lawyer, there are a few things you need to know about these proceedings. You are not on trial here. Nor, for that matter, is Mr. Crawford. This hearing is simply for the court to ascertain if there is sufficient legal reason to keep Mr. Crawford in jail pending a determination by a Grand Jury as to whether he should be indicted and brought to trial. Do you understand what I just said?"

"I think so, Judge Forehand."

"Good. Furthermore, you must answer every question, whether asked by Mr. Matthews or by Mr. Pearson, as honestly and as accurately as you can. Understand?"

"Yes sir."

"However, if you are asked a question, the answer to which you feel may incriminate you, you have the right to refuse to answer that question. Is that clear?"

"I'm not sure, sir."

"In plain language, if either of these gentlemen asks you a question that you think can get you into trouble with the law then you don't have to answer it. That is allowed under the Fifth Amendment to the Constitution. It protects a person from self-incrimination. I'm sure you've studied that in Mr. Tyler's civics class."

I winced at the mention of that name.

"Now do you understand?"

"Yes, sir." Not only did I understand, but I knew the judge had given me a way to avoid telling on Mr. Tyler.

"Good. Proceed, Mr. Matthews."

"Now, Derek, I just want to get at the truth here. I'm not trying to embarrass you or put you in a bad light. I just want the truth. Did Mr. Crawford, at any time, touch you inappropriately or commit any carnal act on you?"

"No, sir, he did not."

"You're sure of that?"

"Objection," Mr. Pearson said. "The witness categorically and forthrightly answered Mr. Matthew's question. His answer cannot be misconstrued."

"Objection sustained. The witness answered the question to my satisfaction. Go on Mr. Matthews."

Dawsey Matthews glowered at the lawyer from Atlanta. He wasn't used to being challenged in his own courtroom. Especially not by some hotshot lawyer from the NAACP.

"All right. Let's try to get at this from another direction."

"Derek, have you ever had sex with a man?"

I blushed and looked for a hole to crawl into. I looked up at the judge. He wasn't offering me any help.

"Judge, is this one of those times I can decide not to answer a question?"

"If, in your own mind, you consider that the answer to the question may incriminate you, then you do not have to answer it."

"Thank you, sir. Then in that case Mr. Dawsey, I will not answer your question."

"Let me get this straight, Derek. You vehemently deny any sexual contact between yourself and Mr. Crawford here, yet you refuse to answer my question about having sex with any other man. That would lead a prudent person to speculate that you *did* have sex with another man."

"Objection, Your Honor. Counsel is making an unwarranted judgment. One which may serve to prejudice the court, or a Grand Jury, assuming this testimony is ultimately passed on to one."

"Objection sustained. The reporter is to strike Mr. Matthews' last comment from the record.

"Two for two," I thought. This guy was good. Dawsey Mathews had steam coming out of his ears.

"I can see that the learned counsel from Atlanta is bent on stymieing my every avenue of questioning of this witness. No further questions your honor."

"Mr. Pearson. Your witness."

"No questions, Your Honor."

"Derek, remember that you are still under oath, and you are subject to recall to the stand. You are not to discuss your testimony, or anything you learn in this courtroom, with anyone else. You may step down."

"Call your next witness, Mr. Matthews."

"I call Sheriff Davis Hudson."

Sheriff Hudson swore the same oath and took the witness chair. Dawsey Matthews began his questioning.

"Sheriff Hudson, can you tell me how you came to believe Derek Barton had been sodomized and how you determined that Mr. Crawford was a logical suspect for such a crime?"

"Derek was seen by Dr. Gordon Sumner at the request of Derek's mother. She thought he was suffering from hemorrhoids. When Dr. Sumner examined Derek, he determined that the bleeding was due to several ruptured blood vessels in his anus. It was his expert opinion that the ruptures were caused by the rough insertion of a foreign object. He told me it was consistent with damage that can be caused by rough anal intercourse. Dr. Sumner signed an affidavit testifying to that conclusion that has been entered into evidence here today."

"Did Dr. Sumner elicit any information from Derek as to who had perpetrated this alleged act of sodomy?"

"No. He said Derek refused to tell him anything. Under persistent questioning from the doctor and his mother the boy refused to say who did it."

"I see. Based on that information, how did you conclude that Mr. Crawford might be implicated?"

"I asked Derek's parents to give me a list of all the people they knew who had the opportunity to be alone with Derek in the days just preceding his examination. They gave me a list of several names. I checked the list out thoroughly to see if there was any possibility of involvement by anyone on the list. I was able to eliminate all but two names. One of those was Mr. Crawford."

"And why could you not eliminate Mr. Crawford?"

"He lives in an old store very near to Derek's house. Derek is known to visit him there quite often. The two also work together on the farm and at the sawmill. They are often alone in the woods and in farm buildings, leaving ample opportunity for such acts to occur."

Mr. Pearson was furiously scribbling notes on a yellow pad and leaning over to confer with Red.

"That hardly seems sufficient to warrant his arrest. Is there more?"

"Yes. Before Mr. Crawford came to work for Mr. Barton he lived in Grady County near Cairo. I investigated whether or not he had a criminal record down there. It turns out he was a suspect in a stabbing for which there was not sufficient evidence to hold him. He was also thought to be involved in some situation with a white woman for whom he was working."

"Objection," Mr. Pearson said. "The evidence in those cases was all hearsay. The sheriff of Grady County never arrested my client on any charges in connection with them. Any connection that Mr. Matthews makes with those incidents and the present situation would be specious at best."

Another one of those words I learned.

"Objection sustained. Hearsay evidence cannot be considered. Anything more?"

Yes, Your Honor. About four or five years ago, two young white boys from Cairo disappeared. One of them was found drowned in the Ochlocknee River about two miles from Mr. Crawford's home. The other boy was found in Florida at his brother's home. Sheriff Pritchard brought the boy back to Cairo and questioned him. He said him and the dead boy got into a fight over money, and he hit the other boy in the head with a brick and rolled him into the river. The sheriff thought it was a simple involuntary manslaughter case until he found the second boy hanging by his belt in his cell.

"On a hunch, he had the coroner autopsy both boys. Turns out the one that drowned had been sodomized. They couldn't tell about the second boy. Too much time had passed. When Sheriff Pritchard started nosing around, he discovered there was a sizable ring of homosexual men and boys that met regularly in a small park near where the drowning victim was found. According to a witness the last person seen with the two boys before the murder was Red Crawford. He said he saw all three of them in a store between his house and the park."

"Thank you Sheriff," Mr. Dawsey said. "Your witness counsel."

"Sheriff Hudson. In your investigation of my client's activities in Grady County, did you question the *so-called* witness from the store sighting?

"Yes, I did."

"And what is your opinion of the credibility of that witness?"

"He's a farmer that lives near Midway. Everyone I spoke to, including the sheriff, said he was an upstanding member of the community."

"Did you ask the sheriff if the witness was in the *delegation* that kidnapped my client for having the temerity to ask a white woman for a drink of water?"

"No. I did not."

"I believe if you'll give him a call he'll confirm it. On that basis I'd say this man's testimony is not only not credible but is patently prejudiced against my client. I believe he saw this as an opportunity to further his grievances toward Mr. Crawford. Aside from this dubious allegation was there any indication that Mr. Crawford was anything more than a normal, heterosexual, law-abiding, citizen of the community?"

"None beyond the instances I have cited."

"The *instances* you have cited are based totally on speculation and hearsay. There is not one shred of hard evidence linking my client to *any* crime in Grady County, nor dare I say, to the present situation. I must say Sheriff Hudson that if this is the *evidence* you plan to use in the indictment of Mr. Crawford, the Grand Jury will laugh you out of town. No further questions, Your Honor."

"You may step down, Davis."

"Do you have other witnesses you wish to call, Mr. Matthews?"

"Yes, Your Honor. I call Roger Barton to the stand."

I had no idea Roger was going to testify. What could he possibly know since nothing had happened in the first place? The bailiff swore Roger in.

"Mr. Barton, I believe there are two instances that, in hindsight, lead you to believe they implicate Mr. Crawford in the crime of sodomy with your brother Derek. Can you tell me about them?"

"Yes, sir. A few weeks ago, my mother asked me to stop by Red's place and tell Derek to come on home. I was walking back to my house, and as I approached the store I could hear them talking. I heard the words *queer,* and *homosexual,* and stuff like that. I didn't think too much about it until later when all this came up. I thought it was just a young boy learning about the facts of life. I reckon now that Derek was learning some facts he didn't need to know."

"What do you mean by that?"

"Well I put two and two together after Doc Sumner said what he did, and I thought maybe Red might be taking advantage of Derek. Especially after what we learned about those two boys in Cairo."

"Go on."

"I went back over to the store a few days after Red was arrested and started looking around. I found that Prince Albert can under his bed. I didn't think anything about it, but when I picked it up it rattled. I opened it up and these pictures fell out."

"Let it be noted that Mr. Barton is referring to this can and the five photographs lying here on the table." Mr. Mathews held up a plastic bag holding a red can. "With the court's permission I'd like to enter them into evidence."

"May I see those?" Judge Forehand said.

The bailiff took the bag from Mr. Matthews and handed it to the judge. He peered at the pictures intently, his face contorting at the sight of something in them that he found extremely disturbing.

"Bailiff, please hand these back to Mr. Matthews. They may be entered as evidence."

"Now, Mr. Barton, will you describe these pictures for me?" Mr. Matthews said.

"They appear to be pictures of naked young boys in various sex acts with grown men."

"I see. And you found these hidden in Mr. Crawford's things?"

"Yes sir."

"I submit to you Judge that these photographs constitute *prima facie* evidence that Mr. Crawford was involved in homosexual activities with boys. *Ipso facto*, I submit he was the perpetrator of criminal sodomy on Derek Barton. Furthermore, I believe he has coerced or otherwise intimidated the young man so that he will not testify against him. I have no other questions of Mr. Roger Barton."

"Mr. Pearson?"

Red's attorney rose slowly from his chair. He rubbed his eyes and looked down at Red. I was dumbfounded by Roger's testimony. There was no way I would ever believe Red had sex with boys, but how could you explain those pictures. Mr. Pearson seemed at a loss for words.

"Your Honor, I must protest. There was no disclosure of these photographs prior to this hearing. That is in direct contradiction of all the rules and ethics of criminal jurisprudence. I can't possibly rebut this evidence until I have had a chance to consult privately with my client and to review it. I beg the court's indulgence in granting a postponement of the balance of this hearing until I have had an opportunity to do so."

Judge Forehand coughed and cleared his throat.

"Mr. Pearson. The revulsion I felt when looking at those pictures inclines me to proceed with all due haste toward arraigning Mr. Crawford and empanelling a Grand Jury. However, in the interest of judicial fairness and in keeping with the strict rules governing disclosure, I must grant your request. Court will re-convene Friday morning at ten o'clock. I must emphasize that no one in this room is to discuss what occurred during this proceeding under penalty of law." He rapped his gavel on the bench.

"All rise." Judge Forehand disappeared out the door behind his desk.

"When did you find those pictures, Roger?" I asked on the drive home thereby utterly disregarding the judge's admonition.

"A day or two after I talked to my friend in Cairo. After he told me about that bunch of *queers* down there, I figured Red was involved. I don't know what I expected to find. I just got lucky. If you had told us the truth right away, we wouldn't have to go through all this folderol. We wouldn't need a hearing. It would be your word against his, and no jury is gonna believe a nigger over a white."

"But it wasn't Red."

"Nobody's gone believe that after we found those pictures. Why don't you admit the truth? What's he holding over you to keep you from talking?"

Further arguing was fruitless. I finished the drive home in silence puzzling over the pictures. Red couldn't be a *homosexual*. He told me all about his women. He went cattin' around almost every Saturday night. *Queers* don't do things like that. But why the pictures?

"Mama, we have to go back to court Friday morning," I said. The aroma of chicken and dumplings coming from the kitchen was overwhelming. The sandwich I ate before we left home for court was long gone.

"Why?"

"They called Roger to testify. He found some dirty pictures in Red's belongings. Since Red's lawyer hadn't been told about them before hand, the judge had to give him time to figure out a response."

"What were the pictures?"

"They wouldn't let me look at them. Mr. Matthews said they showed grown men doing things to young boys. I can't believe Red would be involved in something like that. He likes women too much. I've known him for over three years, and he's never said anything that had anything to do with boys."

"I keep telling you, Derek. If Red didn't abuse you, then all you have to do is tell us who did."

"I can't Mama. It would put all of us in danger. Besides, I think this Mr. Pearson, Red's lawyer, is pretty smart. I figure he'll find a way to get Red off."

The chicken and dumplings tasted real good. Daddy was unusually quiet at the supper table. I figured Mama had told him everything that happened.

"Derek, did you know about those pictures?" he asked after we had gone out to sit on the porch.

"No sir. That was the first I heard of them. Like I told Mama I can't believe Red would have pictures like that. You've heard his stories about his women. Why would he be interested in boys? It doesn't make any sense."

"Maybe not, but you can't dispute those pictures. He kept them around for some reason. You're sure you never saw them?"

"Daddy, how many times do I have to tell you? I never saw them."

"Don't sass me young man. You're not too old to take out behind the woodshed. I'm just trying to make heads or tails of all this, and you're not helping by denying that Red had anything to do with it and then not telling us who did. Both yours and Red's credibility has suffered through all this. I don't want to call my own son a liar, but I don't know what to believe anymore."

Daddy lit a cigarette and walked out toward the chicken house. I think he prayed out there sometimes, too.

Chapter 26

"All rise."

Everyone was seated and ready when Judge Forehand entered the room. We all stood.

"Be seated."

"Mr. Pearson. Have you had sufficient time to consult with Mr. Crawford to determine a response to Wednesday's testimony?"

"I have, Your Honor."

"Then by all means, please proceed."

"I call Mr. Roger Barton back to the stand."

Roger plopped back into the witness chair clearly annoyed that he had to go through this again.

"Now, Mr. Barton, tell the court again how it is you came across these photographs?"

"Like I told you Wednesday I heard about the shenanigans that were going on down in Cairo, and I was curious whether or not Red may have been involved. So I looked through his things, and there they were hidden away in an old Prince Albert tobacco can."

"I see. And you're sure you found them where you say you did?"

"You calling me a liar?" Roger bristled.

"Mr. Barton," the judge said. "Calm down. Just answer the question."

"Yes. That's exactly where I found them." His voice was louder and higher pitched.

"That's strange. I had those photographs and the tobacco can checked for fingerprints yesterday. Guess what? They found your prints as one would expect. They also found one other set of prints. Now one would expect to find my client's prints, or your brother's, if either handled that can and those pictures wouldn't one, Mr. Barton?"

"You sure would," Roger said.

"Well guess what? The other set of prints doesn't match either my client's or your brother's. Now who do you think they may belong to?" He paused to let his words sink in. "I've had the prints sent to the state crime lab in Atlanta. They're going to try to match them up with their archived prints. We should know in a couple of days whose they are. I ask you once again, and remember you're still under oath, are you sure you found those photographs in my client's belongings?"

Roger turned red. Sweat popped out on his forehead and upper lip.

"For the last time," he said with obvious hostility, "that's where I found them."

"No further questions, Your Honor. I'd like to call Sheriff Hudson back to the stand." There was a murmur among the spectators. We all wondered what other tricks Mr. Pearson had up his sleeve.

"Sheriff Hudson," Red's lawyer began, "when were you first aware of these photographs?"

"I believe Roger brought them in last Tuesday."

"So, several days after the arrest of my client and after you knew I was representing him. Is that correct?"

"Yes. I guess that's right."

"And neither you nor Mr. Matthews thought they were relevant enough to mention to Mr. Crawford's counsel." Mr. Pearson looked at Judge Forehand. "In some jurisdictions that might be considered dereliction of duty or even withholding of evidence. But, with that aside, didn't you find it just a little bit curious that these pictures just appeared all of a sudden materializing out of thin air?"

"No. I thought Mr. Barton was just being a good citizen and a good brother. I'm sure his motives were in the interest of seeing justice done."

"I see. Tell me Mr. Hudson, is Roger Barton a sworn officer of the law?"

"No. Not that I'm aware of."

"He's not one of your deputies?"

"Lord, no." He laughed.

"So, neither you, nor anyone that you know, had provided a search warrant to Mr. Barton authorizing him to ransack my client's belongings while looking for incriminating evidence?"

The sheriff blanched. Mr. Matthews coughed. All of a sudden they saw where this line of questioning was going.

Mr. Pearson turned to the bench.

"Judge Forehand. Not only is this evidence of dubious origin, but if it was found by Mr. Barton where he says it was found, it constitutes an illegal search and seizure, and therefore cannot be submitted as evidence in these hearings nor in any subsequent relevant court proceedings."

The courtroom went deadly silent.

"Mr. Pearson. Mr. Matthews. Will both of you approach the bench." Red's lawyer was smiling. Mr. Matthews was not.

"Counselors, I need a little time to brush up on the legal particulars surrounding search and seizure. If I am correct, Mr. Crawford was living in a Barton property, one for which, as I understand it, he was paying no rent. Under those circumstances, I'm not certain of his rights vis-á-vis search and seizure without a warrant. What I am sure of, Mr. Matthews, is that both you and Sheriff Hudson have a lot to answer for in the prosecution of this case. This court is not happy that it has been put in the position of having to rule on these procedural screw-ups. You may return to your seats.

"Mr. Pearson, I will rule on your motion next Monday morning at ten o'clock. In the meantime I am remanding the prisoner into the custody of the sheriff." He stood up.

"All rise."

Judge Forehand left the chamber displaying a high degree of annoyance.

"Red," Mr. Pearson said in a voice that carried to the upper reaches of the balcony, "if I can read the tea leaves correctly, come Monday afternoon you'll be a free man."

Red beamed.

Despite the gag order it didn't take long for the story to get out. What went on in Judge Forehand's courtroom was too juicy to keep under anybody's hat. Especially, those who had scores to settle with either the sheriff or the prosecutor.

Roger was livid on the way home.

"How dare that nigger loving bastard question my honesty? Who does he think he is? Coming down here like this and throwing all this legal shit in our faces."

He continued to mumble under his breath all the way home. I wasn't about to interrupt him. I'd seen him explode before, and it was not a pretty sight. I didn't want to bear the brunt of his fury.

"How'd it go today, Derek?" Mama asked. "Did Judge Forehand rule on Red?"

"No ma'am. They got into a lot of legal mumbo-jumbo that I didn't understand. The judge got real mad at the sheriff and Mr. Matthews. This lawyer from Atlanta, Mr. Pearson, is pretty sharp. He caught Mr. Matthews in some legal screw-ups, and now Judge Forehand has to spend the weekend trying to figure out who's right and who's wrong. That lawyer sure took after Roger. He had him fussing and fuming all the way home. It was sure interesting."

So much time was lost during the week due to the court hearing that I had to work on Saturday. I harnessed Ada and Queen and headed over to apply side-dressing to the tobacco. Daddy drove over with the fertilizer. I helped him unload the eighty-pound bags of ammonium nitrate. The hopper held about forty pounds, and each load would do about four rows. It was past noon when I emptied the last bag into the hopper. There were only a few pounds left when I finished. I unhitched the mules, hooked their traces over the collar staves, and headed home. I stopped to water them in Sikes Creek. I thought of Gobbler. So much had happened in the few short weeks since that terrible day. I would never cross that spot again without thinking of him.

Daddy was already home, and Mama was putting dinner on the table.

Pork chops, corn, snap beans and sliced tomatoes. Boy, was I hungry! Roger came in about half way through.

"I stopped by the pool hall after I dropped the mail off," he said. "Some of the Lavenders and Holmes were there already getting liquored up. It wasn't even noontime. Everybody was talking about the hearing. Louis Lavender said it wasn't right for that lawyer to show me up like that. He said somebody ought to do something about it. I asked him what he had in mind. He said, 'You know, knock some sense in his nigger loving head. Send him packing back to Atlanta with a good coating of tar and feathers.' I told him he'd better watch talk like that. He never knew who might be listening."

"Those boys are always popping off like that," Daddy said. "None of 'em ever went to school a day in their lives. They're a bunch of ignoramuses. Mostly no account white trash. Mean as snakes, too. When they get to drinking like that you better watch out."

Daddy said he was going into Shiloh a little early. He wanted to see what was going on for himself. I figured he might pay a visit to Pop Gullet's place.

"Derek, do you want to go in with me. Maybe you can catch a picture show. It should let out before I finish the mail run."

"Yes, sir, I'd like that."

So much had been going on that I hadn't been to the Ritz in over a month. I got to the show at one thirty. The cartoons were over, and the serial was just starting. It was dark, so I grabbed the first seat I saw. When my eyes became accustomed, I spotted Tommie Person and Warren Cone near the front. I moved down to sit with them. By four thirty, Johnny Mack Brown had thrown the last bad guy in jail. I headed down to the station to meet Daddy.

"Hey, you little *queer*. You the one what's causing all this trouble?"

It was Louis Lavender. He was standing in the doorway of the Pastime Billiard Parlor. I tried to hurry by, but he caught me by the arm. He got right in my face. The beer fumes were overwhelming.

"I asked you a question, boy. Is you the Barton boy what's making Shiloh to look like a piece of shit because of that fancy lawyer? I hear tell the judge may throw out them pictures Roger found in that nigger's bed."

"Let me go! I haven't done anything. Leave me alone."

I jerked my arm away and ran. A police car cruised by, and Louis faded back into the recesses of the pool hall. I was still shaking when I got to the truck.

"What's the matter, Derek? You're as white as a ghost."

"Louis Lavender grabbed me as I was walking past the pool hall. He called me names, and he said he was going to get me for bringing all this shame on Shiloh."

"Don't pay any attention to him. That was just booze talking. He's not so tough when he's sober or when he's not surrounded by all his redneck buddies. I'll take care of him. You stay away from him."

After we dropped the mail off, Daddy stopped at Geeslin's grocery. Mama needed a few things. On Saturday afternoons, every Barton boy since William had dipped ice cream at Geeslins. I helped Jim two summers ago. It was almost a rite of passage. Daddy bought me a cone of black walnut. That was Mama's favorite flavor. I guess I learned to like it from her.

"Here's your groceries, Julia," Daddy called. We took the bags into the kitchen. I still had the cone of ice cream. It was dripping on the linoleum.

"Derek, watch what you're doing. I just scrubbed these floors yesterday."

"I'm sorry, Mama. I was trying to save a bite for you. I know how much you like black walnut."

"Thank you just the same, but get that drippy mess out of here."

I hung over the funnel on the porch and finished my ice cream.

"One of those no-account Lavender boys grabbed Derek when he went past the pool hall. Scared him to death. Called him names and threatened him. Something's got to be done about that bunch of peckerwoods. I'll talk to Davis on Monday. I'm going back to court with Derek. I want to see for myself what all the fuss is about.

Chapter 27

Mama woke me. It was still dark out.

"Derek, get up!"

"What is it, Mama?"

"I don't know for sure, but there's something going on at the jail. Your daddy's already gone over there. I want you to go up to the corner and see what's happening then come back and tell me."

I jumped into my overalls and ran as fast as I could. There were several pickup trucks parked near the courthouse. A flat bed truck was backed up to the jail. A tall wooden cross, wrapped in kerosene soaked burlap sacks, burned on the west lawn. The flames cast dark, fleeting, shadows of men dressed in white sheets and tall hoods as they scurried back and forth. Most wore masks.

Suddenly, the front door of the jail burst open. Two of the robed figures were dragging a man. They threw him onto the bed of the big truck. The driver pulled away. He drove across the south lawn of the courthouse and backed the truck up to the wall. Another man ran inside. He reappeared at a second floor window where a beam protruded from the building. In the past, things too large to fit up the stairs were hauled up to the second floor on a block and tackle. A rusted pulley still dangled from the beam. The man shinnied out on the beam. Someone on the truck threw a rope to him. He threaded it through the pulley and dropped the raw end back to the man below. In the dim light, I could see the other end of the rope. It was a noose, and it was draped around Red Crawford's neck. I screamed and ran across the road to the truck. I jumped up onto the bed. I tried to take the rope off Red.

"Stop! Stop!" I yelled. "He didn't hurt me. Leave him alone."

"Git that boy outta here," the man holding Red shouted. A hand grabbed me and pulled me away.

"You stay back boy, or I'll get another rope for you."

I recognized the voice. It was Louis Lavender. He still reeked of beer. Daddy emerged from the crowd and came over to where I was standing.

"Derek, these men have gone mad. I tried to stop them. They wouldn't listen to me. They've got Buford locked up, and they ripped the phone out of the wall. They aren't smart enough to know it, but that'll set off an alarm down at the telephone office. The sheriff should be out here any minute. You stay back. I'm going to try to reason with these idiots."

"You men need to stop this right now. Let the law take care of him. If he's guilty of anything it'll come out."

"Hiram, you know damn well they ain't gonna convict this nigger. Not with that slick lawyer pulling all his tricks. You heard what he said Friday. He pretty much guaranteed he'd get Red off. He's got Matthews, and Hudson, and the judge buffaloed. If this nigger goes back in that courtroom Monday, he'll walk out a free man. Then what are you gonna do about what he did to yore boy and them other boys in them pictures? Naw, sir. We gotta take care of this ourselfs."

"You can't hide behind those robes. The FBI will be swarming over Wyatt County like ducks on a June bug if you do this. There's a new *federal* law against lynching. President Truman just signed it. You won't just be dealing with the local law here. You won't be able to hide. Too many people know who you are."

"That don't matter none to me, Hiram. We cain't let these folks come down here and tell us how to act. I'd rather die than be run over by a bunch of nigger loving Yankees. 'Sides, they ain't no jury in Wyatt County gonna convict somebody for killing a *buggering* nigger. Ain't gonna happen."

"This won't be a local jury, Louis. This'll be a federal jury. They'll try you someplace else. Quit this foolishness before it's too late."

"You don't know what you're talking about old man. Somebody git him outta here."

A burly arm grabbed Daddy around the neck and dragged him back to where I was standing. It held him there as they tightened the noose around Red's neck. Louis helped Red to his feet. He pulled on the loose end of the rope. The pulley creaked as the rope went taut. Louis tossed it to a man on the ground.

"Tie that rope to that cleat over there," he said. "You got any last words you wanna say, nigger?"

Red turned toward me. The dancing light from the burning cross fell across his face.

"I jest want to say that I ain't never laid a hand on that boy. He been trying to tell you that, but you won't listen. Whoever did what they did to him has made him so scared that he cain't talk about it. He tried to say it won't me, but things got out of hand. He didn't 'spect it would come to this.

"You and me both knows this ain't 'bout Derek and what's been done to him. This 'bout hate. Pure and simple. This 'bout you thinking you is better than a black man. This 'bout blaming somebody else for yo own sorry state. Mark my word. They's a new day acomin'. A day when things like this ain't gone be 'lowed to happen. You can kill me, and you can go on 'bout yo business, but like Mr. Hiram say, you gone have folks bigger than Wyatt County to deal with. They's gonna be a day of reckonin'."

"Somebody shut that nigger up, and let's get on with it."

"I got one more thing I needs to say." Red looked straight at me. "I got a little dog in that store over there, Mr. Hiram. I want Derek to have him if it be all right with you. Derek, will you take care of Pee Wee for me?"

"You know I will, Red," I said through choked back tears.

Daddy tried to break loose from the man's chokehold. He couldn't.

"Stop it! He didn't do it!" I yelled. "It was Mr. Tyler from school! He said he would kill me and my parents if I told on him. He threatened me with a pistol. He beat me with it when we were in Atlanta. Red didn't do it. Let him go."

"You think anybody's gonna believe that now, boy. Nosirree. We all know it was this nigger what did it." Louis tightened the noose.

"God bless you, Red," Daddy said. "I wish I could stop this."

"Okay, that's enough," Louis said. "Everybody off the truck." He started to place a sack over Red's head.

"Don't do that!" Red shouted. "I came into this world with my eyes wide open. I aim to go out the same way. I wants y'all to look me in the eyes when I dies. Then I wants y'all to go home, and try to live with yo'selves knowing you killed an innocent man out of pure, ignorant hate." A flash bulb went off from the upper floor of the jail. Buford was doing his job.

Louis got into the driver's seat. The gears ground and the truck lurched away from the courthouse. Red's feet dragged across the bed of the truck until it slid out from under him. He dropped, and the rope snapped taut. He swung in a wide arc, bouncing off the wall of the courthouse. The oscillations slowed. Red's body stopped twitching. I knew he was dead. I cried and buried my face in my father's chest. I felt his tears falling on my head.

Flashing lights and sirens signaled the arrival of the sheriff. The klansmen had scattered. We stood there bewildered in the fading light from the cross.

"I tried to stop them Davis. They were a drunken mob with their blood up. Nothing anybody said or did was going to stop them."

"You men help me get him down."

Cousin Sim loosened the rope from the cleat. Daddy and the sheriff lowered Red to the ground.

"Who did this, Hiram?"

"They were wearing robes and hoods, but I'll be willing to swear that five of them were Lavenders and Holmes. I was going to talk to you about Louis Lavender. He grabbed Derek on the street yesterday and threatened him. I reckon that don't matter now. That family has been nothing but trouble ever since they moved up here from Mississippi."

"They'll pay for this," the sheriff said. "This was cold-blooded murder. If they had just waited a day or two, they wouldn't have seen the need to do this."

You mean you know *Tyler* did it," Daddy said.

"Yeah. I heard from the sheriff in Duchess County, New York. He sent me a long telegram, and he's sending me some more information. It'll bring this whole case to a close."

"Davis, Derek finally told us it was Tyler," Daddy said. "He said Tyler told him he'd kill him and his folks if Derek told anyone. Louis wouldn't listen. He was hell bent on killing Red. Tyler himself could have been there to back up Derek's story, and it wouldn't have stopped them. They wanted blood, and they got it.

I'll be arresting Tyler soon. Meantime, I've got to do something with Red here." The sheriff walked over to his car and picked up the microphone.

"Charlie, this is the sheriff. Go over to Murray's Funeral Home and ask Aaron to come out to the jail at Corinth. That's right. Thanks."

"Hiram, Sim, if you'll give me a hand we'll get Red over to the jail."

The three men carried Red's body to the jail. I stood with my feet glued to the ground.

"What did the sheriff know? Mr. Tyler came to Shiloh from New York. What history did he have in New York that the school officials here didn't have? Will Mr. Tyler know I've told on him? Will he turn his buddies loose when the sheriff comes after him? Will all this suffering have been in vain? Did Red die for nothing? What have I done?"

The black hearse pulled slowly into the jail yard. The elderly undertaker and his son wheeled Red from the jail and placed him in the hearse. The sheriff stood at the open rear door.

"Aaron, I know Mr. Crawford didn't have any money. He didn't have any family here that I know of. The county will take care of his funeral expenses. We'll bury him in the pauper's section of the Negro Cemetery."

"No!"

It was my father speaking in the sternest voice I could ever remember him using.

"Red did have family here. For the past four years, the Bartons have been his family. I'll take care of his expenses. He'll have a proper funeral, and he'll be buried in the Negro cemetery here in Antioch."

"If that's what you want, Hiram."

"That's what I want."

The taillights of the hearse disappeared toward Shiloh.

"What are you going to do now sheriff?" Daddy asked.

"It's too late to get a warrant for his arrest tonight. I'll call the judge first thing in the morning. As soon as I have it I'll pick him up."

We stopped to pick up Pee Wee. Mama was still up. She had made coffee. "I thought you might need this," she said.

"I sure do, Julia."

"What happened, Hiram? Why do you have Pee Wee?"

There was agony on Daddy's face. The words came out haltingly.

"They lynched Red, Julia. It was the Ku Klux Klan. Red's gone."

"Oh, no!" Mama sobbed. She slumped into a chair. "Why? Why did they do it?"

"It was a bunch of liquored up rednecks. There wasn't any reasoning with them. It was the Holmes boys and the Lavenders mostly. I did my best to stop them, but it was no use. They were bound and determined to hang him no matter what. Pure hate. Pure blood lust. Red just happened to be a handy target. It could have been any black man. Their kind just needs someone to torment. They were trying to make themselves feel bigger. To make themselves feel like they're better than someone else. They're all pathetic excuses for human beings.

"It's been over ten years since a man was lynched in Wyatt County. That was before the war. Things have changed. They won't get away with it now like they did then. Hundreds of Negroes died fighting for this country. Our government can't forget that. It won't turn its back on them. Federal agents will be swarming all over this place."

Daddy stopped his tirade. He was figuring out how to tell Mama what I had told the crowd.

"Julia, Derek told us what happened. Once he saw they were going to hang Red, he just blurted it right out. He told everyone there that it was Mr. Tyler. He said Tyler threatened that him or some of his gang would kill Derek and us if he told anyone. That's why Derek was so afraid to tell us. But that didn't stop 'em. They had their blood up and Red was a convenient victim. None of us could stop them. They weren't going to miss this chance to prove their white superiority.

I had never seen my father so angry. If Leonard Tyler had been standing there in our kitchen at that moment, I'm sure my daddy would have strangled him with his bare hands. He pulled me to him and put his arms around me.

"Derek, I'm so sorry. I'm sorry I wasn't able to protect you from a man like that. We think we don't have to worry about such things in an out-of-the-way place like Wyatt County, but it seems like evil knows no boundaries. I wish you had told us. I know you thought you were doing the right thing. Trying to protect *us*. But we could have protected *you*. I doubt there are any other people who would do his dirty work for him. His threats were just a way to keep a defenseless young boy in line.

"You go on to bed now. Try to get some rest. If it'll make you feel better, I'll lock the doors and keep my double-barreled, twelve gauge by the bed. I don't think we'll need it. People like that are really cowards at heart. They prey on the weak and the helpless to satisfy their own disgusting desires. Go on to bed now. We'll get this all straightened out tomorrow."

Mama sat there crying softly. So much hurt. So much pain. Why? So that one sick, twisted man could satisfy his unspeakable perversions.

I could hear them from my room. Daddy was trying to console my mother. My mother was trying to understand what had happened to her family, trying to imagine what scars her son would carry from this, wondering how his life might be changed, seeking answers to questions that had no answers—not for them—not for me.

Chapter 28

The phone rang early. It was Sheriff Hudson.

"Hello. Yes, Davis, I can be there in fifteen minutes."

"Come on Derek. The sheriff wants us to meet him at Aaron Murray's funeral home."

"What for?"

"He didn't say. He just said to meet him there."

All the way down to the shabby little building behind Pindley's stockyard, I wondered what the sheriff could want. We rattled across the railroad tracks and pulled in behind the black Dodge. Aaron Murray was standing on the porch.

"Come right on in Mr. Barton," the stooped, graying, old man said with a courtly nod. "The sheriff is already here," he said nervously stating the obvious. He took us past the casket-lined parlor into the room at the back. There was an overpowering smell of formaldehyde. We were in the embalming room. Red's body lay on a table with a sheet draped over him. I didn't want to be there.

"Aaron has made an interesting discovery. Show Mr. Barton, Aaron."

The old man pulled back the sheet. Red lay there completely naked, his body stiff. His reddish complexion had turned blue. I had never seen a dead man up close like this before.

"Notice anything unusual?" the sheriff asked.

My father ran his eyes up and down Red's body. Twice. Then he saw it.

"My God! Why didn't he tell us? He could have saved himself."

What did he see that I couldn't?

"I'm not sure he could have, Hiram. Those boys were hell bent on blood. Derek's situation just gave them a credible excuse. No, I think he was just too proud. I think he wanted to go to his grave with his secret."

"What's he talking about, Daddy?"

"Take a closer look, Derek. At his genitals."

Then it struck me. Red had no testicles.

"I don't understand," I said.

"The sheriff down in Cairo stopped those boys from lynching Red when he was accused of messing with one of the white women. It appears they caught up with him later. They castrated him. So you see, he couldn't have sodomized those boys, and he couldn't have abused you."

"But he was always running around with women on the weekends. He told me."

"That was his manhood talking," the sheriff said. "He didn't want anybody to know, so he just carried on as if it never happened."

"Why didn't he tell you?" Daddy said. "Then you would have known he couldn't have done it."

"Same reason. He'd rather die than admit to everyone here that he was less than a man. He thought he would take it to his grave with him. Anyway, I believe he thought Mr. Pearson would get him off and that he'd be turned loose. He thought the truth would come out, and he would go free. He would have too if those idiots hadn't got it in their heads to string him up."

"But what about the pictures," I said. "Where did he get those?"

"He didn't. Red never saw those pictures in his life. They were planted. That other set of prints belonged to that highway patrolman friend of Roger's. There are a lot of unanswered questions. Sheriff Pritchard is checking the rolls of known KKK members in the Cairo area. I have a feeling there'll be a surprise or two on that list. Hiram, tell Roger he's not to leave town until I get to the bottom of this."

Daddy looked shocked.

"I can't believe Roger put those pictures there. Why would he?"

"Where was he last night?" The sheriff asked.

"I don't know."

"I plan on finding out," Sheriff Hudson said. "He has a lot of explaining to do."

"Derek, I received those papers from New York this morning. They confirm the suspicions I had about Tyler all along. I know you thought you were protecting your parents, but your silence may have cost Red his life."

There it was. Plain and simple. The acknowledgment that my silence had led to Red's death. I had been trying to deny it to myself, but deep down inside I knew it was the truth. Could I live with that truth for the rest of my life?"

"The boy was terrified, Davis. He didn't mean for Red to get hurt. He didn't think it would go that far. He tried to stop it, but they wouldn't listen. Derek did what he has always been taught to do. He was trying to protect his family. Now maybe he was misguided, but his intentions were good. He was afraid. Afraid for himself, but more so for his family. Before you pass judgment, you need to stand in his shoes for a while. Sure, things might have turned out different if he'd told us right off, but in his mind they may have turned out bad in other ways. The last thing he wanted was to hurt Red. Red was his best friend. It was others that killed Red not Derek. You need to look to that gang for the guilty ones, not at Derek."

"You may be right, Hiram. I hadn't thought of it like that." I was never prouder of my father in my entire life than I was at that very moment.

"Are you going to arrest Tyler now, Davis?'

"No, I'm not going to arrest Tyler," he said with a half-smile.

"What do you mean?" Daddy said.

"Because, his name isn't Leonard Tyler, it's Leon Tyson. He served ten years in a New York state prison for pedophilia. Some of his associates in prison were excellent forgers. They ginned up a whole new identity for him. When he got out, he headed down this way with a clean resume and a new start. The only problem was he didn't leave his perversions behind."

"Then his story about a homosexual ring in Shiloh isn't true?"

"Not a word of it. He made that up to intimidate Derek and the other boys he abused."

"There were others?"

"At least two, that I've been able to uncover. Forcible rape, threats, all the same things. I have their statements. We'll be able to put Mr. Tyson away for the rest of his natural born life. Too bad it wasn't him in that jail cell instead of Red. I don't think I'd ever catch the guys that strung Tyler up."

"Then you think that if I had told you right away nothing would have happened?" I said.

"I believe that's true son, but like your pa said there was no way for you to know that. None of the other boys came forward for the same reason. Only in their cases nobody else got hurt."

The fact that there were others didn't make me feel much better. Red was still dead, and I felt like I had killed him.

"What are you going to do now Davis?" Daddy asked.

"I'm going back to the courthouse and get that warrant for Tyson's arrest."

"Do you mind if Derek and I go with you?"

"I reckon that will be all right. You'll have to stay down in the lobby of the hotel though. If he's armed like Derek says, it could be dangerous."

Judge Forehand had signed the warrant. It was waiting for the sheriff in his office.

"Come on," the sheriff said. "It's time to take that man off the streets."

We parked on Liberty Street and walked across Main near the Ritz. We stayed close to the buildings. No one observing the street from the hotel could see us. Gary Laird was at the desk.

"Morning, Sheriff. What can I do for you?"

"Gary, is Leonard Tyler in his room?"

"I think so. I haven't seen him since he came back from breakfast. I did go out to the kitchen for a few minutes to get some coffee. He's still up there unless he went out then."

"Gary, give me a key to his room. Hiram, you and Derek stay here. I should be back in a few minutes." He started up the stairs.

"What's this all about?" Gary asked.

"Davis is going to arrest Tyler."

"Good Lord!" Gary said. "I can't believe he'd do something like that. Why he's been living here for over three years, and I haven't heard a peep out of him."

"Yeah," Daddy said. "Sometimes it's the quiet ones you have to look out for."

The sheriff came lumbering back down the stairs.

"He's gone. When was the last time you saw him, Gary?"

"He came down for breakfast about eight o'clock. He went up to the City Café. Came back around nine and went to his room. I haven't seen him since."

"Well, he must have slipped out while you were in the back. I don't know how he could have got wind that I was coming. Us three and the clerk at the courthouse are the only ones who knew except for the judge." He thought for a second. "Wait a minute! Bethel Early at Western Union took down the message from New York. If she blabbed to anyone, I'll skin her alive. Does Tyler have a car?"

"Yes sir," Gary said. "He keeps it parked behind the Sinclair station across the street."

"Come on. I'll bet that bastard got word somehow, and he's skipped town."

We heard the motor running before we rounded the corner of the station. Mr. Tyler's car was parked in its usual spot. I could see him behind the wheel. The car was full of smoke.

"My God! He's trying to kill himself," Daddy said.

A flexible hose hooked to the exhaust pipe ran through a back window. The rolled up window held it in place.

"Stand back!" Sheriff Hudson shouted.

He ran to the car and jerked on the door. It was locked. He picked up a piece of scrap iron and knocked out the window. He reached inside, unlocked the door, and dragged the limp body of Leon Tyson from the car. Daddy turned off the ignition.

"Is he still alive?" Daddy asked.

"I don't know. I can't feel a pulse. Derek, run back over to the hotel and tell Gary to call an ambulance."

I took off. The sheriff and Daddy were trying to revive Mr. Tyson. It didn't look good. Five minutes went by before we heard the siren. The ambulance attendant and nurse took over from Daddy and the sheriff. The nurse pumped on Mr. Tyson's chest while the attendant held his nose and breathed into his mouth. They did this for another ten minutes before the nurse looked up and shook her head. She took the stethoscope from her ears.

"I'm afraid we were too late. There's no pulse. I can't detect a heartbeat. He's dead."

"Thank you, Mary Margaret. You did all you could. I'll call Gordon to come down here to officially determine the cause of death and certify it for the records. You two can head on back over to the hospital.

"Hiram, you and Derek might as well go on home. There's nothing more you can do here. I'm sorry you had to see this, Derek. It's a sorry end to a very sick life. He took the coward's way out. He's been responsible for a lot of misery and heartache both here and where he came from. I hope we'll be able to put this all behind us now. I know it'll take a long time for everyone involved to come to terms with what happened, but I do know this. We live in a loving, caring, forgiving community. In God's good time, he heals all wounds. He'll heal this one too."

"Thank you, Davis," my father said. He shook the sheriff's hand. He put his arm around my shoulder. We walked away. We left the past behind.

The End